JULIA F

Julia Franck was born in Berlin in 1970. Her novel *The Blind Side of the Heart* won the German Book Prize and sold over a million copies in Germany alone. It was shortlisted for the Independent Foreign Fiction Prize and the Jewish Quarterly–Wingate Literary Prize, and was named one of the best books of the year by the *Guardian*. *West* is her third novel to be translated into English.

JULIA FRANCK

West

TRANSLATED FROM THE GERMAN BY
Anthea Bell

VINTAGE

1 3 5 7 9 10 8 6 4 2

Vintage
20 Vauxhall Bridge Road,
London SW1V 2SA

Vintage is part of the Penguin Random House group of companies
whose addresses can be found at global.penguinrandomhouse.com

Penguin
Random House
UK

First published in Vintage in 2015

First published in trade paperback by Harvill Secker in 2014

First published with the title *Lagerfeuer* in 2003 by DuMont, Cologne

www.vintage-books.co.uk

A CIP catalogue record for this book is available from the British Library

ISBN 9780099554325

Published with the support of the Culture Programme of the European Union

This project has been funded with support from the European Commission.
This publication reflects the views only of the author, and the Commission
cannot be held responsible for any use which may be made of the
information contained herein

 Culture

Typeset in Jenson by Palimpsest Book Production Limited,
Falkirk, Stirlingshire

Printed and bound by Clays Ltd, St Ives Plc

For Oscar, Emilie and Uli

Nelly Senff drives over a bridge

The children wearily lowered their arms; they had been tenaciously waving, at first with enthusiasm in spite of the lack of any response, then probably out of habit and the pushiness of children. They must have been waving for an hour, their mouths pressed against the windows where they left wet kiss marks in the condensation on the glass; they had also rubbed their noses on the glass, they had continued waving until Katya told her brother, 'I can't keep this up any more, come on, let's stop,' and Aleksei nodded as if giving up at last, bringing their farewell to an end, was a good idea. The car took us a little further forward again; the brake lights of the small van in front of us went off. Under the flat-roofed super-structure a uniformed man stood in the twilight, indicating that we were to come closer, and then immediately raised both arms in the air. We stopped with a jolt, the engine stuttered and flooded. It had been like that for four hours; maybe we had covered three metres in those four hours, maybe ten. The Bornholm bridge must be a few metres ahead of us, I knew that, but we couldn't see it; a plain, broad building with a narrow carriageway passing through it hid everything coming towards us from view. The small van was waved over and guided into another lane. The lights flickered and came on, except for one of them on the right that stayed dark. I wondered when they ever got time to do any repairs in this place. Perhaps between twelve midnight and two in the morning. You could see how the shadow ahead of us came closer until it disappeared under the bonnet of the car. Soon after that it was climbing over the windscreen, over our faces, and at last it ruthlessly swallowed up the car like everything else: the shadow of that broad roof, of the building that bridged the carriageway and hid the view ahead. The building consisted entirely of cardboard and corrugated iron. The sun in front of us sank behind the houses and shone once more in the window of the guardhouse tower high above us, as if with the enticing promise that, by following it, we would be sure to see it again in the West tomorrow. Then it was gone, leaving us here in the twilight with only a few fiery streaks in the sky, and the shadows were swallowing up not only us but the entire city behind us, when Gerd ground out his cigarette, breathed in deeply, held his breath, and told me he had wondered ten years ago when I would finally make this journey. He whistled through his teeth as if casually, but at the time, he pointed out, I had only just met that man, and he could tell me that today, now that I was sitting in his car and my journey led only in this one direction. I couldn't get out, whereupon he laughed; he had always, he said, imagined holding me naked in his arms.

Gerd lit another cigarette, curling his tongue round it from below, started the engine, stopped it, started it again; the ashtray was brimming over. I collected the cigarette ends with my bare hand and stuffed them into a small plastic bag that I had been careful to bring with me in case the children felt sick. I was the one who felt sick now. I didn't want to be naked in Gerd's arms. I'd been successfully fending off that idea until this moment when, with a little whistle through his teeth and a few harmless words, he made my efforts ridiculous. Even the fact that I was in his car, with my children on the back seat of it kissing the windows, and we were in the process of crossing this bridge didn't make it an exciting prospect.

Katya held her nose and asked if she could open the window. I nodded, and ignored Gerd's groan. I had imagined for some time that Gerd would spare me having to listen to what he wanted out of thoughtfulness, and in the knowledge that I didn't want him to touch me at all. Then again, I'd hoped that he had forgotten my body as far as possible. Not very well, maybe, but still I hoped he'd made the effort. An effort that I had appreciated, but now he wasn't making that effort at all, or if he had then it failed at this moment. The man whose name he certainly had not forgotten, although he didn't speak it, had been the father of my children. But that wasn't the reason why I suddenly felt repelled by Gerd. I was repelled by his refusal to acknowledge why we were sitting in his car. We were sitting in it solely to get across this bridge, and maybe also for another reason, but definitely not with the aim of sitting together undisturbed in a very small space. Cool air came in from outside, smelling of petrol and slightly of summer, but more of night and the coming cold. Twilight. A uniformed police officer came over to the car and bent down on Gerd's side so that he could get a better view of the interior. His torch shone a little light on our faces; the beam was faint and flickered, as if it would go out any moment. He checked our names and faces in turn. I looked into a pallid face with a broad, low forehead; his eyes were deep-set, forced all the way back into their sockets by his cheekbones, a Pomeranian face, no longer youthful although he was still young. He tapped the back door with his flashlight and said we couldn't stop here with the windows open, they had to be closed for safety reasons. After he had checked the children's papers, he said, 'Get out.' My door stuck; I shook it until it sprang open and got out.

'No,' the uniformed police officer called to me over the roof of the car, 'not you, only the children.'

I sat down in the car again and turned round. 'He wants you two to get out,' I repeated, at the same time reaching for Aleksei's hand to hold it tight. But my own hand met thin air; only now did I notice that I was trembling. The doors closed. The man said something to my children that I couldn't make out, as he pointed to our car, shook his head and clapped Aleksei's thin shoulder. Then I saw them following him into the low building. There was a neon light on above the dark window. I waited for a light to appear, but the window stayed black. Perhaps a roller blind had come down inside it. Or there was a special layer on the glass to prevent you from seeing in, while it was possible to see out from inside, just as you could see through the bronze mirror windows of the Palace of the Republic. The king looked out and could see his people, but those outside saw blank panes, were dazzled by their brightness and could not see through them. If they had been on the same level as the king and his windows, looking straight at the mirror glass, they could at least have seen their reflections and met the unconcealed curiosity of their own gaze. But the little people stood down below in the square, seeing nothing but the sky reflected up there in the windows. Their glance was not returned. However, the panes of the window here were particularly black, deep black, black as coal, raven black, and the longer I looked at the window the more unnatural it seemed to me. No brightness, no orange glow. All the light soaked up long ago. No raven, no coal, no depths. Only black. The window was nothing but a dummy. Gerd ground out his cigarette and lit another.

'Nice and quiet here.' He was enjoying these minutes alone with me. They'll ask Katya and Aleksei why we wanted to cross the bridge, I thought. They'll take them separately into a room without any windows, sit each child down on a chair and say: We want to know something, and you must tell us the truth, do you hear? And Katya will nod, while Aleksei will look at his shoes. Look at me, the servant of the state will tell Aleksei as he pats him on the back, like an old friend, a colleague, someone to be trusted. Not knowing that even if Aleksei did raise his head he could see only the man's vague outline, because his glasses weren't much good any more. He liked looking at his shoes; they were the furthest part of him from his eyes, yet they belonged to him, he knew just what his shoes looked like. Perhaps the official would threaten him, perhaps he would tug at his arm so that Aleksei wouldn't forget how much stronger a man like him was. Perhaps there would be three of them facing Aleksei, five of them, the whole room could be full of uniformed servants of the state, members of the People's Police, of State Security, border soldiers, men in high places, apprentices, assistants – but then that individual man would lose some of his authority. Why does your mother want to cross the bridge? Has she known the man with you for long? Does she love him? Have you seen him kissing her? And her kissing him? How do they kiss each other? Would you like to have a father from the West? Has he brought you children presents? What kind of presents? Ah, then he's a capitalist. Isn't he? Silence. What could Aleksei say? There were only wrong answers. Something was darting about at the base of my spine; I could call it fear, but it was only a flickering sensation. Wrong answers. Aleksei didn't even know that, but maybe he was beginning to guess it. Will they detain us? What would that piece of paper, that permit, count for if they simply made me disappear and put the children in a home? Compulsory adoption. There were rumours of such things. Enemies of the state in particular, but also enemies of socialist democracy, and more especially people who fled the country, were those whose children were taken into the care of the state. Irretrievably and never to be found again. Later they could always say I had died of a pulmonary embolism. They could say that about whomever they chose. The stories you heard hardly differed – only the names of the people in the stories differed. Why would anyone here bother to make up an imaginative story, and for whose benefit? Since facts are also inventions and subject to a consensus of opinion, no one will be able to prove that I didn't create an uproar and I wasn't ill – only Gerd could do that. In so far as he wasn't one of them, it was a good thing that I was sitting here with him in the car, that it was his car. Keep the darting sensation down, don't panic. He couldn't disappear just like that, the king would be in difficulty, great difficulty, we weren't all that important to him, not even Aleksei, not even Katya. Little fishes. Tiny little fishes. True, they had swum away from the shoal, they weren't swimming with the current any more, but they were tiny enough to be overlooked. What do you think capitalism has in store for you? That's what Katya's teacher had asked a few weeks ago, when she kept Katya back in the classroom after lessons for a private talk. Doesn't your family believe in peace? You do remember, Katya, don't you? Didn't you too want to help the poor children in Vietnam? Didn't you bring rice to school and collect raw materials? And whose fault is the poverty in Vietnam? Well, whose fault? Who lets so many children in the world go hungry? Haven't you learned anything at school? In kindergarten, in the day nursery? Don't you know that capitalists are your enemies? Katya had come home with swollen eyelids. She didn't want other children to go hungry because of us, she didn't want to go away to live with people who let other children go hungry. She cried half the night. She would certainly be interrogated along those lines now. And what did you say your future father was? No, a cabinet-maker isn't quite right. He's a capitalist. Yes, an enemy. What about your real father? What happened to him?

I knocked on the window.

'Why are you knocking on the window? Stop knocking on the window.' Gerd leaned back, avoiding my eyes; he was probably terrified of losing his nerve.

I knocked on the window.

'Stop it.'

I knocked twice, copying the rhythm of his order.

He groaned, and I passed the palm of my hand over the pane.

'How long have they been in there?' I asked, staring at the black window of the low building.

'No idea, I didn't look at the time. Twenty minutes, maybe.'

'Longer than that.'

Gerd didn't reply; he was smoking. Since the uniformed police officer had gone away with my children, the door hadn't opened once. No one had gone into the building, no one had come out of it. The door was so firmly closed that I wondered if I'd been mistaken, and my children had gone into an entirely different building with a door I'd been overlooking all this time. Or maybe they'd been taken into the building I was watching and then taken out again somewhere else, and I'd never noticed. Through a back door. Maybe an underground passage led to a remote police camp, straight to the Central Committee, to the dark, blue-green vaults of State Security. There'd be only one way out of those vaults, and it would lead to a dungeon in the copper palace. There might be another intricate labyrinth with special dungeons under the square where the palace stood, dungeons where the children of refugees and fugitives were locked up and made to improve themselves. Until they were ready to be taken into socialist families by citizens loyal to the state. Into families that couldn't exist, maybe. And I was waiting here in vain for my children.

'Did you see them going in too? There. Do you see that hut? They're in there.' I heard the uncertainty in my voice, but I pointed to the hut with the dummy window.

Gerd's eyes followed my finger. He laughed, letting out air once with a brief, vigorous snort, and shrugged his shoulders wearily. 'I don't know.' He glanced around. 'They all look the same.'

The huts stood in a straight row, all with a narrow door on the left, a dummy window on the right and a neon light over it. Except for the huts at the ends of the row. As far as I could see, their windows were not dummies, and light shone out of them. Gerd snorted again as he breathed out. 'You don't think they're going to keep your children there, do you?'

Keep them there. Not here. In his thoughts Gerd was already on the other side of the bridge. I wasn't. Gerd laughed. 'You're a funny one – you really think they have nothing better to do than take little kids into custody?'

'Not just little kids.' I tried to laugh with him, not really successfully. 'In our country you never know.'

'In our country?' Gerd laughed again, and tears suddenly rose to my eyes. I turned away to keep him from seeing them. 'In our country the first thing I'm going to do is invite you all out to eat. A huge plateful of *pommes frites*. I'm ravenous.'

I was just mopping tears off my face with my sleeve, and had turned to the window so that Gerd wouldn't laugh at me for crying on top of everything else, when a doughy face appeared right in front of mine. Another uniformed man knocked on the glass from outside.

'Window,' I heard him say, his thumb pointing insistently down. I turned the handle; the window squealed as it descended into the side of the car.

'Open the boot.'

I looked at Gerd, who was still grinning. He took the key out of the ignition. 'Here you are.' He reached his arm out in front of me and towards the man, who took the key from his hand and disappeared. Although the fresh air was pleasantly mild, I wound the window up again. I could hear the boot being opened. Things were taken out; there was knocking at the underside of the car. Soon after that I saw two officers disappear into one of the huts with our cases.

A fly was buzzing at the bottom corner of the windscreen; it flew into the glass again and again, its small body seemed to hit it with a muted, dull, heavy sound, but it still kept going, buzzed, stopped for a moment, rammed the glass and fell silent. Then more buzzing. I felt the shelf below the dashboard, and soon located the exhausted but buzzing body of the fly under my hand. I slowly let my hand lie flat until the fly was tickling me between my forefinger and ring finger, its delicate little wings still moving all the time, buzzing, tickling me so much that I pressed those two fingers together as firmly as possible on the shelf. It struggled, but it couldn't escape. The space between my fingers and the plastic seemed too large; at intervals, I could still feel the struggling wings. I thought of the whitish fluid that would be squeezed out of the fly if I pressed hard. Suddenly there was a loud knock on the window. I saw only the fist, no face, a uniform; the door was opened. I almost knocked into the man as I fell out. He caught me.

'How often do I have to say it?'

'What?'

'Come with me.' The officer roughly took my bare arm and hauled me along beside him. I stumbled over the shallow step. Inside, a corridor stretched ahead, looking much too long for the hut; maybe it ran all the way through two or three huts. My guard pushed me into a room on the left, where they seemed to be expecting us already. Two almost identical men sat behind the narrow table. They too wore uniforms, but not the uniforms of the People's Police. It wasn't worth the trouble of trying to work out which state service they belonged to. Games of hide-and-seek, illusions, were all a part of dressing up in uniforms. They were so similar that they had to be twins, or at least brothers.

'Sit down. So you're leaving the country to marry Herr Gerd Becker?'

'Yes.'

'You're moving into an apartment in West Berlin together, I suppose?'

'Of course.'

'And your future husband has already furnished it, has he? He's been living there for some time, I believe?'

I nodded confidently. 'Yes, of course.'

While the twin on the right was asking the questions, his brother leafed through the files, apparently looking for something.

'Look, all this is down in my application forms. Only last week I went to see State Security, and all their questioning was about Herr Becker.'

'Really? What questioning, Fräulein – Frau Senff? Nelly Senff. You've been married before?'

'No, you know I haven't.'

'Not even to the father of your children?'

I shook my head.

'What did you say?'

'No.'

'But now of all times you want to try marriage, do you?'

Now of all times? Patience, I told myself, patience, don't lose your nerve now, and I said, 'Yes, I do.'

'How about the father of your children?'

I looked straight at the right-hand brother. 'You know about that.'

'What? What do we know about? Aren't you going to answer us?'

They're trying to get on your nerves, I thought, that's all, they just want to get on your nerves. What kind of satisfaction did these petty officials, self-important as they were, get out of such questions and answers?

'So a man from the West is a better prospect, is he?'

I nodded, shrugging one shoulder. What did I know about men from the West in general or a particular specimen of the genre, and his suitability for what purposes? Gerd was helping me with the illusion; he was very good at that.

'Your mother didn't marry either. Seems to run in your family, eh? Living in sin. Illegitimate children. You really expect us to believe that you're getting married over there?'

'It couldn't be done, just like that.'

'What do you mean?'

'For my mother. It couldn't be done, just like that. Different laws, different customs. First they couldn't get married, then they didn't want to any more.'

The twins looked at me blankly. Until the one on the right, without turning his head, said to the one on the left, 'Jews.' The one on the left leafed through the papers, tapped one page with his finger, and muttered something that sounded like, 'I don't believe it . . . not these days.'

'Your mother was Jewish?' The one on the right was staring at me, open-mouthed.

'She still is. Yes. No, I mean she isn't a believer. Not any more. Not in God, anyway. She believes in communism, but you know that.'

'Did you know that?' he asked the other officer. 'Was she famous?' As soon as a German hears of a Jew who is still alive he thinks the Jew must be famous. The imputation of fame seemed the only way for the Jew in question to have escaped the Germans' own killing strategies. Anyone who did escape must be famous, not least because he or she had escaped. The man on the left leafed through the file and pointed to various pages. 'Your mother was born in '24, your father in '22, but he died in France in 1950. What's this? During their return from exile?' The man on the left turned the page, the man on the right stared at me. 'Then your grandmother went back to Berlin with your pregnant mother? And you were born here.'

I didn't reply. After all, these things must be in their files.

'Why Berlin?'

'I told you, she believes in communism now.'

'Communism is not a matter of faith,' observed the man on the right.

'It isn't?'

'No, it's a matter of conviction, of a proper frame of mind. You didn't attend a socialist school? What school did you go to, then?'

What school did I go to? Did he think there were still schools specially for Jewish children, or did he think Jews simply didn't go to school?

'The Marshal I. S. Konev School,' said the man on the left, laughing and punching his brother in the ribs.

His brother, who obviously couldn't believe it, checked by glancing at the file.

'Five years before us,' the one on the left whispered to the one on the right.

A certificate for good studies at a socialist school. Maybe they didn't have them yet in my time. Katya had any number of such certificates, *for good studies and exemplary social out-of-school activities*, and she had insisted on taking those certificates to the West with her, even though they were hardly likely to be childhood milestones in the career of a potential heroine there. After all, she hadn't collected all that waste paper for nothing, as she explained to me, although when I asked she couldn't tell me what else it had been for. The children weren't even allowed to take home the originals of their school reports. Copies were handed out so that what belonged to the state would remain with the state.

I crossed my legs and didn't answer.

'You don't look Jewish, though.'

'What?'

'You don't look like a Jewish woman. Or, well, let's say not a typical Jewish woman. But you must be Jewish if your mother is Jewish.'

'What does a typical Jewish woman look like, then?'

'You should know better than anyone, Fräulein Senff. Senff – that's a Jewish name, is it?'

I couldn't suppress a groan. 'It's my mother's surname.'

'Sounds kind of German,' muttered the man on the left, immersing himself in a red page of the file in front of him again.

I bit my lip and breathed out for as long as possible. If I didn't breathe in, I tried to persuade myself, if I emptied myself of as much air as I could, then an explosion was practically impossible, or at least it would be a lot more difficult. The man on the left stood up, holding the file, and left the room, leaving behind the man on the right, who wasn't the man on the right any longer but the only man sitting opposite me at the table, while three others whose rank and function were presumably of no significance stood on guard beside him. Without turning their heads, without moving a muscle, they were following every movement, or at least every movement of mine, out of the corners of their eyes. The only officer left closed the files, paused for effect, relishing the silence he had enjoined on the rest of us, finally smiled with his bloodshot eyes, which now disappeared entirely, and looked at me.

'Frau Senff, what I don't understand is why you should pack toothpaste and soap when you are arriving at your future husband's apartment this evening – the apartment where you are going to live together. We're wasting our time here if you hold us up any longer with these stories. Doesn't he have any soap? Your fiancé, Herr Becker?'

I looked at the man in his unidentifiable uniform, felt the blood rush into my face, and closed my mouth. My tongue was sticking to my gums.

'At a loss for words, Senff? Now then, come with me.'

I stood up and followed the only officer left down a narrow corridor and into another room. These rooms had no windows. The plastic flooring on which the soles of our shoes squeaked had a sharp, vaguely sweetish smell. A smell that reminded me of my children's school satchels. Imitation leather. Embossed plastic. The same three models for years on end, generally only in two colours, brown and leaf green; the combination of yellow and orange was unusual. Years ago there must have been red ones.

I heard my heels on the plastic floor, felt myself unexpectedly putting one foot in front of another with a certain verve, a verve that might be thought to be cheerful, my skirt swirled round my thighs, I was almost dancing along, as if I were going to a ball and looking forward to it. A uniformed man opened the door, I gave him a civil and lively nod, another man closed the door behind me.

Inside this room I found myself facing about ten more officers. The air was full of smoke, one of the officers looked me up and down, my skirt came to rest. I folded my arms.

'Sit down.'

'Thank you, but this place of yours isn't exactly comfortable.'

'Sit,' insisted the man who might be the senior officer present. I smiled confidentially at him. I was the only woman in the room. I was thinking that I would visit my uncle Leonard in Paris. He was living with his third wife on the outskirts of the Marais district. He had lived in America with his second, north of San Francisco on a small hill in the middle of the woods. Hummingbirds came flying to the big window looking out on his terrace, to drink the sugared water that he had hung under the roof in little containers. They beat their wings so fast that you could see how swiftly time passes. He felt that was reassuring. When he looked out of the window there was only woodland, and a little further down the slope they could see the eastern banks of the little lake behind the cedars. In summer there was often mist in the valley. The last time I had seen my uncle, three years ago, he told me that back in Paris with his third wife, he could forget everything even better; at good moments he could forget his own past, and sometimes himself. Perhaps Uncle Leonard would show me aspects of Paris not to be found on any picture postcard, the Charcuterie Panzer and the goods on display, not standing outside shops as they did here but hanging from the roofs on ropes. He would eat fresh mussels with me. I'd meet his two American sons, who pursued various professions, doing a little of this and that without fully understanding anything, he said. That's what freedom makes of people, he said again and again, looking at me half pityingly, half enviously, because I seemed to have no freedom at all, and there was nothing for it but to embark on a scientific career. So close to my journey's end, I didn't feel the least inclination to take any more orders. But I was not going to do anything stupid. I sat down.

'You're a chemist?'

'You know I am.'

'You worked at the Academy of Sciences for four years.'

'I started there after finishing my studies, yes. But I haven't worked there for two years. I work for the Dorotheenstadt cemetery.'

'The cemetery?'

'Recently, yes. Because I applied for an exit permit.' I was surprised to find how little these border officials seemed to know. I had been asked the same questions several times in the last few months – and other people I knew had been asked them too. I knew it from their own mouths in some cases, in others I could only guess.

The uniformed man looked on through the files.

'Stand up again.'

'You want me to stand up?'

'That's what we just said, yes. And no questions. We ask the questions.'

I stood up. My skirt was sticking to my behind.

'You applied for an exit permit in April the year before last. From May onwards, limits were placed on your contacts. You were carrying secrets?'

'No. I mean yes, another limit *was* to be imposed, but I wasn't carrying secrets.'

'Our information differs. Are you trying to lie to us?'

'No.'

'What were you working on at the Academy of Sciences?'

My shoes were pinching; I stepped from foot to foot and looked around.

'Are you going to be much longer about it?'

'What am I supposed to tell you? I've forgotten. And what I haven't forgotten I have to keep quiet about, and you wouldn't understand the things I don't have to keep quiet about anyway. You're not scientists, gentlemen.'

'Oh, very clever.' The official closed the file lying in front of him and whispered to the senior officer present, who was sitting just behind him.

'Take her away.' The senior officer nodded to a tall man with an unusually small head. The man was so tall that his trousers had clearly had to be let down; the dark green at the hem of the legs was like a border. The tall man took my upper arm and led me into a nearby room. Also without any windows.

'Where are my children?'

'Didn't you hear? We ask the questions.'

I would have liked to sit down here, but there was no chair and no table in the room, and I wasn't going to sit down on the floor in my skirt in front of this servant of the state. I looked at my watch. It was just after six. Aleksei and Katya would be getting hungry. Waiting without knowing what they were waiting for.

When I looked at my watch again it was ten past six, and then I was looking at it about every three minutes, the last time at five to seven, when an official came in with a woman in uniform.

'Any incidents?' The official looked enquiringly at the tall man.

'No incidents,' he said from high up in the air. By way of a salute, the very tall man put his hand to his small head.

'Get undressed.' The older official nodded to me with relish.

'What?'

'When you've taken off your clothes you can give them to my colleague here.' His female colleague looked at me without expression. No names were given. For a moment I wondered what a guard like mine, a young if tall but small-headed officer, was called, what department he belonged to, what rank he might hold. Perhaps his actual name was Hauptmann, captain, his small head and low rank notwithstanding. But it must be possible to avoid such a confusing name, it could be changed by law, thus solving the problem, because a name like that would clearly be a professional disadvantage, making him look ridiculous, a disadvantage intolerable in a world of rank and order. The older official snapped at me, 'Are you going to take much longer?'

'Why should I get undressed?'

'We ask the questions here, not you,' repeated the tall man, with an encouraging grin.

'What, get undressed in front of you?' The border officers here probably learned only four or five sentences to be used as occasion demanded. Sentences that concealed their identities, but were enough for issuing the necessary instructions. I almost laughed.

'Do you see anyone else here?' The tall man with the small head stroked the little black pistol nestling close to his body. The laugh that burst out of me at this couldn't be suppressed. 'You want me to . . . ?'

'Come on, come on, we're only human beings like you.' The older officer sounded bored.

'Human beings?' I laughed nervously.

The door opened, and another uniformed man came in.

'What's up now? Where are her things?' His voice sounded hoarse.

'She's being difficult.'

'Shall we fetch reinforcements?'

'No.' I took my shoes off first. 'No.' Then my dress. The woman officer held out her hand, and I had to take the things over to her.

'Everything.'

I could do without another *Are you going to take much longer?* I decided not to think at all for a moment, took off my tights and underwear and gave those to the woman officer as well. I arranged the tights neatly before draping them over her arm.

'Your jewellery too.'

I took off my necklace and handed it to the woman officer, who remained entirely impassive. And why would she feel involved in any of this?

'Your watch.' The tall man with the little head was stroking his pistol. 'And your glasses.'

I looked at the watch once more: ten past seven. They didn't have much time left. Suddenly I was sure that they would have been told to let us cross the border before midnight. Otherwise they would be breaking their own rules. There must be treaties between the two states making such stipulations.

'Your ring.'

I looked at the uniformed man as if I hadn't understood him. He pointed to my hand. I looked at my hand and shook my head.

'The ring.'

'I can't, it won't come off.'

'Any ring will come off. Soap!'

I shook my head harder than ever. An officer left the room, presumably to get some soap.

'If soap won't do it, there are other methods here,' the uniformed man whispered to me. I pretended not to hear him. I hadn't taken the ring off since Vassily's death, not when I went to bed, not when I went swimming, not when I was washing up, not when I was turning over earth in the cemetery and pulling up weeds, not when I washed my hands afterwards. Never.

The other officer came back with a piece of hard soap.

'Are you going to take much longer?'

'Please don't.'

The officer reached for my hand and tugged at the ring.

'Please don't.' My voice was strangely calm, as if it didn't belong to me. I clenched my hand into a fist. The officer tried to open it up again, pushing each finger upwards separately.

'Please. Don't.'

In slow motion, I saw the ring being pressed, pushed, forced up my finger bit by bit, and disappearing into the officer's hand. The soap was not used. I could feel neither the ring nor my hand. A little way off I heard a voice: 'Please don't. Please don't. Please don't.' The older officer, the one still standing by the door, the one who usually gave orders, must have been imitating me.

'You stay here,' he told the younger man, so that the boy would keep an eye on me. Then he signed to his woman colleague, who followed him with my things. The ring hadn't even left an impression on my middle finger. The boy was leaning beside the door, and looked as if he were enjoying himself. I suddenly thought of my brother, who had wanted nothing more before his adolescence than to wear a uniform, preferably a police or military uniform, but he was also fascinated by firefighters, pilots and sailors. He liked gold stars better than the silver or red ones. His professional ambitions were turned exclusively in that direction. I am sure he would have made a bad policeman. Not because of any inability to give orders and intervene spontaneously in a situation, those things came easily to him, but he found it hard to take orders, and wouldn't tolerate them from anyone but my mother. So he was obliged to become an unskilled milling-machine operator. The boy here obeyed orders only too willingly, not least if they entailed keeping an eye on a naked woman. His eyes flickered restlessly over my body and its surroundings, they were so tenaciously watchful that I couldn't even have sunk unnoticed into the ground in my shame. I measured him up. Small head. Young. Very tall. I couldn't see any more striking details, nothing unique and individual about him. Maybe his skin was pale, but anyone's skin would look pale in that light. I wasn't even to know his name; I could only guess at it. His rank remained a secret; knowing it would have helped me to get my bearings. Only his outward appearance, to which I had been exposed for some time now, created what was certainly an unintended sense of familiarity. My nakedness seemed to embarrass him more than me. Suddenly the place turned pitch dark, and then the light came on again.

'Sorry,' said the tall boy, hardly able to conceal his amusement. He must have leaned back against the light switch. I folded my arms again.

After a while the door was opened, and the older officer said, 'Come this way.' The woman officer appeared in the doorway, presumably accompanying us for the sake of decency. To preserve discipline and good order. She had brought a hand towel for me, but it was too small to cover everything, my breasts and my private parts, and I would also have liked to cover the large mole just above the back of my knee, which I hated and found embarrassing. I wanted them to see that even less than my breasts and private parts. Our way led down the corridor into another room, where a man in a greyish-blue apron and glasses was waiting. He was putting a tube with an angle in it on a shelf, perhaps he was a handyman who kept the place in order and did repairs. 'There she is,' said the older officer, of me.

The man in the grey-blue apron didn't look at me, just wearily indicated the chair in the room with his head and told me to sit down on it.

'Why?'

'Routine.'

The chair was like a kind of throne, with broad armrests and a firmly fixed, high base.

'Up there.'

'I need the lavatory first.'

'What, now?'

'Yes.'

'The toilets are at the other end of the corridor, you can't go there now.' The officer was staring thoughtfully at my breasts, which wouldn't stay covered by the towel.

'There's a bucket in the corner,' said the man in the grey-blue apron, pointing to a white enamel bucket.

I squatted over the bucket, the towel slipped to the floor, and with one hand I clung to the nearest end of it, as if that connection made a difference to my nakedness.

My eyes fell on the one man who had come into the room without my noticing. I couldn't decide whether this was the original right-hand man or left-hand man. That made it easier not to take his presence personally. The woman officer handed me some cellulose wadding.

'Now, get up there.'

The upholstery of the throne was torn in several places, and foam stuffing was coming out of it. The foam was losing its consistency, fragmenting on the surface where it came into contact with air and fluids, anything rubbing it made little pieces of foam flake off. I couldn't stop thinking. I thought to myself: Some women have had very different experiences. In the war. I looked around the room and saw one of the black panes opposite me; its frame was set flush with the wall, so that it could hardly have been a window to the outside world. Anyway, it was in the right angle between the door and the corridor along which we had come, so that it must be more likely to look into another room.

How dark was the night outside by now? The room had no other windows. I could see no clock, no instrument however small or improvised for measuring the passage of time, let alone showing the location of the room. On a shelf beside me, over an arm's length away, lay various instruments side by side, some looking like syringes, empty syringes of various sizes, syringes filled with transparent fluid, syringes filled with bluish fluid, a small pair of forceps, a kind of knife reminiscent of a razor, two pairs of scissors, one with blunt ends, finally something that looked like an ice-cream scoop, but a little smaller, and needles. Only we were not at war with anyone. At least, until now I hadn't entirely believed in the way the word *war* was used these days. Or in the adjective *cold* that went with it. What did that mean, cold? I had gooseflesh, but cold? I wasn't cold. I felt nothing. Even my feet, now sticking up in the air, were numb. By war, I imagined something different, something outside my experience, and what was said about it conjured up only curiously disjointed images. My eyes lingered on the black pane. There couldn't be anything behind it. Just as the copper palace could be a stage set, the wrappings of a dream with only a great void inside, a large, empty space, filled only with air and a few iron struts that served to hold up the scenery. Sand on the floor. If red carpets were laid on the way into it, and ministers of state walked over them and disappeared from the visible world, then as they went on down underground passages they reached no better place than the blue-green vaults of State Security. And their faces paled there, and fear made its way so far into them that even on returning to their own distant countries they did not want to talk about the inside of the palace. Memory failed them. But here things were still in working order, unlike the structure of the foam stuffing sticking to my thigh.

I really had not noticed, until now, that we were living through a war. I felt ashamed of myself for that. But it was certainly not shame they were looking for inside me. Instruments were thrust back and forth. Was there going to be a hot war? I couldn't help thinking of my grandmother, who three years ago, at the age of eighty-seven and after crossing the border several times without any trouble, had been stopped at the border the day before Hanukkah, taken into a small room, told to undress and open her mouth, so that all her crowns and bridgework could be removed under a similar pretext to the one they were now using on me. Only they must have been hoping to find material from some Western secret service that she was presumably trying to smuggle into the country, whereas in my case they were certainly afraid I might have been spying, for Western science, on the laughable results of their research. The masterpieces of Professor Schumann, doctor of dentistry, were destroyed bit by bit in less than two hours, and then my grandmother was made to wait for several hours more before finally being sent home with no false teeth and a box full of the ruins of her crowns. Perhaps my grandmother hadn't told me the rest of it. It must be a burning pain, or at least my brain was telling me something of that kind. Burning although I didn't feel it burning. And why would this man in the blue-grey apron go carefully with me? He was a handyman, not a lover. And as he was obviously sure what he was looking for, but couldn't find it, he took his time over his investigation. The burning pain went away, but it was as if my head had been placed in a pair of metal pincers, so that I couldn't see anything lower than my navel. And it was not a search on which the handyman here was engaged. He was constructing something inside me, adding something, making me the carrier of his DIY work. They wouldn't be letting me go, they were sending me in as a Trojan Horse.

After what happened to his mother, Uncle Leonard had sent her a short letter. In the first sentence he expressed his horror. He devoted the few sentences that followed to wondering why on earth she had returned to Germany, and to the Russian sector at that. She had grown up in Bavaria, so on that point she couldn't even argue that she had gone back in search of the scenes of her childhood, although, as he said, she kept trying to do so. No, he wrote, he could not understand the step she had taken. It was no way to let people treat you. And he was asking her, once more, he said, to come to him in Paris, where he would buy her a little apartment. He would be glad if she would phone him and tell him when she was arriving, so that he could meet her at the airport.

But my grandmother didn't phone him. She showed us the letter and smiled a tired smile. He's forgotten how to write German, she said wearily. Can't even get the spelling quite right, look. His own mother tongue gone, just like that. Oh dear. What would I do in Paris? That's what she asked us. We didn't have any answer, and didn't try to find one, so it was easy for her to end any conversation about the kind of life she lived here and would live there with that remark. I hadn't seen Uncle Leonard since he wrote that letter. And if I really thought about it, I doubted whether he would come to Berlin again. It had been a long time since he last came there, longer than the time between any of his earlier visits. Perhaps he was afraid that he too might be drawn physically closer to the family. Although my grandmother was still alive, she would never travel all the way to see her son again. In the first few months after the incident, she used every opportunity of going to Wilmersdorf in the West, where Dr Schumann junior, with instructions from his old father, tried to reconstruct what Dr Schumann senior had for decades considered his masterpiece, until he gave up and my grandmother had dentures made. I thought of what Uncle Leonard had written to my grandmother: it was no way to let people treat you.

'Relax,' snapped the man whose head now surfaced from between my legs. 'Relax, will you, or we'll never get anywhere.'

I didn't want to find out where he wanted to get. Maybe the man searching about inside me had only been looking for that flicker of fear, and had found it and torn it out, hence the burning sensation that I couldn't feel any more. A scraping and tearing sound came, muted, to my ears. I could see the bald patch at the back of the man's head between my legs, until he straightened up with a smile on his face, not a mischievous smile, no, he hadn't stolen anything out of me, it was more as if he had achieved something. He put my legs together and turned away to rearrange his instruments, apparently deep in thought; perhaps it was satisfaction that I saw in his face, or perhaps disappointment as he silently and slowly put instruments back in their containers, making further arrangements just as if he were waiting for the next person on whom he could try out his routine. He took three cotton wool balls out of a packet wrapped in cellophane lying on the lower shelf, put two small containers of fluid and two tins with lids on at a certain distance from them, pushed them back and forth, until he remembered, glancing at my knees, that I was still sitting on the chair naked, with my legs together, and obviously waiting for the instruction that he now gave me. 'You can go away.' Or perhaps he meant that the officers were to go away with me. My arms and legs, even part of my buttocks and my labia had gone to sleep. One of the officers helped me out of the pincer-shaped depression that had been holding my head down.

Back in the room without windows, a table or a chair, I faced the grinning youth again. I felt he was almost on the point of introducing himself: My name is Hauptmann, and maybe he would have given me a little bow, not without making his head look even smaller, and I would have rewarded this approach with silence. Or rather with deafness, but to him it would have been silence. I wasn't interested any more in his rank and the disadvantages that he might be contending with. The young officer enjoyed his profession. The pistol seemed not entirely unconnected with this enjoyment; he patted its butt with what were certainly damp hands. After a while my clothes were returned. A dress with a pattern of large flowers, pale sandals with small heels already beginning to tilt sideways, a lace-trimmed bra that my grandmother had brought back from the West a few years ago, a plain pair of panties, and the nylon tights that Uncle Leonard had sent me from Paris. For fear of spoiling them I had kept them in my stocking drawer until the time for packing came, finally putting them on for the first time this morning, carefully in spite of my haste when I was getting up. The woman officer held out a white plastic bowl containing my watch, necklace, earrings and ring. I put everything on. I didn't feel the ring. Or the watch. Or the tights. Or myself. I looked at the time. It was twenty past eight.

'My children will be hungry.'

No one answered me.

'Follow us.' I followed them.

The two officers took me into a room with a small cubicle in it. A man in a white coat was waiting there. His orders were brief. Dress, tights, underwear. I was to get undressed again. As if organic fibres interfered with X-rays. Shoes, watch, jewellery. I was to stand in the tiny cubicle with my heels on the red line. The door was closed. I couldn't see anything, no X-ray device, no pictures. Maybe they were checking that the handyman had done his job properly. I thought of secret reports of the huge amount of radiation used in cubicles like this. But all I felt was the plastic flooring under my bare feet. The door was opened. My clothes were lying over the woman officer's arm. I didn't ask any more questions. I did as I was told until I was ordered to follow the officers again. We went out into the open air.

It was a good deal cooler now. Dark. I looked for Gerd's car. Lukewarm water was trickling from my eyes, and I wiped it away. My shoes pinched. I could feel my watch again, and the ring.

Everything seemed to be in its proper place. Gerd was sitting in his car, had wound the window down and was blowing smoke my way. I saw Katya and Aleksei sitting on the back seat, quarrelling. They both sighed theatrically as I got in.

'At last, Mama. We always have to wait ages for you.'

'But now for those *pommes frites*,' said Gerd.

I turned round to my children and felt like hugging them tight, but there was too much space between us.

'Are you two all right?'

'Yes, but now for those *pommes frites*,' said Katya, imitating the way Gerd said it very well, and with a certain pride that I'd noticed quite often in her recently; she probably didn't know what *pommes frites* were, but she liked using the term.

'Mama, they asked really funny questions. They wanted to know if we were going to have Gerd's surname.' Katya tapped her forehead.

'And?'

'I didn't say anything. Did you?'

Aleksei shook his head. 'No.' He pressed his glasses firmly down on his nose. Not much to be done about the fit, the optician had said regretfully, models of frames have been like that for the last few years, and his is the best fit available, there was once a model that might have fitted better, it was called the Dove of Peace, but it went out of use years ago, a real shame, and he has such a small nose. No, the frame for girls is just as wide over the bridge of the nose, the only difference is that it's pink.

'We simply didn't say anything, and we said we didn't know anything either. It's a secret, right?'

'A secret, yes.' I smiled.

'But are you two really getting married?'

'Who knows?' said Gerd, trying to join in this conversation.

'No, I've already told you so.' Not for nothing had I explained

28

the difference between wrong answers and better answers to Katya and Aleksei.

'They wanted me to get undressed.'

I turned abruptly round and reached for Aleksei's hand again. 'What?'

'Yes.' He sounded bored. 'They thought we couldn't take all those new underclothes with us. They wanted to know if we'd bought a lot of new stuff at the Strausberger Platz on purpose.'

'Yes, that's right. They wanted to keep my underclothes as well. They thought there was sure to be plenty for us over on the other side.' Katya chuckled.

'Did they examine you?'

'Examine us? We're not ill.' They both shook their heads.

'No, only they thought it was funny that we were wearing two sets of underclothes. It was funny, too. They kept one set.'

'They kept both mine.' Aleksei pushed up his sweater so that we could see his bare stomach.

Gerd drove at walking speed past the border guards, who signalled with their guns, one after the other, that we could drive on. We went through the border building, and as expected the bridge lay ahead. A simple structure, much smaller and shorter than I had imagined it.

'Are the cases back in the boot?'

'Of course – did you think they'd keep them?' Gerd laughed at me.

The barrier was raised; a soldier waved us past. Thud, thud went the car as its wheels went over a tarred surface, a dull thud, thud. I guessed at the depths below. When I looked to the right out of my window, I saw the beams of the headlights pulsating on the black water. 'I wonder if the water's deep?'

'There's no water down there. Only railway tracks.' Gerd turned on the radio. *When the wicked carried us away in captivity, required from us a song. Now how shall we sing the Lord's song in a strange land?*

I looked round. A soldier was closing the barrier again behind us.

On the other side of the bridge stood brightly lit huts. A border officer wearing what had to be a Western uniform came out of the door of one and signed to us to stop. Gerd turned the radio down. This officer also wanted to see our papers.

'Good evening. Thank you, yes. These are the children's papers?' The officer looked through them. 'Where will you be reporting to?'

'Reporting to?' Puzzled, I looked at Gerd.

'Marienfelde – we're going to the reception camp there first.' Gerd gave the thumbs-up sign, as if it were something secretly agreed with the officer in advance.

'Although the family's already been reunited?' The officer couldn't repress a smile. It looked conspiratorial. 'So you'll be staying in Berlin for now?'

The idea that Gerd might be in league with these men and the guards on the other side of the bridge suddenly seemed to me very natural. It would explain why Gerd said, so confidently, that we were going to a camp. We wouldn't have needed to do that if we were Gerd's real family. Gerd's home would be open to us, soap and everything freely available. But Gerd's apartment in Schöneberg was small, not even two rooms, as he said emphatically, indicating that a room you had to walk through to reach the other didn't count as a self-contained room. He could and would happily take me in, but not my children. The officer took a step back.

'Wait a moment – can I use the toilet in there?'

'Of course.' The officer opened the car door for Gerd and closed it after him. As they walked away, I saw him put his arm round Gerd's shoulders. The two of them disappeared inside one of the huts. I slid a little further down in my seat. The second hand of the car clock jerked and stayed put; obviously an impulse was reaching it but something prevented it from moving on. The officer came back with Gerd, both of them talking and laughing, then they stopped, put their heads close together, and a small flame lit up their faces. When they straightened their necks again, they were drawing on cigarettes, and they walked on to the car. The officer looked into my side of the car, gave me a friendly nod and handed me the papers. 'Well, good luck and safe journey.' He raised his hand in farewell, and just as I was thinking he was about to wave, his hand moved, tapped the bonnet, and he held the open palm up to Gerd as a greeting.

Gerd turned on the ignition. 'Guess what, I was at school with him in Wiesbaden, and now we meet again like this at the border crossing.' He turned the radio up to full volume, looked for another station and sang along: *There we sat down, yea, we wept, when we remembered Zion.* I was overcome by a great weariness, I felt dizzy, I tried to keep my eyes open and suppressed yawn after yawn. *By the rivers of Babylon, there we sat down.* All the stations seemed to be playing the same song.

'Mama, I'm hungry.'

Krystyna Jabłonovska holds her brother's hand

I heard the familiar grunting from the top bunk of the bed; my father was breathing regularly, it was just that he seemed to be choking on air from time to time. His breath stopped briefly now and then, making me think he didn't have to breathe at all. At the age of seventy-eight you don't have to breathe regularly, you don't have to do anything any more. It was still dark outside. But the light of the lamps that stood at brief intervals between the blocks, so that the camp could be seen even by night and in darkness, was enough for me to undress and pack Jerzy's clean underpants in the bag. There wasn't much I could do for Jerzy. I wasn't allowed to take him food or anything to drink in the hospital. I had once smuggled in some of our sausage rations for him, but he didn't want to eat the sausage, and the nurses were cross when they found it in his locker. He didn't wear the underpants, but I washed them all the same from week to week. Quietly, so that my father wouldn't wake and call down from the bed, 'Krystyna, you clumsy thing,' I opened the door. Most of the people in the apartment seemed to be still asleep. I didn't meet anyone on the way to the porter's lodge either. It was too soon for schoolchildren to be up and about; hardly anyone left the camp so early.

When I reached the hospital dawn was breaking.

'Can't you at least put on a proper pair of pyjamas? Why do you think I brought you clean clothes?' Jerzy's clothes cupboard

33

was chaotic. I put his ironed underpants in the drawer. In between the shirts and pyjamas that he hadn't worn once so far, I found a packet of cigarettes and a German women's magazine.

'Do you read this sort of thing?'

'Why would I be reading it? It was lying about the waiting room, so I took it with me.'

'But why?'

'There are beautiful women in it, that's why.'

'Beautiful women,' I said, putting the magazine in an empty drawer under the pyjamas. It looked to me more like a secret, and Jerzy didn't have any secrets from me. Maybe he did in the past, in the years of his marriage, but he could hardly have kept anything secret since he moved in with Father and me again.

I didn't want to watch him cleaning his fingernails by running one of them under the others.

'Come over here.' The manicure set was in the drawer of the bedside locker; I sat down on the chair beside his bed again and reached for his hand.

'No, don't.' Jerzy tried to pull his hand away, but I held it firmly, together with the cannula that had a plaster over it to keep it in place better. Pulling the hand away would have hurt him so much that he kept still. His skin was white and cracked, and reminded me of the bark of an old tree. The skin over his veins was covered with marks where injections had gone in.

'What about your pyjamas?'

'No one here wears pyjamas. Look around the place, Krystyna. Do you see any of these men in pyjamas?'

I turned and looked at the men sitting up in their beds, every one of them wearing the same white nightshirts.

'So?' I was cutting Jerzy's nails close to the skin with the scissors. 'You don't have to wear those things just because they do.'

Jerzy did not reply to that. He was chewing a toothpick and

examining the nails of his other hand. Out of the corner of my eye I saw a nurse change the nightshirt that the man in the bed next to him was wearing. She rubbed his back with alcoholic liniment and massaged the man, who was quite young and whose veins stood out, tinged with blue, all over his body. The touch of her hands made him whimper quietly.

'Is that why?' I whispered to Jerzy, but he seemed totally absorbed in the contemplation of his nails. 'Is that why you don't want to wear pyjamas? Jerzy, tell me.'

Jerzy looked at me with a blank expression on his face. 'What did you say?'

'Don't go acting as if you can't hear properly again. You can hear perfectly well, Jerzy, perfectly well. You want her to undress you, that's why you want to wear this silly hospital nightshirt. So that she'll undress you, not for any other reason.'

'What's Father doing?'

'What do you think he's doing? He rests all day. From morning to evening.'

'You ought to go for walks with him.'

'You think so? I'd rather come and see you, Jerzy. If he's not going to move about of his own accord I'm not going to help him.'

'Ouch! Careful what you're doing.'

'I am being careful, Jerzy. That's an ingrown fingernail.'

'I told you to be careful what you're doing.' Jerzy tried to pull his hand away from me, but I held it tightly.

'The nail,' I said, cutting his little fingernail. Then I tried to inject patience into my voice. 'I can change your things too, Jerzy, if you need help.' He had had heavy bluish rings around his eyes since he'd been in here, and his face seemed to have fallen in. So they were letting him go hungry. 'I can do it. Just say the word and I'll change your things. You don't need those nurses, Jerzy, you have me.' I heard the wooden clatter of the nurse's clogs behind me as she crossed the room, calling out brightly to an old man, 'Well, and how are we today?' I heard her shaking out a blanket, and I saw Jerzy's eyes following her all round the room, ignoring me and my offer.

'You're avoiding the subject,' he said, without deigning to give me a glance.

I cut his nail so close to the fingertip that it must have hurt him. 'What subject?'

'You know what I mean.' He was attentively following the clatter of the clogs behind my back.

I didn't go on asking. After all, I knew he didn't mean my concern or lack of it for Father. He meant that his sister was wasting herself and her life. He disapproved of any kind of waste. It annoyed him that I'd sold my cello instead of making myself into what he thought I was capable of. Not just capable of it, as he had been saying all along, he thought it was my duty to make the most of my abilities. But little as he wanted my concern for him, I wanted his for me even less. 'We didn't leave Stettin in order to –'

'Why don't you go, Krystyna? Leave me on my own. Look, the nurses are getting supper ready.'

'I'll stay. Just a moment longer.' I held Jerzy's thin, cold hand firmly even though he was trying to pull it away. For the first time in our lives I was stronger than he was. 'They aren't giving you proper food, Jerzy, I can see that. They're letting you go hungry. I can tell from the way you look.'

'Go away, please. Go away. Go back to Father in the camp, why don't you? He gets scared in the dark.'

'I know, but it's always dark in autumn. If I wasn't going to leave him alone I couldn't come to see you at all in winter,' I said, trying not to sound threatening or pleading, and I felt my own fear of leaving Jerzy here in the hospital to the nurses, and the day and the night, and the drip they had attached him to at the beginning of the week, my fear of the way home in the dark and the neon-lit double-decker bus, home to the camp because our other home wasn't ours any more. Although the house would certainly be well kept and still standing upright in its place, not at all impressed by our absence. It was countless kilometres away now, two borders further east, on the other side of the River Oder. Home was out of reach. I had to keep telling Father so, to get him to remember it, and to shed a few tears.

Jerzy sighed.

'Why do you always sigh so loudly?' I asked. I didn't want to hear him sighing.

Jerzy sighed again.

'Please don't.' I held his hand tightly.

'I'm not sighing, I'm groaning. That's what I'm here for. It makes breathing easier.' Jerzy laughed. 'What's that?' He looked in alarm at our hands, withdrawing his own hand with all his strength, and I opened mine. The nails I had cut came into view. Yellow half-moons. I nodded and put my fur coat on. After all the years in which first my mother and then I had worn it, its lustre was dulled. The fur left fine black hairs behind on the sheets of Jerzy's bed. I picked the hairs off the sheets with one hand while I went on holding Jerzy's fingers with the other.

'Is there anything you'd like?' I stroked his cold, gleaming forehead.

'I'd like you to go away.' Jerzy turned his head to the window. The beds of his seven companions in the ward were reflected in its panes. I let go of his hand.

When I opened the door into the corridor, the blonde nurse was standing in the niche in front of a large double door with her back to me. The greenish light from the emergency exit made her hair shine, and she was straightening her underclothes beneath her nurse's coat.

I wished her, 'Good evening.'

'Good evening to you, too,' she murmured back, and she bent and adjusted her stockings. Reluctantly, I went along the corridor and down the stairs. The banister rail felt sticky under my hand. Down in the entrance area the little cafe had already closed, or I would have sat down to eat an ice cream, a brightly coloured one on a stick, and I'd have drunk a hot chocolate with it. But I did have a small green bottle of fizzy lemonade that I'd bought off the shelf when the cafe was still open, and I let the sweet lemonade run down my throat. I licked the last few drops out of the neck of the bottle with the tip of my tongue.

The main lights in the cafe were switched off, and the only illumination came from the chilled shelf and above the cash desk. I heard the murmur of the chilling unit through the thick glass pane. My feet felt heavy and my tongue was furred; I could still taste the coffee that the nurse had offered to me instead of Jerzy. I drank Jerzy's coffee every afternoon, with two extra sugar lumps. At regular intervals I heard a pushing sound, wood on wood. The cleaning lady was making her way along the corridor, with her long-handled scrubbing brush moving alternately from left to right over the skirting boards. Her cart squealed as she pushed it a little further forward. I went aimlessly up one of the back staircases again to the first floor. There were trays on the windowsills opposite many of the doors, with plates and teapots on them. So as not to be discovered close to Jerzy's door, I went along the corridor in the other direction. A door might open, letting a doctor out. I would be able to stop him and ask how Jerzy was doing. The thoughts of the doctors on duty in the wards were elsewhere, but they always said something like: You'll have your brother home for Christmas. It was this hope that had drawn us to the Federal Republic, equipped with information about forebears of German origin. For no other reason. The papers had been expensive.

Ahead of me, the nurse pushed a door open with her elbow and carried a tray out of the room. She placed the tray on the windowsill and bent over it, lifting a lid. With her fingertips, she took a handful of grapes from the dish under the lid and put it in the pocket of her white coat. Then she tore a bag open, tipped her head back and poured the contents of the bag into her mouth. She took no notice of me. I would have liked a doctor to come out of one of the doors so that I could ask him a question. But no doctor was going to show up while I was pacing up and down the corridor. Tired out, I tightened the scarf I was wearing over my head.

The drizzling rain outside slowed the cars down. A class of schoolchildren carrying skates sat in the double-decker bus. There had been no frosts yet, so they must be on their way to an artificial ice rink. The children were pushing and shoving each other, sometimes in my direction, but I looked out of the window. One child told another to watch out for the old lady. Since there was no one else on the top deck of the bus but the children and their two teachers, the child must have meant me. He opened a bag of sweets. They rolled all over the bus, and the children scrabbled for the glittering sweets on the floor. I bent down, without any haste, and fished up one that had come to rest right beside my foot. The sweet was soft and stuck to my teeth and gums.

The mere thought of going straight back to the camp, rather than taking the long way round, and then persuading my father to eat supper made me uneasy. I had no money; there was only a two-mark piece for emergencies in my wallet.

When I got out at Marienfelder Allee, I crossed the road to the little Edeka market. I looked at the magazines until a saleswoman told me I ought to buy them before I read them. I stood in front of the display of household goods and compared two bottle openers. One had a plastic handle and cost a lot. The party ware, cardboard plates and white plastic beakers, seemed to me much too expensive for its shoddy quality. Suddenly the background music stopped.

It was just before six. I put the empty shopping basket on top of the tower of other baskets and went back out into the drizzle.

From outside, the camp looked like a modern fortress. Orange street lights illuminated the new building, which had small windows set in the smooth facade. Most of the inmates were in their apartments at this time of the evening, eating supper. Their plates were white, their cups had little roses on the sides, the teapots were made of silvery metal.

The porter stopped me at the barrier. He was a new porter, and it was the first time I had seen him.

'Where are you going?'

'I live here.'

'Name?'

'Jabłonovska. Krystyna Jabłonovska.'

He looked through his card index and asked to see my pass.

I showed him the temporary pass, not without pride; it was adorned by a passport photo in colour. When I'd registered I had been told that I could change my name, or at least the spelling of my first name. Young people often did. At over fifty, however, I felt too old for such changes. Krystyna was fine so far as I was concerned.

The porter asked what was in my bag.

'No one's ever wanted to know that before,' I replied, and told him it contained my brother's dirty washing. He was in hospital, I added, and I had been to see him. The porter nodded. Then I went on my way, past the first two blocks and up the second flight of stairs you came to in the third. The damp air in the stairwell smelled of humanity.

Before going into our room I took refuge in the kitchen. The plastic covering the hanging cupboard was probably meant to look like wood; it was the same with the cooker and the sink. The fridge was empty. Someone had been looting my provisions again.

'Krystyna!' As if he had heard my quiet entrance into the apartment, even though he was hard of hearing, as if he could smell me, or had been waiting for my appearance for hours, calling my name again and again at intervals, his hollow voice came from our room. I took a deep breath.

My father was lying on the bed, like Oblomov on the stove. In the darkness of the room I heard the metal bunk bed squeal, and reached for the light switch. He didn't seem to have moved from the spot since I had left him that morning.

'So there you are.' He turned over onto his side so that he could see me better. 'Have you brought anything to drink?'

'Lemonade.' I took the bottle out of my bag and put it on the little table between the two bunk beds. I hung the bag over the arm of the chair.

'I don't like lemonade,' said my father, in a tone of surprise, as if he were saying it for the first time and as if I didn't already know that he didn't like it.

I had difficulty in unscrewing the top. The fine bubbles tickled my nose, and I breathed in the aroma of sweet lemon, then put the bottle to my mouth and took a hefty swig.

'You fat girl,' grunted my father behind me, and I felt like reminding him that I was getting old, and it was none of his business how fat or thin I was. But I said nothing. My father was lucky we hadn't simply left him behind in our big house in Stettin.

'You've eaten all your brother's food, that's why he's so ill.' It was a long time since I'd been able to take my father seriously.

He thought that cancer was caused by starvation, and people got it from not having enough to eat.

Later I lay on the bottom bunk of the bed, below him, and stared into the darkness. I heard him saying quietly, 'What a fat girl you are,' but before he had finished saying 'girl' a curious kind of laughter crept into his throat, a diabolical laughter intended to condemn me to an infernal fate. He dreamed and talked in his sleep. My eyes were wide open when the door of the room was opened and someone switched the light on. Above me, I saw the metal springs of the top bunk bed and the brown mattress with its beige stripes. For a moment I doubted whether my father was lying up there and whether he had spoken. I turned to the wall and looked at the tiny places where the paint was lifting off it. Right at eye level, a previous occupant had drawn a penis in thick, black felt pen. Over the last few weeks I had abstracted all kinds of cleaning materials from work, putting them in my bag, and had tried to remove the graffiti here.

'Sorry,' babbled the voice of a neighbour who had obviously found the wrong door. He went away again, and I had to get up to switch the light off.

How John Bird eavesdrops on his own wife and listens to someone else as well

Even from the garage I could hear her laughter through the open window. I looked through the gap between the window frame and the curtain. Eunice had put her bare feet up on the low table beside the sofa, and was holding the telephone receiver wedged between shoulder and chin. She had rolled-up paper tissues between her toes. Recently she had taken to wearing black nails. There was paper on the low table in front of her, and she was holding three pencils at once in her right hand. Eunice was sitting with her back to me and couldn't see me. My key stuck in the lock, so I had to knock at the door. Her laughter was full-throated, like something breaking out of her, something she'd had difficulty in restraining, a wild beast, a captive animal, and I couldn't help knocking harder, competing with her laughter, until I heard a window closing behind me, and out of the corner of my eye I saw our elderly neighbour, only a shadow, but I knew she was watching me even if she couldn't make anything out. My knuckles hurt; I lit a cigarette and pressed the doorbell. Eunice didn't hear it; she laughed and told whoever was on the line that she couldn't believe it, she just could not believe it. She must be talking to Sally or her sister. She phoned one or other of them almost daily, assuring them that she would soon be back, and I would some-times find her crying when I came home, sitting on the sofa and crying. Only last week I'd told her that now she was twenty-seven she didn't have to rely on her mother, me or anyone else to make decisions for her; she could go back to Knoxville any time she liked. A single glance had shown me how much distance she was putting between us. How could I think of such a thing, she had screamed, adding that I was wrong if I assumed she expected other people to tell her what to do, and she had kicked the low table by the sofa.

But today she was laughing again, so loud that she didn't hear the doorbell or my knocking, and I had to ring a second time. She was laughing uninhibitedly, entirely out of control. The key was turned; she had locked the door on the inside, and now she let me in, speaking into the receiver with her back to me. Eunice disappeared into the large living room. One black nail remained stuck on the pale carpet. As she moved away I asked quietly what there was for supper. As I might have expected, she didn't answer but just went on laughing down the phone, then she suddenly shrieked, and pointed to the TV set, where the sound was muted, and told the receiver what was happening on the screen.

Taking my shoes off, I said, 'I'm going into the kitchen, Eunice.' At least, I wasn't actually saying it to her, I was saying it merely in order to know I had said it. In the kitchen I got a beer out of the fridge and put a piece of dry bread into the toaster. She was laughing and laughing. My comparison with the wild animal is a lame one, I thought, there'd never be room for so many wild animals in Eunice, there wouldn't be room in her for one, not a single one. A great sense of peace spread through me. A sense of satisfaction. I stood there munching dry white toast and telling myself it was my own fault, I could simply have gone in and admired her nails, or the wild animals that had fled out of her, passing over her hands and the coloured pencils, ready for her to put them down on the sheet of paper. It occurred to me that I once used to take her feet in my own hands, years ago probably, small, soft feet. Once she had lost a nail, and it was so painful that she had shut herself in the bathroom right away to stick it on again. Soft, milk-white feet. Had I kissed them? I had only to act as if I were part of it, part of her life, part of the couple we were at the time.

I wondered when I had first felt that sense of being in the way, a foreign body. Perhaps when we moved into the new house. Her drawings made me uneasy. At first her tigers were colourful and her butterflies black and white, then people thought they would like bats in her tattoo designs, and Eunice drew bats with wings as delicate as cobwebs and the faces of tiny devils. Finally they wanted her pictures anyway, never mind what subjects other artists were asked to draw, Eunice could draw anything she liked, and whatever it was her customers were ready to immortalise the design in their skin with needles. She drew dragons with bleeding wings, and I felt guilty of shedding their blood; she drew leopards with white eyes looking as if they been gouged out, and teeth wanting to tear someone – me – to pieces.

She put her head round the kitchen door, saw me and closed the door again.

'Hey, wait a minute.' I opened the door, and she looked round with a question in her eyes.

'Hello,' I said, but I wasn't as self-confident as my voice suggested.

'Hello?' She looked up at me in surprise. Then she turned, and I followed her along the corridor to the stairs leading to the upper floor.

'Are we going to have something to eat?'

'Oh, I forgot to say – we're invited out. Kate and her husband are celebrating because they're leaving, so I thought we'd go there later, darling, I've bought some flowers to take. You wouldn't have made it in time for supper anyway. Kate's glad to be going, and so is Tom. They hated Germany so much, and now they're happy, darling. They're going home. Did you know they come from Baton Rouge? Both of them. Imagine, from Baton Rouge to Berlin! What could be worse? So I thought we'd go round later and have a drink with them.'

Eunice talked at Mickey Mouse speed, like a wound-up clockwork toy, and her voice rose higher and higher the faster she spoke. I managed to grasp her arm, but she shook my hand off.

'I'm going to get ready, darling.'

'Have you eaten already, then?'

'You never notice anything. I've been eating nothing but red food since Sunday.'

'Red?'

'First green, then red.'

'I thought that was on Sunday ten days ago.'

'Yes, it's for two weeks this time, didn't I tell you? No? Well, anyway, I'm going to get ready, darling.'

She called me darling as if it were a name, or the full stop at the end of her sentences. Full stop. Darling. She disappeared into the bathroom, leaving the door ajar, and in the mirror I could see her plucking her eyebrows. She had stuck a piece of paper up beside the mirror with Sellotape, and every few seconds she marked a line on it, plucked a hair out, made a mark, plucked the next hair out, made the next mark.

I finished the last of my beer from the bottle.

'What is it?' She was looking at me over the top of the mirror. I smiled at her.

'You don't feel like smiling. I can tell.'

We'd had a woman to interview at the assessment office today, a woman who wouldn't tell us her reasons for being here.

'I don't want to see your pretend smile any more, understand?

46

You look miserable as sin and then you smile at me.' Eunice grimaced, stretching her face, opening her mouth only briefly. 'Can you imagine what it's like living with a stranger?' She made several more marks one by one. 'No, you can't.'

'Your drawings are larger these days,' I commented, and thought of that woman. Her name was Nelly Senff, and she hadn't wanted to give us any political reasons for coming over. A curious sort of pride, although once she'd applied for an exit permit she hadn't been able to practise her profession. There were any number of possible reasons in our files why she would want to leave. She wasn't using any of them.

'Talking about my drawings, John? How reassuring for you that my work is so visible, isn't it? You always know what I'm doing. Always.' Eunice turned to me and looked into my eyes. 'While I don't know anything about you.'

'Eunice, you did know how it would be, right from the start.'

'Not from the start.'

'As soon as I was able to tell you.'

'Huh, as soon as you were able to tell me that I'd never get to know any more about you.' Tears came into her eyes. 'But then it was too late.'

'Too late?'

Eunice pushed me aside and looked in the cupboard on the wall for the right face cream. 'I'd fallen in love by then. Too late because I'd fallen in love by then. How was I to know you weren't a sales rep after all? I wasn't prepared for you to say one day: *Oh, none of that is true. I work for the Secret Service, but you'll never hear any more about it from me.*'

'You could still have said no.'

'That's what you think. But I didn't know, understand? And I didn't believe it either. Why would I? How can anyone imagine never knowing anything about the other person in her life?'

47

'That's not true, Eunice. You know I like scrambled eggs. You know I like Ella Fitzgerald. You know everything personal about me.'

'Everything personal? What does that mean?' Eunice screamed, she screamed to show how desperate she was, but although I saw that it didn't touch me. It touched me less than the silent despair of Nelly Senff, the woman whose refusal to give us any information I had thought I understood. 'Stop these accusations, Eunice. They aren't getting us anywhere.'

Eunice cried for a bit. Then she blew her nose and looked at me as if determined to be brave. 'Darling, can you get my underclothes off the line for me? The salmon-pink set.'

I went out on the terrace and searched through the garments that I had hung out in the morning. Eunice owned exclusively salmon-pink underwear, nylon trimmed with lace. She thought underclothes ought not to be machine-washed, so I washed her nylon underwear. She was allergic to washing powder, and wouldn't accept my suggestion of machine-washing her underwear without detergent. So I had been washing her underclothes for years, without any passion but with a sense of duty, as if it were a service I owed her. I felt guilty about all that I had to deny her in our marriage, and even guiltier about what I didn't have to deny her, but increasingly I withheld it all the same.

'Here.' I held the underclothes out to her.

'Do you think I should get my hair straightened?' Her hand passed over the paper on which she was drawing, and I saw the head of a cute little kitten. Leaning forward in surprise, I saw her hand move aside to reveal the kitten's open chest. Its entrails were hanging out.

'You have lovely wavy hair.'

'Frizzy, darling, I have frizzy hair like all of us black people. Wavy hair is different.' She ran her hand through her hair,

48

looking in the mirror to see whether I was really looking as well. Then her eyes went back to the cute kitten and its never-ending entrails.

If Nelly Senff had been at all cooperative, she'd have qualified for guaranteed refugee status right away. But she obviously had reasons for not telling us her reasons, and that made us suspicious.

'Or should I colour it?'

'Colouring sounds like a good idea,' I said, wondering whether it was possible that Nelly Senff had a better notion of her friend Vassily's whereabouts than we did.

'Red because I'm only eating red food?'

'Red.' As a rule we knew more about the people we questioned than they knew themselves. Just sometimes, and only in cases like Nelly Senff's, did it seem that we might yet find out something else.

'Are you crazy, John? You're not listening to me at all. Red? I said that for a joke.' Eunice sobbed. 'So you say red. What would that look like? A black woman with red hair?'

'Sorry, Eunice.'

'Sorry, sorry. There's nothing to be sorry about.' She took hold of me to push me out of the bathroom. 'You can be glad I'm still here. But not much longer, do you hear? Not much longer.' Tears fell from her eyes. 'What kind of life would you have then, darling?'

'You're only staying here because of me.' I was making a statement, not asking a question. She wanted me to be grateful to her, she thought I loved her for staying. I stood in the doorway and watched her turning round and crying as she went on drawing her kitten.

'What do you think?'

In the mirror, I saw Eunice smiling at her kitten picture and drawing its paws going into its chest. The cute little animal with the big round eyes was tearing its own guts out.

'Shit, I only just put mascara on my new lashes.' Eunice blew her nose on a piece of toilet paper. 'Do you still remember what it was like at first, darling, when we arrived here?' Eunice was sobbing, doing her best to sound composed. She was fighting, she wanted me to appreciate her fight. Hard to tell whether Nelly Senff was fighting a battle with herself. We had put her through the wringer for eight hours today. She had become increasingly uncommunicative and finally asked for a break, saying she wanted to go out and collect the promised food coupons so that she could get food for her children. But she couldn't have gone out anyway. Only approved applicants could go out, and she had to prove her suitability for acceptance in this interview. The pastor was in charge of her children during the day while she went through the application process. They couldn't go to school until we were through with it, probably after Monday. Eunice was sobbing.

'Dear heart.' I put my hands on her strong shoulders, but Eunice was clutching her pencil as if it were all she had to cling to.

'Just whose hearts are you interested in?' Eunice made the kitten take its heart in its claws. It suddenly occurred to me that she might draw me.

'I checked the speedometer of your car yesterday to see how many kilometres you'd done.' Eunice looked at me sullenly.

'You what?'

'I wanted to know how far you drive to work, even if I don't know where that actually is.'

'You're spying on me? My own wife?'

Eunice began a new drawing. She was sobbing.

'It's sending me crazy, can't you see that? I know nothing,

50

absolutely nothing. Two hundred and seven kilometres in a day. How do you rack up all that distance inside the city wall? That's what I ask myself. Maybe you drive across the border every day and work over there.'

I shook my head. Eunice was talking like a woman possessed. Sometimes she seemed to forget me and my profession for weeks, but outbursts like this were getting more and more frequent. Outbursts of boundless suspicion.

'Could be there's something wrong with the speedometer,' she said quietly, as if to herself.

'Stop it, Eunice.' I took hold of her upper arms, left and right.

Eunice shook her head. 'The way you touch me, John, it's like you were holding a pair of pincers and I had some kind of infection – do you realise that?'

I dropped my hands impatiently. Eunice turned over the sheet of paper with the kitten picture, and on the other side of it I saw two snakes devouring one another. Each had the other's tail in its mouth. Eunice stuck the picture in place and picked up a jar of make-up.

Nelly Senff had two children, and their father, Vassily Batalov, was said to have killed himself three years ago.

I touched Eunice's hair; it was stiff and bristly. 'It's beautiful the way it is,' I said, letting go.

The only reason Nelly Senff had given us for her wish to cross the border was for a change of scene. After Batalov's death, she said, she had felt unable to go on living. She had been buried alive with all her memories, she told us. That was why she'd wanted to come here. To get rid of her memories. But reasons of that kind didn't carry much weight. She could consider herself lucky if she was kept here and allowed into the Federal Republic.

'I'm ready. We can go.' Eunice had put on too much rouge for my liking.

'I'm tired. You should have told me earlier that we were invited out.'

Eunice opened her swollen eyes. 'You bastard.' Baffled, she shook her head. I was well acquainted with this volte-face of hers between great sadness and despair and pure self-pity in the middle of her rage. I shrugged.

She closed the door in my face, and I heard her cursing inside. 'Tired? What makes you so tired?' I went over to the stairs and heard her screaming, 'It's always about you, isn't it? Your wonderful secret life, your hunger, your sex, your sleep. Wow, are you ever important!' She uttered a shrill cry. I knew her accusations inside out, but I really was so tired that I could hardly stand on my feet. Every time we asked the people who wanted to cross the border a question, we had to be careful to give nothing away. Drop no hints, show no sympathy. It was stressful.

Had Eunice not noticed that we hadn't slept together for months? Where did she dredge up that angry comment about sex? The idea of touching her was far from my mind. Everything about her had resolved itself into a pattern, a set of images that I had probably seen years ago but could no longer make out clearly, and it wasn't renewed because I knew what the pattern felt like and had no more curiosity about it. Slowly, I went downstairs. The TV was on with the sound muted. I recognised our President, visiting Berlin and hoping to pick up a few more voters here amid all the jubilation. The TV guide lay open on the table. On West III a programme entitled *What Can a Man Do?* was about to begin. The Germans were rediscovering our social critic and moralist Upton Sinclair. I'd have been interested in watching it, but we got poor reception on that station. Our President waved, and American flags fluttered over the screen. After a little while I closed my eyes, and once again I saw that woman Nelly Senff in front of me. Unusual name, Nelly. It suited her. The way she'd slipped a hand under the shoulder strap of her dress, rubbing the white skin over her collarbone, and forgetting to cover her mouth with her hand when she yawned. Something about her had intrigued me from the first, as soon as I entered the room where Harold had been waiting with her. There was an aroma both sweet and sharp in the air, like fruit. When I walked round her chair later I realised that it came from her.

A door banged. Eunice ran along the corridor upstairs. I had spoilt her evening. As far as I knew she had never gone out on her own here. She was probably about to shut herself up in the bedroom. There were sure to be large sheets of paper on my side of the bed; I would have to move them out of the way if I wanted to get into the bedroom myself and lie down.

I leaned my head against the back of the chair, breathed out and took my left slipper off with my right foot, my right slipper off with my left foot. I relished the peace of being alone. I missed being alone. In spite of the isolation of it, I did miss having a few moments to spend without other people. I enjoyed driving the car in the morning and evening – but there were many days when I would also have liked to be in this house on my own. As soon as I saw Eunice and one of her drawings, I knew I was in the way. Perhaps that woman Nelly Senff really did believe that a single black impulse had enticed her lover to the next world. Or the few little quarrels they might have had. What could those quarrels have been about?

The smell of grass being smoked rose to my nostrils. Penetrating. I didn't know where Eunice got hold of the stuff, she wasn't saying, and it probably wouldn't have done me much good to know. She had spent almost every evening for over a year sitting up there. She drew and she filled our bedroom with cannabis smoke. Did she think that tempted me? The moments when I thought it would be good for her and pleasant for me if she finally went back to Knoxville without me were getting more and more frequent.

We had offered Nelly Senff Marlboros and Camels. But this Senff woman, Nelly Senff, didn't smoke cigarettes at all. We had offered them to her hoping it would make things easier, but she refused. She stood up and asked to be allowed to go to the toilet. The smell of her was driving me crazy. I had to excuse myself for a moment. When I came back she was sitting on her chair again, sipping from the can of Coca-Cola we had given her, and looking at me as directly as if she'd guessed the effect she had on me. Yet that was hardly possible, given the way she presented herself, no make-up, hair carelessly pinned on top of her head. It showed her neck to good advantage, a long, white neck, immaculate. Her skin glistened slightly. When Harold left the room to get another Thermos jug, I sat down at the table opposite her and said, 'You're not afraid any more, are you, Frau Senff? You know that you're safe here?'

'Safe?' She looked at me enquiringly, and then added quietly, 'It's not about that, not at all.' She shook her head, and I thought a soft breath of wind carried her scent straight to my nose. 'Do you know what a woman once said to me? There's no safer place in the whole world than a communist country surrounded by a wall like ours.' Nelly laughed. Her laughter was so unexpected, light and bubbling, that I gave a start.

A strong pulling sensation forced me to stand up, more of a reflex action than the result of thought, and I took a step round the table, stopped in front of her and said, 'We only want the best for you.' My voice sounded hoarse.

'Communist.' She laughed. 'Imagine, my mother really thinks it had something to do with her communist ideas. As if the country had developed in line with her revolutionary notions.'

Slowly, the laughter in her voice ebbed away. 'But it was socialist, wasn't it? And socialism has nothing to do with communism.'

I nodded vigorously, and then shook my head. 'No, indeed it doesn't.'

I heard the door open and close behind me. Harold put the Thermos jug down on the table and held a Mars bar out to Nelly.

'You give your victims such expensive things?' Her hand was still clutching the Coca-Cola can. She was hardly drinking from it; it looked more as if she were doing us a favour by seeming to, but she was really just sipping tiny drops from the small opening. The chance of holding the can seemed to her more important than the chance of drinking from it.

'Victims?' Harold gave her a questioning look, let his outstretched arm drop, and then looked at me even more questioningly. 'You're not our victim. We're interviewing you in order to assess whether you were suffering persecution. So what was the friend's name? You said that he was a friend of Batalov.'

'No, I have not been persecuted.' She shook her head with determination and wound a strand of hair round her finger. 'Definitely not. I haven't been able to work since I applied for a visa to leave the country, but that was standard, especially for people working in scientific research. Or in the media or education, and I don't know what else. That was perfectly normal.'

'The friend's name?'

'What friend?'

'Just now you mentioned a friend whom he met now and then through his translations.'

'Did I? No, I don't know any friend of Vassily's.'

'Listen, don't think we're stupid.' Harold was losing patience. When he was annoyed, he raised his voice. 'As soon as we ask you for names you don't know any.'

Nelly did not reply.

'If you're not going to cooperate, we can't help you.'

Nelly reached for a strand of hair again and wound it round her finger. She was watching Harold attentively.

'The question is, who's supposed to be helping whom,' she said calmly, letting go of the strand of hair.

Harold was breathing heavily; then he turned to the girl taking the minutes, looked at her neckline – a low one, as usual – and snapped, 'You don't have to record that sort of thing.'

The girl taking the minutes looked up. 'Shall I cross it out?'

'Well.' Harold settled into the safety of his chair behind the desk. 'Let's go back to before you applied for an exit visa. You said you wanted to travel because . . . because there were certain problems between you and your friend.' Harold opened his folder again and waited for her to reply.

Nelly looked at Harold with a question in her eyes. Her skin looked to me as white as marble, her eyes were reddened, and the bags under them were tinged pink.

'Problems? But I told you, he took his own life. After that it made no sense for me to stay there any longer. He'd left his mark on everything, and there was nowhere new for me. I wanted to be in another country with the same language, but without all the places where he'd been – that's why I'm here. Don't you understand?'

'I'm sorry,' said Harold, his tone matter-of-fact, 'but you won't get your friend back by coming here either.'

Tears came into Nelly's eyes, she swallowed audibly, and breathed deeply. Her nostrils were quivering. She was not crying, or not really, not like Eunice. Nelly didn't seem to have to struggle to keep from crying; tears just happened to trickle into her eyes but did not fall. Harold gave me a look full of meaning.

'You said Vassily Batalov threw himself off a building, without leaving any real goodbye letter. But you found a note in his papers. Quite a recent note, I suppose?'

'It could have been a draft of a letter, yes.'

'And you didn't bring this note with you? His last note, your last sign of life from him, you just left it behind?'

'Didn't I tell you before that I'm not interested in these material things? I must have left it there.'

'You call that material? Surely it had some other value for you.' Harold pushed a sheet of paper over the table to Nelly. 'Here, write down what the note said.'

'I can't.'

'Yes, you can. If you don't cooperate we can't help you.' Harold looked injured, then changed his tone of voice and said impatiently, 'Do try to understand, your permit to enter the Federal Republic is at stake. You do want that permit, don't you?'

Nelly nodded, looked doubtfully at me and then at Harold.

'Go on.' Harold held the ballpoint out to her.

Nelly's hands stayed in her lap. Once again she looked at me undecidedly. I felt as if she were expecting my support.

Now Harold was pushing the point of the pen down on the paper. 'Here. He indicated that he had lost hope. Here, write it. And he ended by saying you mustn't take it personally, didn't he? Here.'

Nelly looked at me again.

'Here.'

The expectation in her eyes made me ask something, and it was only as I said it that I heard what it was. 'How do you interpret that remark – that you weren't to take it personally?' I took care to make my voice sound sympathetic. After all, I had to ask.

Nelly folded her arms over her breasts and looked at me with wide, bright eyes. She didn't answer.

57

'Here.' Harold was digging the ballpoint into the paper. He leaned forward. 'Frau Senff?'

'There was nothing like that in any note.'

'What?' Harold put a hand to his ear. 'Then you've been lying to us, is that so?'

'No, I didn't put it like that.'

Harold was leafing through his folder. 'Frau Senff, we're only asking these questions so that we can find out what repressive measures you've been subjected to.'

Nelly nodded. 'Yes, you said that before.' She spoke so quietly that I could hardly make out what she said. 'I'm really exhausted, you know, maybe I just can't think of anything else.' She put her head on one side and moistened her lips. 'You see, I've been questioned by State Security half my life, today it's you asking the questions, it'll be the British tomorrow, and the French the day after that – unless you haven't finished with me yet. Oh, and when does the Federal German Secret Service get its turn? I'd forgotten them. And I was questioned at the border by our own servants of the state, no idea who they were exactly, maybe State Security in a uniform to look like police. My head is empty, you've no idea how empty, I can't remember what I told you and what I told the others. This is cross-examination, that's all. Are you planning to have another go at me tomorrow?' Her voice sounded almost pleading.

'Have you been cross-examined?' Harold was not impressed by her exhaustion. I looked at the time. We'd been questioning her in alternating shifts for seven hours now, and if I knew McNeill and Fleischman they wouldn't let her leave before five.

Nelly laughed hysterically. 'Have I been cross-examined? Is that a joke? I've been cross-examined non-stop. You interrogate me, other people interrogate me, I've come out with everything

I know, don't you see? There's nothing left in my head, it's empty, it's all come out, every last little thing.' Nelly knocked her head with her fist. I'd have liked to stop her, if doing so wouldn't have made me look ridiculous. Yet her voice was firm and friendly, in fact it was in curious contrast to her alleged exhaustion.

'In the past, however, before you applied for an exit permit? Were you repeatedly interrogated then, too?'

'Of course I was, there must have been seven or ten or fifteen or heaven knows how many such meetings with State Security, some of them on People's Police premises. I had to go to those meetings if I wanted to be allowed to study, and then, later, to take up my position at the Academy of Sciences. And in between times they found opportunities to call me in for more questioning.'

'Where exactly did that take place? Who was in charge of the interrogations?'

'So what's your name again?'

'Why mine? I was just asking you for the names of the State Security interrogators.' Harold's patience had been exhausted long ago. He wasn't even trying to put on a show of friendliness now.

'You think they tell us names? Surely you know that at least. No names. And even if they *had* introduced themselves, how would anyone remember names in a situation like that?'

'Where were you interrogated?'

'Where am I now?'

'I see, where are you now? Have you just come round from a fainting fit, young lady? Building P, that's where you are.'

'Building P. It was in all sorts of different places.'

'Which places?'

'I don't remember.'

'Here.' Once again, Harold turned to the sheet of paper, boring a hole in it with the ballpoint. 'Write down the names of the places and people concerned. Draw a sketch of the places.'

Nelly did not move.

Breathing heavily, Harold lit himself a Marlboro, and tapped the pack to knock another cigarette out of it. 'Won't you have one after all?'

'No, thank you.'

'Hmm. Or a Camel?' Harold took a pack of Camels out of his shirt pocket. He held it out to her. 'You can have the whole pack. Camels. Genuine American cigarettes.' Nelly shook her head. Harold drew on his cigarette three times in quick succession. 'Have you been asked to work with us?'

'Yes, I've been asked that, too. Didn't you ask me before? I've been offered different kinds of work. But they didn't appeal to me.' Nelly laughed. She laughed like a young girl who has understood a suggestive joke but isn't sure whether she ought to show that she understands it, and in the end keeps quiet to appear decorous and thus at least deny that she might have understood. 'You see, I always had a good argument to protect me from State Security. I said I came from a Jewish family. And also my scientific ambition wasn't wide-ranging enough. So they could only roll little stones my way.'

'But what kind of effect did your Jewish faith have on them? Can you tell us that more specifically?' Harold lit another cigarette from the one that he hadn't quite finished, and blew the smoke in Nelly's face. He doesn't do that kind of thing on purpose, it's the result of his concentration on what has to be heard, to be asked, to be left unmentioned.

'I have no idea. It wasn't about any faith. I simply said I came from a Jewish family, and it sounded like an apology. As if it were understandable that anyone from a Jewish family wouldn't want to work with them. Or perhaps as if they themselves wouldn't be interested in working closely with people like me. Religious faith doesn't have much to do with it, but that didn't interest State Security. You see, I'm not political, I'm not religious, it's just that my head is empty and I didn't want to stay in that prison any longer.'

'When you talk about prison, what do you mean?'

'Well, all those places.'

'What places?' Once again Harold bored a hole in the paper with his ballpoint. By now there were several holes in it, but Nelly hadn't shown the slightest sign of even putting her hand out to the pen.

'The Müggelsee. We lived less than ten minutes away, in Friedrichshagen. Vasya was a fantastic swimmer. The cafes down in the building where Vasya told me one evening that he'd like to marry me. He'd forgotten about it next day. He said he'd just been drunk.'

Harold rolled his eyes, propped his head on his hand and looked at the ceiling. Nelly didn't seem to notice his disappointment, she simply went on talking undaunted.

'Don't you see, I was surrounded. All the places here – well, I mean over there – make me remember. And every memory means telling lies, or so it sometimes seems to me when I hear my children or other people. Only now I'm telling lies all on my own, you see, and there's a difference between knowing there are two of you involved in what happens and the kind of life they present to us as lies, nice lies or nasty ones, there's a difference between that and having to keep it all going by yourself. It's a heavy weight to bear. Weight. Yes, think of it like this, memories weigh as heavily as a child. How heavy do you think a child can be if you're carrying it by yourself?'

I was watching Nelly Senff with curiosity. I wanted to see some sign of her unhappiness, a sign of pain in her smooth young face. Nothing. Now she put a strand of hair behind her ear. That was all.

'You didn't feel imprisoned by the Wall?' Harold ventured. He too seemed to want to find some evidence of good refugee status in her.

But Nelly Senff smiled light-heartedly and interrupted his question. 'You mean because we weren't allowed to travel and couldn't study anything we liked? Thank God, that's all I can say, thank God for the Wall, or there'd probably be a thousand places to remember in your half of the city as well. My grandmother can travel, she's always been able to. They don't make anyone who was persecuted by the Nazi regime stay here. They seem to have come of their own free will and to stay here of their own free will, too. My mother says they had no choice. Anyone who wanted to come back after the war had to go to the East. But I think it was just a mirage. A Utopia. Something like what the West is for many of us today, I mean many of us in the East. The better side of a land laid waste, a failure of a country. I'd rather say that from a distance she was anaesthetised by the socialist ideal.'

'Why do you say anaesthetised?'

'Isn't it a kind of anaesthetic? Imagine that because of your origins you're persecuted and mistreated, you live in camps or in exile, always afraid? You can't stop to think about God then. She had no time for him, my grandmother always said, she just had no time and probably not the necessary patience to think of him either. And then imagine you finally discover other movements, revolutionaries, even ardent communists – people who simply have the gift of never losing hope because they've stored it up on their own account and want to force it on an entire nation . . .'

'Take it easy, take it easy, Frau Senff, we can't quite keep up with you.' I could see that the girl taking the minutes was sitting there without typing, baffled by this torrent of words. Her fingers lay on the keys as if frozen rigid.

'Don't you have bugs here, then?' Nelly blinked at us.

'Bugs?' Harold shook his head. 'You mean recorders? Do you feel that we are persecuting you?'

'Not as long as you sit where you are, no, I don't, and then what would you be after? My empty head?'

'Your little head isn't as empty as all that,' said Harold, probably meaning *little* in the sense of *pretty*, for her head was anything but little. 'Just go rather more slowly, please, Frau Senff. You mean that socialist anaesthesia, as you put it, was a consequence of the persecution of the Jews? Or the failure of the Nazis?'

'It isn't as simple as that. There were hardly any Jews here whom that would apply to. I just think that communism is a substitute for religion.' She added, quietly, 'And perhaps for the Weimar Republic, but that's another story.'

'You think so?' Harold couldn't hide his incredulous grin, so it was as well that Nelly wasn't paying him any attention.

'It particularly affected the kind of people who weren't just able to believe in an idea but who found belief was a kind of personal necessity, and one way or another their faith had been destroyed. Just as they lost their relations they lost their faith. Look at it another way, and I'm sure that loss is also true of the Nazis. The outcome of the war must have hurt them. You see, they'd believed heart and soul in the National Socialist idea. Communism as everyone coming together to live in a community only looks as if it were the opposite of exclusion, devouring and death. Aren't they both symptoms of fear? Fear of what's strange?'

Now Harold was laughing openly. 'She's studied that much philosophy! Turn it around: what do you think of lust? The lust for power?'

'Not fear?' Nelly Senff studied her crossed legs. Her eyes were

63

bright as she looked at Harold. 'Take away what someone believes in, and the pain and sense of injustice leave a longing for compensation behind, for being absorbed in a new ideology that can cope with the loss of the old one. Communism filled that gap for a short time – and when no one wanted to look very closely, for fear of being hurt again and because they knew what pain was like, communism turned into socialism. Or at least that's what they called it. And what its name promises was only for appearances. Scars are often numb, didn't you know that?'

Harold and I were both sitting there open-mouthed, listening to this woman who, for all the emptiness she thought her head contained, was talking all kinds of confused stuff. Before I realised what I was doing, I stroked the long scar on my forehead. She was right, the scar itself felt nothing, it was only my fingers that felt it like a foreign body in the middle of my forehead.

'One last question, Frau Senff. Take the question as a chance, or if you like as an indication: are you sure that you want your application to the government here to be accepted?' Harold lit a cigarette and watched for her reaction, but she showed none. 'I expect you know that applications for a permit to live here are sometimes rejected? Do you know what it's like in the camps for those whose applications are not accepted?'

Nelly Senff looked at us wearily. She didn't bat an eyelid. It almost seemed as if she didn't notice Harold's attempt to threaten her. Her silence, and the reluctance that it expressed to give us the information he had asked for, seemed to be more important to her than a secure, comfortable permit to come to the Federal Republic.

'The emergency reception procedure will decide whether, in your case, moving to the West is a matter of your predicament or a conflict of conscience. It looks as if you may have difficulties. Yes, we are in Germany, but we are not actively looking for people from the East. I'm just making that clear. And if you haven't proved your point, I'd say you can forget about your entitlement to stay.'

Nelly Senff shrugged and suppressed a yawn.

'If you'll excuse us, our colleagues will be with you in a minute to ask you some more questions.' Harold knocked more than three centimetres of ash off his filter-tip cigarette and dropped the butt into his over-full ashtray. Its closing mechanism had stopped working because the butts had jammed the scissor-like opening. Harold tore the wrapping off a chocolate bar, put half of it in his mouth and bit into it. With apparent difficulty he got to his feet, and I followed him, unasked. I nodded to Nelly Senff in passing. She looked down at the floor, and I breathed her perfume in.

Outside, Harold said, 'Really, I ask you! Someone like that was all I needed – a woman to lecture us about anaesthetised feelings or some such thing. Are you all right? Did you see her legs? These German women don't even shave their legs – they're all the same, from East and West alike.'

'Maybe if they do shave them they won't get anything here but food coupons.'

'For Christ's sake, John, where do you live? Haven't you ever looked at German women's legs? I'll tell you right now, they don't shave anywhere else either. You have to go to cute little kids if you want a bit of smooth skin.'

Instead of answering that, I asked him whether he really thought that Nelly Senff knew anything about our suspicions of Batalov. Without a moment's hesitation Harold said no, he didn't think so. She was prudish and stupid but that was all. The others could have gone along with Stasi attempts to recruit them, we might as well ask her again when exactly that was and what she had told them.

We went into the discussion room and greeted our colleagues, who seemed to be well informed already. 'Tough nut to crack, was she?'

'More of an empty nutshell.' Harold laughed and went to the toilet.

McNeill clapped me on the shoulder. 'We'll have her out of here tomorrow anyway. This has to go higher up.'

Sometimes it annoyed me that the elite of the CIA, who never set foot in the camp, thought themselves a cut above those of us who were on duty there almost daily. But then, I hoped to belong to that elite myself some day, and not have to pass the barrier and go to Building P on the part of the campsite boarded off from the rest. There were already days when they said they needed me outside in Argentinische Allee. Officially as a liaison man, but it was easy to suspect that they wanted to observe the way we worked and look for possible candidates to join them. For instance tomorrow, when my colleague had the day off and I was to be present at the further interrogation of the woman Nelly Senff.

'Listen, I'm talking to you. Did you drop off to sleep just sitting there?' Eunice hit my upper arm. She looked worn out; her eyes were reddened and small. Probably from the grass she'd been smoking rather than tears. 'The darkness here will kill me.' She dropped to the sofa beside me and nestled her head into my shoulder. 'Don't you think they could give you a job back in the States?' Her breath was stale, as if she hadn't opened her mouth in a century.

'I want to go back, I want to go back – you're not a baby any more, Eunice. Coming here was a chance for you, too; you could have learned German, you could have begun studying.'

'Could have, could have. Why would I study? I'm a graphic

artist. Learn German? I'd sooner be a cannibal. Why would I learn German when there's no one for me to talk to?'

'No one you want to talk to, Eunice. Don't twist the meaning in retrospect. As if I'd made you come.'

'But you did make me come. You know you did.'

'How?'

'You didn't even ask me, you just said the situation is such-and-such, we're moving to Berlin, Germany.'

'Well, it's not Siberia.'

'No, it's Germany, darling. My friend Sally only had to ask her husband once, and he took her straight back to New Orleans.'

'Please, Eunice, don't start on about Sally again. But for her, no Dutch Morial. You must be joking.'

'Still, a black mayor. We're at the ends of the earth here. My girlfriends –'

'Are unhappy too, you say so yourself. And I'm tired. I thought you wanted to sleep on your own?'

'I do.' Proud and defiant, she turned and went upstairs again. Indistinctly, she said something that sounded like: Has it occurred to you that I don't need you any more? But I wasn't listening, and her murmuring disappeared to the top floor with her. I heard rushing water from the bathroom. The pink rug that Eunice wrapped round her during the day while she watched TV and did her drawings was lying on the end of the sofa. I spread it over me and tried to remember the aroma of Nelly. If I'd been Vassily Batalov, I thought, I wouldn't have told her anything either. If you have your wits about you, you don't let someone whose thinking is as skewed as Nelly Senff's into any secrets. But maybe he hadn't had his wits about him. Maybe she'd turned them long before. And finally my instinct told me – it had already told me what questions the British Secret Service would ask, and I could deduce from that what they knew from us and from the French – that Vassily Batalov's espionage activities were nothing but a sham. We'd have known about them, particularly if he'd been working for us as a double agent, which was what the others suspected. But we knew no such thing. Or at least, not as far as I was aware. Regular humming, as if of a small engine, intruded on my thoughts. I opened my eyes and stared into the dark. Maybe Eunice was brushing her teeth with the electric toothbrush that we'd brought from the States. Or whatever. Then I heard her soft moaning. I didn't want to think whether Eunice was moaning with pleasure or pain. Maybe she was in tears again. I breathed out through my nose. If the snakes were eating each other, swallowing one another's bodies bit by bit, the question was which would be left. The snake who was younger and stronger and swallowed bits of the other faster, or the snake with more stamina and a better brain? My earplugs were in the mirrored wall cupboard in the bathroom, but I didn't want to go up and disturb her in her isolation. I hesitated, then took a tissue and pulled it into shape until it would fit in my ears.

Hans Pischke in luck

The baby was crying. I had stuffed every crack in the door of my room, I had put chewing gum round the key in the keyhole, the baby kept crying. I had hung a blanket over the door, I had pushed the metal bunk bed over to the other side of the wall, although that was against the rules, and the baby kept crying. I'd put a blanket over my head, and still the baby kept crying. I was breathing only through the tiniest airspaces in the vault of the blanket, I was taking shallow breaths, hardly breathing at all, because the crying was getting on my nerves, flinging me abruptly into daytime in the morning.

I got out of bed, humming a tune to drown out the baby's crying, and took the water bottle off the table to pee into it.

'Shut up, will you?' growled a voice from the lower bed. I turned in alarm. The blanket on the bed below mine moved, and I recognised my new room-mate's shock of hair.

'Sorry, I forgot about you,' I whispered, putting the bottle down again and getting my trousers on.

'Just keep your mouth shut. Good heavens, you've been talking all night and all this morning.' He pulled the blanket further over his head until even his hair was no longer in sight. There were bloodstains on his blanket, the floor and finally on the handkerchief lying in front of our bunk bed. For most of the last two days I had seen him only sitting on a chair with his head tipped back to stop his nosebleed. But clearly there was no stopping it, either sitting or lying down, either awake or asleep. 'You must be feeling terrible.'

'I said just shut up,' he bellowed from under his blanket.

To avoid leaving the room first thing in the morning I had bought a portable immersion heater that I held in my cup only briefly, until the water seemed hot enough for me to tip brown instant coffee powder into it and stir. The baby's cries came through from the next room. I watched the walls to see if they were shaking, warping slightly under the anguish of those cries. But nothing was shaking or warping, except in me – in me it was warping so badly that I felt sick. I wasn't going to be driven out by a baby, certainly not, I wasn't going to the toilet either if I could manage it, I was doing as little of that as possible; I might meet the baby's mother there, or the baby's father, or one of the Russians, three men and a woman, who claimed to be siblings and slept in the two bunk beds in the second large room, while I slept in the little room next to it, curled up and trying not to go to the toilet, not to puke, not to express myself ever again in any way whatsoever. But I wasn't going to let myself be driven out any more. When I thought about it, Nescafé was the finest achievement of the Western world.

'Did you say Smurf?' Suddenly my room-mate sat up in the lower bed and stared at me. 'Say that again.'

'Sorry. What was that?'

'Say it again. Smurf?'

'Me? No, I didn't say a thing. Honestly I didn't.' I put my head under the blanket, turned my back to him, and hoped that the bumping noise behind me meant he was lying down again.

I often did talk out loud to myself without noticing it. I must have talked about the Smurf that Birgit and Cesare had brought when they came to see me here in the camp on my birthday. They hadn't set foot here before; they must be afraid of the porter and

70

the check-ups. They didn't visit until my birthday, as if I made a great thing of that. Cesare took a jar of Nescafé out of his jacket pocket, tipped out the contents on my little table, and as if by magic Birgit produced from her bag a thumb-sized blue child's model figure with a floppy hat and a trumpet. The plastic figure wore a piece of red fabric round its neck, a little scarf that she had obviously made for it. The torso of the figure, otherwise blue, was painted the same red as Birgit's fingernails. Birgit called it the Red Guard Smurf; she put it on top of the hill of instant coffee and beamed at me. Probably unconsciously, she pressed both her breasts together and recited the nursery rhyme in a sing-song voice, like reciting a magic formula: *Little Hans, all alone, travels over stick and stone. Hat on head and stick in hand, the happiest boy in all the land.* Birgit didn't go on to the next lines, about his mama shedding tears, but bit her lip instead.

The baby didn't understand sing-song, the baby didn't say a word. It had only one means of communication: crying.

Birgit was my cousin. Her aunt had met my uncle when I was sixteen. The pair of them had swiftly decided to take me out of the home where I'd been living until then and give me proper family care for two full years. Since then I had met Birgit at infrequent intervals when members of her family met, and I was always introduced to them all over again as if I had only just become a member of it myself, although I felt I was a stranger to them until the last. But not only for that reason. Birgit was an artist, and made sure that no one ever forgot it. In Cesare she had obviously found someone who was not only impressed by her artistic identity but would proudly give her a hand at this, that or the other 'happening'. He called himself a communist, and it was easy to imagine that he liked having a German girlfriend from the East. When I met Birgit with him in the Weltlaterne restaurant, shortly after my arrival, he used her visit to the Ladies to tell me how happy he was with her. She had actually run away from the GDR, so brave of her, he told me with shining eyes, while I thought of my own failed attempt at flight, and felt humiliated by his beaming expression. After all, her flight had been successful, if not quite as I had always assumed. However, Cesare explained to me that Birgit's ideas were more communist, or at least more revolutionary, than socialist ideas. She had painted the Lenin memorial red from top to bottom – he exhaled appreciatively – and without being caught. I nodded, and thought of the night when I had climbed it myself, all alone, clinging to Lenin's head three metres up in the air, at the same time trying to prevent the bucket of paint dangling from my waist by a rope tipping over, until I slipped and lost my hold just as the search-lights came on, slid down Lenin's bronze armour to the ground, curling up my feet in anticipation of the impact – which was definitely a mistake, because it meant I broke bones in both of them – and collapsed like an amateur. Like an amateur, which I certainly was not. Even if only Lenin's head was red, because of course I'd wanted to start at the top, and I hadn't got as far as the bottom. To that extent *from top to bottom* was sheer exaggeration, and it had cost me several months in prison, which Birgit simply suppressed in the heroic tale she had appropriated as her own. Perhaps prison seemed to her too difficult to imagine. I couldn't bear Birgit a grudge for stealing my story and making it her own; after all, it obviously had the desired effect. Cesare was at her feet. 'A strong woman, Birgit, a strong woman.' Birgit came back from the Ladies wearing black lipstick, and looked challeng-ingly at Cesare. '*Mamma mia*, am I disturbing you two?' With which she sat on his lap and bit his cheek. She was good at improving her image; she probably thought it chic to have an Italian boyfriend – or at least so her favourite expression of the time, *Mamma mia*, suggested.

Birgit's obligatory question was sure to follow: had I finally found a job or a place to live? That idea struck me as an illusion.

'Damn it all,' someone bellowed in my ear, and two hands went around my throat. 'I'm a peace-loving man, peace-loving, damn it all.'

'Sorry.' I tried to free myself from his clutches, but my room-mate tightened his hands on my windpipe.

Without advance warning, he let go, and I had to cling to the chair for support.

'I want another room,' cursed my room-mate, and he tied his shoes. 'This is too much, just too much.'

'I'm sorry,' I repeated before he jumped up, snatched his jacket from the back of the chair and slammed the door behind him.

Birgit and Cesare were the only acquaintances I had in Berlin; look at it more closely, and they were the *only* acquaintances I had in the West, although I could admit to myself that there hadn't been all that many in the East, either. Not if you don't want to strip the word *acquaintance* of a certain sense of friendship.

We had drunk coffee to celebrate my birthday – in fact it was the first Nescafé I ever drank, and we had offered some to my room-mate of the time, but he was about to go for a first interview, in a shirt and tie. Birgit said what a nice view I had of the new building opposite, which was just the same as mine, and into the rooms of the other camp inmates. You had to take risks in life, repeated Cesare for the second time, looking admiringly at the double bunk bed, and compared the cramped room where I still – he counted on his fingers – had several months to vegetate with the conditions in which a beast of prey was kept, something that he obviously thought he knew from the inside.

'Done it,' laughed my room-mate as he rushed back into the

room, holding a handkerchief under his nose and stuffing his clothes into his bag with one hand. 'You can keep these,' he said, pushing a cigarette packet that he had already opened to me over the table. 'Good luck.' The man disappeared, and I had the room to myself again.

Finally Birgit had reached for Cesare's hand, as if she had to pluck up courage for her question. She wanted to abduct me and take me to a party, she said. But it didn't begin until midnight, Cesare added.

'Too late,' I said, not letting my relief show. 'At this time of day, and for a whole night, I wouldn't get permission.' I tried scraping the lacquer off the Smurf figurine with my thumbnail.

'Permission?' Cesare looked round, laughed and said, 'Good heavens, I thought you were pushing forty. Where's your mummy, then? Permission?'

I looked at Cesare in surprise. Birgit pinched his hand and explained, not sure whether to express her indignation loudly or keep her voice down, 'He has to apply to the management here, Cesare, if he wants to be out all night.' Birgit's moral undertone seemed to echo through the room long after she had finished her sentence. I stood up as if I had to make my bed, straightening the blanket, and feeling more ashamed of the pointlessness of what I was doing than of my obviously pitiful situation.

There was a soft rushing sound in my left ear. Silence reigned between the three of us until Birgit said, 'We'll be going now,' and the two of them left.

I opened the window and saw them come out of the entrance to the building downstairs. So as not to be seen, I didn't sit on the windowsill with my cigarette as usual, one foot propped on the frame. The pallid neon lighting falling on them from the entrance was too weak to show their faces.

'Left?' I heard Cesare ask incredulously. 'Just like that? How could I have thought of such a thing? Surely a woman could never do that, never.'

They stopped, and I saw Birgit clinging to Cesare. 'Mamma mia, there's no understanding it,' she whispered. 'No one knows why, he never saw her again.'

'She must have been sick,' suggested Cesare.

'She wasn't.'

'She had a lover, then!'

'Good idea. But is that enough?'

'When was this?'

The sound in my ear grew louder; above the beating and rushing that reminded me of the pistons of engines in the belly of a ship I heard a singing, ringing, rustling sound, a chafing tickle that I was to bear calmly – as long as there was no metallic clicking and clacking like keys turning in locks, and no voices, Keep calm, Herr Pischke, or it won't go away. And there were moments like those when I positively enjoyed the noise, the scraping and murmuring that protected me from loud voices outside, got in their way, filled my aural passages too much for me to hear Birgit's answer, hear her telling a stranger what motivated my life, what went to make me up, and I saw how Birgit took his hand and drew him on, while he shook his head and said, as they went away, something like: Perhaps that's why he's the way he is. And: I don't believe it, I don't believe it.

I stubbed the cigarette out on the windowsill and threw it out of the window; the noise had subsided. I could hear even the cigarette falling on the ground as if my ear were lying on the paving. The air was damp. I almost thought I heard a faint hissing, like a last spark of fire going out. I turned round, picking up my deputy from the table and threw the little Red Guard Smurf into the waste-paper basket. Not that the childish figurine annoyed me, not at all, I simply didn't want it in my room. What had really annoyed me was the spilt Nescafé, which I tried to clear away as thoroughly as possible, but days later I was still finding small remains under the table, on my sweater, even outside the toilet.

The baby on the other side of the wall was crying non-stop, and in addition I now heard its mother's voice; it sounded shrill, and although I closed my ears and tried not to listen, I heard her telling the man that he hadn't got up once in the night to pacify the baby. I could hear his voice only as a deep growling sound, an attempt at an answer, not long enough to be an explanation, certainly not reassuring, for at once I heard her again repeating a sentence that I had heard her make for the last seven days.

'I can't stand it any more, do you hear, I can't stand it any more.'

'Then go away,' I whispered into my cup, and perhaps her husband had said something like that, at least she began crying, she cried like a glockenspiel with high, short, jerky sounds. 'A prison,' I heard her gasp. There was a rumble, a thump, sound as if the baby were being thrown at the wall or at least a chair wrecked and a bare behind smacked. Then it was strangely quiet, I couldn't even hear an outcry or a whimper from her, and so I imagined her lying at her husband's feet with her face distorted, and him, exhausted, kneeling beside her, relieved to have stopped her reproaches, and overwhelmed by a coldness that made what he had done bearable. The baby seemed to have recovered and was bawling at the top of its voice. My last sip of coffee was cold. I put my cap on, pulling it down over my temples to left and right like blinkers, so that as little as possible of my face could be seen, and listened at the door of the room before I opened it. The corridor was empty, the door of the next room ajar, but apart from the baby there didn't seem to be anyone in the apartment. All the same I tiptoed out, closed the door of

76

my room carefully so that no creak, none at all, could be heard. I plucked out a hair from where it was longest at the back of my head and caught it in the crack of the closed door. How else could I know for sure whether anyone opened the door to the room while I was out, to come in and look around? Hastily, I left the apartment.

John Bird is a witness

Next morning I drove out into Argentinische Allee in my Mercedes. I adjusted the volume of the radio. *Take a chance on me*. RIAS Berlin. The eight o'clock news. Nelly. I was still hearing the song in my head as I passed the security officers, let them take my jacket off, gave the secretary a friendly nod and greeted the superior officers.

So I was there again when Nelly Senff was asked more questions. This time Fleischman was conducting the interrogation. He was one of the oldest and most experienced of us. She was wearing the same dress as yesterday. Her chair stood by itself in the room, no table in front of her, no Coca-Cola can to clutch.

'Are your children being well looked after?' Fleischman began indirectly. His voice was warm and husky.

'My children are in the camp with the pastor. They're painting.'

'Do they like painting, then?'

'School doesn't begin for another week. But I'm sure you know that. First I have to answer your questions, and you have to find out whether any of us has an infectious illness, right? Then we'll be allowed to mingle with the people outside.' Nelly Senff was telling us our own conditions. There was no trace of disappointment and bitterness in her tone, and self-pity also seemed foreign to her. Perhaps there was a touch of mockery directed at all the security precautions she had encountered here, but she wasn't letting them discourage her.

'Oh yes, right.' Still standing, Fleischman leafed through her file. 'Yesterday my colleagues Harold and John Bird here' – he gestured towards me – 'were asking you about your partner, Vassily Batalov. You met him in Berlin?'

'We didn't live together.'

'But he's the father of your children. Did you meet him in Berlin?'

'Yes.' Nelly looked attentively from Fleischman to me, and suddenly smiled.

Fleischman moved a little closer to her. 'You did?' His voice was almost friendly, tempting her with warmth, with the understanding of an older man.

'Oh, never mind. I couldn't help thinking of something else.'

'What was it?'

'I'd rather not say. I don't have to, do I?' She put a strand of hair back from her face and smiled again. Perhaps she had recognised me as an old acquaintance because we had already met yesterday – and at the time that probably seemed to her like being unusually close to someone. I was her old, familiar friend. Her shoe jiggled restlessly up and down. Her legs, which had black hairs on them, were a matt, slightly ochre colour, and by comparison with her otherwise clear, almost white skin, seemed to have been tinted, so there was only one possible explanation: with that flowered dress made of light fabric (I imagined you could see through it in the sunlight), its main colour a pale lemon yellow, she was wearing ochre nylon tights. The blue sandals were not quite right for the outfit either.

'No, you don't have to do anything.' Fleischman's apparent friendliness didn't let up; he showed no disappointment at her reserve. 'However, I can tell you what you were thinking of. You were thinking you hadn't met Batalov in Berlin at all.'

'No?' Nelly gave a start, her leg stopped moving up and

down, and she looked at Fleischman in surprise, almost with curiosity.

'You met him in Ahrenshoop. Number 29 Hohes Ufer. Do you remember?'

'What?' Nelly coughed.

'The daughter of the family there had invited you and some friends to visit, and that's where you first met Batalov.'

'In Ahrenshoop?' Nelly went red.

'A blue house, thatched roof. The eleventh of April 1967. You arrived in the morning after going to Ribnitz by train, and from there on by bus to Ahrenshoop. A sandy path, poplars, sea buckthorn. Several people from East Berlin were there: Karin, daughter of the owner of the holiday house, with her husband Lehnert; Elfriede, a translator; Robert and Peter, two Berlin artists. You yourself were doing your final school exams at the time. And from Leipzig there was Frank Nause, a construction engineer with his girlfriend Bärbel, a medical student; and finally the translator Batalov from Leningrad.'

Nelly did not reply. The red blotches on her face had moved down to her neckline, and she was looking intently at the toes of her shoes.

'Don't forget that we want to help you. We'd like to be able to form an accurate idea of your situation. You realise how much may depend on that?' Fleischman leaned against the desk. He was visibly enjoying driving Nelly into a corner by showing her how much more he knew than she and others thought. The files of the CIA contained information that other secret services could only dream of. Fleischman's apparent friendliness must now seem to Nelly unpredictable and dangerous. 'How well did you know these friends through whom you met Batalov?'

'H-how well did I know them?' Nelly Senff stammered.

For a moment Nelly Senff and Fleischman looked at each

other in surprise, as if a third party had been asking them questions and neither of them knew any answer.

Miss Killeybegs cautiously opened the door and carried in a tray with a Thermos jug and cups on it. The aroma of coffee filled the room. When she was about to pour the coffee, Fleischman took the jug from her. 'May I? Oh, and would you be so kind as to bring us another cup, Miss Killeybegs?' Miss Killeybegs went away, and Fleischman poured coffee into a cup. 'Sugar? Milk?'

'No thank you, just black.' Nelly cleared her throat, took the cup from him and blew on it.

'Don't pretend to be stupid, Frau Senff. If you answer my questions with more questions, I'll use other methods, and finally I'll have you gently sent back.'

'I knew Karin, not the others.' Nelly tried to balance the cup on her knee. After a short attempt, she gave up and held it in mid-air.

'Did Batalov speak fluent German right away?' Fleischman poured milk and coffee into another cup, put three sugar lumps on the side of the saucer, and placed it on the table for Frau Schröder.

'He had a slight accent, but many people thought it was South German. His mother was German-born, and he grew up with the language.' Nelly stirred her coffee and looked at Fleischman. 'Correct?' Her own statements must seem to her slight now, and capable of being checked against the state of Fleischman's knowledge at any time.

Fleischman nodded. For me, there was coffee with only a drop of milk; Fleischman could tell the right kind of coffee to suit every face. As long as Fleischman was conducting the interrogation I wouldn't be able to ask a single question. Yet I would very much have liked to find out from her how long she thought

Batalov had lived in the country, and how she would have described his Russian identity. Couldn't he really have had a South German accent, not a Russian one at all? Although she hadn't actually claimed that he was Russian. People's origins tend to reveal themselves, and we were far from knowing all there was to know about his. The doubts that existed were our reason for considering Nelly important. It was perfectly possible that she could tell us things that reinforced or weakened various suspicions. Batalov was said to have come to the country to work as a translator, but we had been unable to find a single publication under his name. We had studied all the lists of positions as state translators, and even among the names of other translators and similar employees his did not appear. The story that he had not completed the process of applying for naturalisation yet, which had been given as the reason for his inability to marry Nelly, was very probably a lie. At least, we had been unable to find any such application with his name on it.

When Miss Killeybegs brought the fourth cup, Fleischman thanked her courteously, but at the same time dismissed her from the room again with an impatient wave of his hand. He stirred his coffee, looked at Nelly, his glasses steamed up with condensation, and he held the cup a little further off until the mist before his eyes dispersed. Neither bafflement nor a question could be seen in his eyes, as if he knew Nelly's answers and was asking the questions only for the sake of civility and a sense of order.

'Did you and Batalov spend the night of 11 April at the Blue House and come close to one another on that occasion?'

'I'm not telling you that.' Nelly regretfully shook her head.

'You spent the night there, in the attic storey. The two lower bedrooms were occupied by the other guests.' Fleischman took a large gulp of coffee.

The whites of Nelly's eyes were flushed with red. Maybe little veins had burst from the strain of following Fleischman's information and not crying with fear and horror.

'The two of you became really close, however, two weeks later in another friend's apartment.' Fleischman was still smiling. 'What was that friend's name?'

Nelly dropped her coffee cup. She took no notice of the brown splashes that the coffee left on her dress and her tights. There was no telling, from her reaction, whether she had dropped the cup on purpose or by accident. She wasn't looking at Fleischman but straight past him. However, she said, 'Your colleague wasted a lot of time asking about names yesterday. I don't want to name any names. You're treating me just as the Stasi did. Names, names, names. To you, human beings are nothing but carriers of information. I didn't give the Stasi any names, and I won't give you any either.'

Fleischman looked at her half amused, half interested, and then he nodded as if she were quite right. Frau Schröder stood up and poured him more coffee. No one moved to clear away the broken pieces of Nelly's coffee cup. She was not offered any more coffee. Fleischman's cup was steaming. He tried a tiny sip, but it was obviously still too hot. Then he raised a finger as if the next question had only just occurred to him. 'You said yesterday that Vassily Batalov threw himself off the top of a building.'

Nelly shook her head.

The clattering of the typewriter stopped, but Frau Schröder couldn't remember any statements made yesterday. She hadn't been present then, she did her job exclusively in the distinguished halls and rooms of the CIA. Indifferently, as if she didn't hear the meaning of the spoken words, she stared ahead of her into space.

'No, it was your colleague who said that. I didn't contradict him. But Vassily didn't fall off any building. I don't believe it. He was afraid of heights, he wouldn't climb a roof just for fun and throw himself off it.'

'Committing suicide isn't fun.' Fleischman looked at the hot coffee in his cup appreciatively, and drank it without any blowing or slurping. Frau Schröder clattered, went down to the next line, clattered, made a correction and stopped.

Nelly crossed her leg and bit one of her fingernails. 'You don't happen to have a pair of nail scissors, do you? I broke a nail a little while ago, and I can't find my nail scissors. I probably forgot to bring them.'

Fleischman and I looked at Frau Schröder, who didn't notice for several seconds. 'What? Excuse me, but what did you say? Nail scissors – that's a genuine question, isn't it? I mean, I don't have to make a note of it?'

'My dear, we never ask anything but genuine questions here – but no, indeed, you don't have to make a note of this one. Perhaps you could answer it.' Fleischman had an almost considerate relationship with Frau Schröder, who certainly had no idea that but for his thoughtfulness she would have lost her job with us some time ago.

'I . . . well, I'd have to go and look . . . wait a moment, oh no, here's my handbag.' She took her bag off the arm of her chair and searched its contents.

Sure enough, she did produce a small manicure case and put it carefully down beside her typewriter. Nelly got to her feet, picked up the case, thanked Frau Schröder and sat down with it on her chair again. She unzipped it. The scissors had gilt handles. 'The death certificate said: *Died of a broken neck after suicide by throwing himself off a rooftop.* The space where a doctor was supposed to sign was struck through.' She drew in air through her teeth; obviously she had cut herself, or perhaps the damage to the nail had gone deeper than she thought and the cuticle was torn.

Fleischman cast me a triumphant glance.

Nelly looked at her sandals, then raised her head and looked me straight in the eye. I smiled, but of course she did not smile back. She put the scissors away in the manicure case.

'What do you mean by that?'

'I mean exactly what I said. That was recorded on the death certificate I had to sign. It was remarkably detailed, considering that there didn't seem to be any known witnesses.' She zipped up the manicure case. 'And I wasn't to bother about the rest of the formalities of his funeral because he wasn't a citizen of the state yet. But I expect you know all about that, don't you? The funeral arrangements were a matter for the authorities, so to speak. All the same, they'd put a bunch of carnations on the coffin, and there was a showy flower display – you know, with flowers that haven't been available here for years. Hadn't been available over there, I mean. White roses, enormous lilies looking almost artificial, double carnations. Not what you'd call tasteful. It was an impressive arrangement, though, particularly as the card tucked into the bow of ribbon just said *In farewell to a faithful comrade*, and no one could find out who had sent it.' Nelly stood up. She had to wait a minute until the clattering stopped and she could give Frau Schröder her manicure case back.

'Maybe the Artists' Association?' Fleischman went off at a tangent.

'Are you asking me? I can imagine you know who it was.'

'Who was it?' Fleischman dwelt on the question in such a way that I myself couldn't decide whether he knew who had sent the flowers or not.

'I don't know.' Nelly shook her head, rubbed her eyes and crossed her legs the other way. A piece of broken china crunched under the sole of one sandal.'Certainly not the Artists' Association. He wasn't a member. Do you think that as a translator and a Russian he could walk into it just like that?' Nelly raised one arm to brush the hair back from her face. Only now did I notice the large patches of sweat that had formed on her dress under her armpit. 'Do you know what surprised me? His parents didn't come to the funeral. A young man dies, and not a single family member comes. His father must already have been very infirm by then. Vassily told me he'd been ill a long time. They had probably kept in touch by letters. Then the authorities promised me to let his parents know. I couldn't come by anything myself – no address, nothing, his apartment was sealed – I had no rights.' Nelly shook her head, passed the palms of her hands over her face and looked at me for help. 'Could you give me a glass of water?'

I was about to stand up and get her some water when Fleischman, who didn't seem to have noticed my movement yet, said sternly,'We'll be stopping for a break soon. Go on with what you were saying for now, Frau Senff. You had no rights?'

I could tell from her voice how dry Nelly's mouth was. 'Unmarried. Later they delivered a few personal things for me and the children. But neither his father nor his mother came to the funeral. I've always wondered whether they were refused a travel permit.'

Now at the latest I would have asked Nelly how she accounted to herself for the fact that she and her lover Batalov were still living apart. She would certainly have said it was because his apartment was also his workplace. But that made it all the more surprising that she had no address of any kind for his family – there had never been a meeting with them earlier. It was perfectly possible that the story of his German-born mother who was said to have married in Russia was pure invention. I imagined the horror that Nelly Senff might feel if we told her about such suppositions, how she would wind all her strands of hair round her fingers at once, and keep smacking her dry lips, how she would finally collapse and one of us would have to catch her as she fell. I wouldn't hesitate for long. In that case I wouldn't fail to admire her pretty dress. For a fraction of a second I thought of stripping off that dress to relieve her of the patches of sweat, which must be uncomfortable for her. And I need say nothing about her tights and much else that I could do, which surely would strike her as a good deed and unhoped-for protection.

However, Fleischman seemed to be a stranger to both attraction and pity. He was a professional through and through, and I could see not the slightest personal emotion in him. He would not let Nelly Senff know any of the important details that were very probably known only to the CIA. After all, the other secret services would have their turn after us, and it would have been incautious to let Nelly know any more.

Fleischman sighed. 'What could the absence of a doctor's name on the death certificate mean?'

'It meant that I wasn't to have any name or address I could turn to if I wanted to find out what exactly might have happened. It meant there was no one who would tell me that he was certainly the man who fell from that roof, that he threw himself off it. And what else does it mean?' Nelly glanced at her wristwatch. 'At night I dream of him coming back, he appears from behind a building and draws me into a corner. He confesses that he's still alive, only it would be better for everyone to believe that he's dead.'

'And could that be the truth?'

Nelly laughed, a child's laugh so far as I, a childless man, could judge.

Fleischman looked at her challengingly.

'My mother says that often happened to her generation. Her friends, still young girls if they survived, had all lost some man or other – sometimes all the men they knew. And a man coming back was a common dream, they all had it. It's nothing unusual, you see, you're probably comforting yourself by conjuring up that mirage. The time and place are different, and that's something in common to the dream as well. As if you were in a system of coordinates of points of the compass all over the world, a system in common to everyone.'

'You may be right there.' Fleischman put his head on one side and scratched himself. 'I never thought of it like that before. But the fact is that you don't know if what the death certificate says is true.'

'There are a lot of things we don't know.'

'He could still be alive.'

'If they could invite his parents to stand beside an empty grave, yes. Or he could be dead. Fallen off that very roof. Except that he'd hardly have jumped off it himself, he'd have been pushed.'

'Who'd have had any interest in pushing him off the roof?' Fleischman was acting stupid.

Nelly shrugged her shoulders and yawned.

'What makes you think of an idea like that? Is there anything to support it?'

'The fact that he didn't leave a farewell letter.'

'A very personal motive for such an insinuation.'

'No, a motive would be different,' Nelly informed him. 'It's an idea, nothing but an idea. I mean, aren't we talking about our ideas?' She leaned forward, hunching her shoulders, put her hands over her face and took a deep breath. I'd been wondering how long it would be before she shed tears. Fleischman looked at me, and I thought I saw satisfaction in his eyes. Contentment. Up to this point Nelly Senff had seemed entirely indifferent, her manner as easy as that of a girl passing on rumours that may be cruel in their way but don't touch her, leave no trace at all in the girl's appearance or behaviour. She went on sitting in that hunched position.

'Were you able to see him? Did they offer to let you see him one last time?'

'No, what use would that have been? It seems he was badly disfigured. Do you think they'd have anaesthetised him and made up his face, and then put him in front of me anaesthetised and with his face made up, and I'd have believed them? You think I'd assume he was dead, and the last I saw of him would have been that distorted illusion?' Her voice came from deep inside her. She must be freezing in her lightweight summer dress.

She didn't look at us, she didn't straighten up. 'Will you let me leave now? I can't talk to you any longer. You didn't know Vassily; what business of yours is his death?'

'Did you think all that at the time? That his death might be a spectacle specially staged for you?' Fleischman interrupted her, disregarding her plea to be allowed to leave.

She raised her head and shoulders; still bending forward, she smoothed the dress over her legs and ran her thumb over the fabric, where there was a large coffee stain. She said to the coffee stain, not to Fleischman or to me, 'Such ideas do come into your mind when you've been in a situation like ours, where there's no indication of possible suicide. Vassily didn't kill himself at home. The dead person isn't found by friends or relations but picked up by strangers.'

'The dead person. You speak as if this sort of thing often happened.'

'There are such cases, yes. Are you trying to make out you don't know?' Now she straightened right up. She had not been crying. She looked at us, first Fleischman, then me, then

Fleischman again. 'You surely know that people disappear in strange ways. Some turn up again in prison, others are said to have committed suicide. The combination of prison and so-called suicide isn't unusual, either.'

'Supposing your suspicion is correct, just supposing, then Batalov didn't kill himself but was abducted or murdered. What motive could the state have for that?'

'What do you want me to say? I knew Vassily, and I think I know that he had no intention of committing suicide. But do you think I know a state? Maybe they didn't like his Russian nose. You misunderstood me if you think I suspected he'd been abducted or murdered.'

'Isn't that what you were just saying?'

'No. I only suggested that there are many possibilities. What else could I do but think about it? How could I decide about a person supposed to be dead, how could I presume to decide about Vassily and whether he died of his own free will, so it was his own responsibility – or whether someone else, an amorphous grey blob called the state was responsible? I can't make that decision.' Nelly's eyes were watering now. 'There are moments when I think he did it himself – and then I'm glad and proud, and I think at least he made his own decision, he liked to take responsibility with no grey blob in the way. But then again it soothes the pain in me and I feel that my pride in him hurts me and our children, and I tell myself he wasn't as crazy, as ir-responsible, as tired as all that. At such moments I hate the whole country, I see a potential murderer in every person on the street following his usual routine in silence so as to do his duty some day. I see a father fetching his child from school, and I can't help thinking he might wear a uniform on duty, he could have been the one who killed Vassily, perhaps with a blow to the back of the neck, perhaps with a shot. I see the man tossing his child in the air, and then I look away, I see my own son and take hold of him and try to toss him in the air, but he's too big and heavy – and he doesn't have a father to toss him in the air, only a mother to hug him . . .'

Nelly's eyes were swimming. Fleischman did not allow himself to show any satisfaction.

'. . . and I avoid looking at that other father. After all, the man could be a baker and I could be eating his rolls every morning, if you see what I mean. Then I go crazy myself. That's how it is. And when I'm exhausted I think: You're making it too easy for yourself. An indefinable Something is to blame – even if it takes no responsibility. Then, at the latest, the moment has come when I have to go, I can't stay where I am any longer. That's why I went and why I'm sitting here now.'

'You think you'll simply be able to shake off a past like that here?' Fleischman smiled, an accomplished smile, a studied, a sharply cutting smile, and Nelly withstood that smile as if it didn't hurt; she shook her head, and her eyes sprayed contempt.

Krystyna Jabłonovska's brother makes plans

One day, the day after Jerzy's operation, I went to the hospital and found myself standing by an empty bed.

The young blonde nurse came in.

'Where is he, please, Nurse?'

'Don't worry, Frau Jabłonovska, he came through it all very well. We had to take your brother into the washroom for a little while. He had a slight epileptic fit and soiled himself. Sit down and wait a minute, the male nurse will bring him back straight away.'

Large drops of water were dripping off my fur coat onto the linoleum flooring. They formed small lakes. I sat there waiting. I could sense that Jerzy's neighbour in the ward was looking at me, devouring me with his eyes. I looked out of the window, and he said, his eyes still on me, 'Pretty cold today, right?' I looked at the tree, black with rain, with only a few leaves left on its branches, but many raindrops. 'Nice crisp weather,' he said, clicking his tongue. Then I heard him slurping from his spout cup, and ventured to glance at him surreptitiously. He was staring at my neckline, and I drew the fur coat closer and watched a black bird sitting on the tree and cawing. 'Fat as butter,' I heard Jerzy's neighbour say, and, 'What a little podge,' and I watched a second black bird arrive, perch beside the first, and the first flew away. When my brother was brought in, the male nurse lifted him out of the wheelchair and put him on his bed. Nurse Hildegard, who was approaching retirement, plumped up the pillow and straightened Jerzy's nightshirt. He seemed to have become thoroughly entangled in it while he was being moved about, they had to turn him over from left to right, and for a brief moment my eyes fell on the dark, soft piece of flesh lying wrinkled up on his thigh; it was small, as small as my little finger, and it took me another moment to work out what it was. A click of the tongue came from the bed next to his, but no one except me seemed to notice. My brother's glazed eyes met mine as if he noticed me watching him. I quickly looked away and told myself that I could hardly have seen it. My opportunities of seeing such things were limited. Was the bird out on the tree holding a worm in its beak? Nurse Hildegard put my brother's bed socks on him before covering him up with the nightshirt.

'Five marks, yes,' the male nurse told her, 'and that after three weeks of all-round care. Generous, I call it.'

She snorted. 'Drop the subject. You'll get used to it.'

'I won't. I'd sooner start going to evening classes.' The male nurse adjusted Jerzy's blanket until it was wrapped round and under his feet and smooth on top of them.

'You've been saying that ever since I've known you, dear, and that's at least four years.'

The blonde nurse came over. 'Can I help?'

'You can lift him and the two of us will pull the sheet; it's still creased.' The male nurse obeyed Nurse Hildegard's instructions, raised Jerzy above the bed, and the blonde young nurse and Nurse Hildegard straightened the sheet.

'You wash them day in, day out, you do things for them when no one else wants to touch them – and five marks is all the thanks you get.' The male nurse was talking like a waterfall.

'No idea of what's right and proper, these people, no idea

at all.' The blonde nurse appeared to know exactly what he meant.

'They might as well not give us anything at all, isn't that so, Doro?' asked the male nurse, and the young nurse nodded and laughed in an unseemly manner. 'When you're right,' she said, 'you're right,' the other two added in chorus, and the three of them pulled at the covers, taking care that they showed no creases in spite of being tucked in like that, tugging at them again and again.

I felt for my purse in the pocket of my fur coat; there were only a few marks left in it, nothing like enough there to give even one of the nurses five of them. The young blonde whom the male nurse had called Doro patted my brother's cheek as if he were a child, and said, 'Well, are we feeling better now?' She went away, giggling. I was embarrassed by her lack of respect, even more so because I knew how little my brother could notice it.

I heard that click of the tongue again, and now that Jerzy had landed safely in his bed and I felt his slender, cool hand in mine, I looked at the man in the next bed, summoning up all my self-confidence. 'The older the bolder,' he said, clicking his tongue again, and he gave me a startled but at the same time friendly smile.

The operation had been successful, Jerzy had come round from the anaesthetic. He asked, in Polish, if I was his mother.

'No, Jerzy,' I said, wondering whether I had to tell him that our mother had died seventeen years ago, presumably of the same disease that he had now. 'I'm Krystyna.'

'That's good.' He nodded, lost in thought, and I wondered whether he knew who Krystyna was. Maybe he was simply hiding his uncertainty behind the nod. He felt that he got his bearings when he nodded, so he kept on nodding at regular intervals.

'Yes.' I showed him the photo of our father sitting on the double bunk bed waving to Jerzy. 'Father sends his love.'

'Where is he?'

'In the camp. You know he doesn't like moving about. He lies in bed all day. A week ago, just before your operation, he sat up and asked me to find someone to take a photo of him. So that you won't forget him, he said. But he's the one who keeps forgetting you're in hospital. He complains because you don't come to see him often, but then thinks you're away working to get us an apartment, and sometimes he gets impatient and asks when you're going to come and get us out of the camp.'

'We're in the camp?'

'Mmm.' I gave Jerzy the photo.

Jerzy turned the drip and shook his head over the photo, at a loss. 'But that was a long time ago, right? I thought our time in the camp was over. They let Father and me go, Krystyna. The war really is over now, isn't it?' Jerzy looked uncertainly at me, then laughed as if he'd caught me out telling a lie. It wasn't only our father who forgot where his son was and that we had come to Germany because of him, so that he could get good treatment. The doctor had warned me that the progress of the disease, and also the operation and the anaesthetic it entailed, could lead to mental confusion. It would probably go away again, he said, but he couldn't be absolutely sure of that in advance.

'What year is this, Jerzy?'

'Why are you asking? Do you think I don't know?' Jerzy looked out of the window. His feelings were injured. I went over to the wardrobe and took the women's magazine out. He could read its date of publication on the cover and spare me the embarrassment of having to ask him.

'Look, here's your paper, Jerzy.' The cover showed a blonde woman with pink lips in silk underwear. *Agneta chooses her own clothes*, said a caption in small lettering under the picture.

Jerzy cast me an angry glance, and then his face cleared. 'No, you're wrong, Krystyna, that isn't mine.'

We said nothing for a while.

'You look so pale, Krystyna. Are you sad?' My brother, as white as the wall himself, was looking at me in concern.

'It doesn't matter.'

'You're having trouble with that piece by Liszt, aren't you? You're still practising the solo. It's too expressive for you, Krystyna. It needs to be played passionately, it needs passion.'

I shook my head. He didn't even seem to remember that I had sold my cello to pay for the German papers. 'I'm not playing Liszt these days.'

'Have you begun on the Brahms sonata, number 2 in F major, opus 99?' Even he seemed to doubt that.

'No, Jerzy.'

'Krystyna, don't say another word. Chopin's sonata for cello and piano in G minor, that's it, Krystyna.'

I could have given my life for Jerzy. Just playing the cello, if only he could take it in.

'I knew it, Krystyna. Oh, I knew you'd begin to work on that one some day! And you think of that young man when you play it, am I right? The redhead. What was his name? In your mind, you're thinking of that young pianist.'

'I'm not thinking of anything at all, Jerzy. What young man? Any young man could easily be my son.'

'Your son? But you aren't even married, Krystyna, how could he be your son?'

'Exactly.'

'What son are you talking about, Krystyna?'

'I'm not talking about any son. I'm talking about the son I don't have.' I was beginning to lose patience.

'Then why are you so angry?'

'Oh, for goodness' sake, I'm not angry.'

As the door behind me opened, Jerzy plucked at my blouse. 'Psst, quick, hide, Krystyna.'

I lowered the magazine and looked round. The young blonde nurse came in with one of the other men from Jerzy's ward and led him over to his bed.

'Hide!' Jerzy impatiently tugged my sleeve.

'There's no reason for me to hide,' I said, freeing myself from his grasp. I had to prise his fingers open one by one, he was clutching my sleeve so hard.

'Go on, hurry up.' Jerzy was furious, and I looked at him in surprise. I had never yet needed to hide. My resistance seemed to be causing him real distress; he rolled his eyes, took a deep breath, and finally tried pushing me a little way off. Then I saw a smile on his face, a gentle, enraptured smile. But it wasn't meant for me; he was smiling at something in the room beyond me. I turned, and saw the nurse removing a few faded flowers from the other patient's vase and taking them out of the ward. When I looked at my brother again, he was smiling abstractedly with his gaze on the door. He even seemed to have forgotten how to nod.

'Jerzy?' I raised the magazine. 'Jerzy?'

My brother seemed to be frozen in mid-smile. 'That's Dorothea. We're in love.'

'Who's Dorothea?'

'The pretty girl. Didn't you see her? She wears a white dress every day, just for me. Do-ro-thea.'

I looked into his mouth, which was wide open. They didn't even clean his teeth for him properly here.

'We're in love.' He closed his mouth and smacked his lips with relish, as if he were eating a delicious dessert.

I nodded.

'It'll be on Monday,' whispered Jerzy.

'Oh yes?'

'The twentieth of October, that's a good date.'

'It is?'

'I'm going to ask her to marry me.'

'Ah.' Exhausted, I let myself drop into the chair beside his bed. We said nothing for a while. He smiled and nodded, and I looked out of the window to avoid his smile. There was no bird in the tree any more.

'Something like this doesn't often happen in life, Krystyna. Maybe just once. And then you mustn't let the opportunity pass.'

'Why did you want me to hide?'

'Who knows, she might have been jealous. She doesn't know anything about you.'

'She doesn't know anything about me?'

'Shhh.'

I hesitated for a moment, and then tapped the magazine. 'Look, Jerzy, this magazine –'

'Oh, it's not mine.' He tried to lie on his side. 'You've missed the train, Krystyna, I don't expect you'll get a husband at all now.' He raised his head. 'But anyway, it's probably better for a woman cellist not to have a husband. No children, no husband, at the most . . .' he couldn't manage to turn in bed '. . . at the most an unhappy love affair.'

I stood up to help him turn.

'No, don't. Dorothea will do that when she comes back. And no son, do you hear, Krystyna? You're too old anyway. And the man in the next bed says too fat. But what does he know about cellists?'

'Leave me alone, Jerzy.' I sat down again.

'I tell you what, you should try the Mendelssohn sonata as well. Number 2, opus 58.'

'I've tried it already. It's not the sort of thing I can play.'

'That's why you should try it. You ought always to try things that you can't do yet.'

'Jerzy, I don't like Mendelssohn's sonata number 2.'

'That makes no difference, Krystyna. The chance of a great passion doesn't come to everyone of its own accord – a lot of people have to look for it.'

'You could say the same of yourself,' I commented, and opened the magazine.

'What?'

'What is the date today, Jerzy?'

'Well, of course it's the nineteenth of October, Krystyna, if tomorrow is the twentieth.'

'And what year?'

'You don't know anything.' Jerzy looked at me in concern, and shook his head.

'I do know what year it is, but maybe you don't.'

'Weren't you just going to leave, Krystyna?'

'No, why?'

'You stood up.'

'I did, but now I'm sitting down again,' I said, and thought: I won't be leaving in a hurry today. In fact there was nothing for me to do in the camp but sit about. In which case I'd rather sit here. The tongue-clicking sound from the next bed made me nervous, but not unpleasantly so. Sometimes there was a little conversation with one of the others in Jerzy's ward. I heard his neighbour whisper, 'What a little podge,' again, and it had a gentle, caressing sound. I remembered the German of what he said; I'd look it up in the dictionary when I was back in the camp and make sure of the meaning before I ventured to look at his surprised face again.

I could give my whole life for Jerzy if only I was playing the cello. Instead I'd brought him to Germany and this hospital, I'd sold my cello, and all I could do now was hold his hand. I stroked that hand and said, 'See you tomorrow.'

Nelly Senff is asked to dance

With Aleksei holding my right hand and Katya holding my left hand, I rang the Polish woman's doorbell, a floor below ours. I'd met her only yesterday on the staircase. They said her father spent all day in bed asleep, so she must be at home.

'Excuse me, please. I hope you weren't still asleep?'

The Polish woman dried her plump, wet hands on her apron and held one of them out to me. 'It's Sunday, isn't it?'

'Yes, nine o'clock. I'm sorry to call so early.' Maybe I'd have done better not to ring the bell. 'I thought I'd just try you. There's no school on Sunday, and I have to go out, but I can't take the children.'

'Come along in.'

Aleksei shook himself under the pressure of her large paw, and Katya retreated half a metre and clung to my hand. A penetrating odour of cabbage and pork met us. We went in.

'My father's still asleep,' she said apologetically, but all the same she asked us to sit down at her little table, which was just the same as ours upstairs. In fact the entire room was identical to ours. The same metal bunk beds, the same compressed wood chairs, the same flooring. The arrangement of the furniture looked identical as well. The green waste-paper basket stood, like ours, right between the door and the wardrobe. Even the bedlinen, checked blue and white, was exactly like ours, which was not surprising, since everyone went to the same place to collect it.

'We used to go to church every Sunday,' she said. 'But the Catholic church here is so different, and a long way off. My father can't walk there any more. We're believers, you see.' She lit a candle on the table and straightened up the little picture of the Virgin leaning against the candle. 'Are you new here?' The Polish woman pulled the chair back and let first me and then the children sit down at the table.

'Yes, we've been here since Monday.'

'Would you like a coffee? Excuse me, I was preparing lunch, I must just add a little water and stir the pan. Please wait.' I glanced at the time, but the Polish woman was already passing a cup over my shoulder. 'It's black, you'll need plenty of sugar.' She gave me a friendly smile, and without asking me spooned teaspoon after teaspoon into my cup.

'Stop, that's plenty, thank you.' I held my hand over the cup while sugar fell between my fingers.

'Oh, did I introduce myself? I'm Krystyna. As you can hear, my father is sleeping peacefully.' Just as she said that her father half choked on a snore, cleared his throat and turned over in the top bunk.

'Coca-Cola for the children?' Before I could open my mouth to point out that it was not only Sunday, but Sunday morning, she disappeared into the kitchen. Looking pleased and embarrassed, my children nibbled their lips as they looked forward to the Coca-Cola.

'New here, are you?' The old man leaned over the side of the top bunk.

'Good morning. Excuse us, please, we didn't mean to wake you.'

'Oh, nobody wakes me. I'm an early riser, always have been.' The Polish woman's father sat up in bed and passed the flat of his hand over the white hair on his chest.

'Do you like music?' He showed us a small radio that he obviously kept on top of the bunk bed, and turned it on. *There we sat down, yea, we wept, when we remembered Zion. By the rivers of Babylon.* He nodded his head and turned the little wheel to tune the radio with his thumb. As soon as he had found a different piece with a faster rhythm, he turned up the volume and climbed down from his bed. 'Would you like to dance?' And he was reaching for my hand to pull me up from the chair, just as his daughter came into the room with the bottle of Coca-Cola.

'Father, don't do that.' Frau Jabłonovska put her hands over her ears.

'You know, I was the best dancer for miles around, no one could dance better than me.' The old man smelled of sleep, and pushed me round the room with his paunch. 'There were wonderful dances, you know' – his eyes were shining – 'and the girls, ah, there they stood, each more charming than the next. You see, they were all just waiting for me to ask them to dance.'

'Father.' Seeing her father dancing, Frau Jabłonovska had gone red in the face and was trying to grab hold of his pyjamas. 'Father, stop it. This lady is our guest.'

'That's why, my plump little pigeon, that's why.' He danced round his daughter as if she were nothing but a decorative pillar in the ballroom, 'And a one, two, three – there, you see, it's easy.' His paunch led the dance, making sure that I didn't tread on his feet, his hands kept us both balanced.

'I'm Vładisłav,' he whispered, 'and may I ask your name?' The old man's lips brushed my ear.

'Nelly.'

'What?'

'My name is Nelly.'

'What a pretty waist you have. You must go dancing often.'

'No, not at all.' His courtesy was touching. As a good dancer himself, after all, he must have noticed by now that I didn't know any of his steps, let alone my own.

'Father, the lady would like to leave, do let go of her.'

'The lady would like to leave? Oh, I don't think so.' Holding me firmly, he whirled me round until I felt dizzy. 'Yes, I was the best dancer. I once won the big prize in Stettin – guess who my partner was? And no, she wasn't Krystyna's mother.' He paused for effect. 'Cilly Auerbach, no less. What a dancer she was!' He guided me through the room before him as if I were a shield.

A loud knocking on the wall made Frau Jabłonovska turn down the music.

'Father, please.' But Frau Jabłonovska was shooed from one corner of the room to the next by her father, along with me and his elbow. 'The neighbours, Father. It's Sunday morning.'

'And guess what? She wanted to marry me.' He laughed out loud. 'She was still almost a child, she'd just made her first successful films, and she wanted to marry me! And a one, a one, two, three!'

The music ended, and the woman announcer launched into a news item of some length about the rising rate of unemployment.

He sat down beside Katya and took hold of her chin, 'So who's this pretty little girl?' However, he didn't wait for an answer, but turned back to me and said, 'How they admired us in those days, after the First World War! We were mere children – that amazes you, eh? How old do you think the gentleman you've just been dancing with is?'

I didn't want to hurt his feelings, so although I was sure he must be over seventy I shrugged my shoulders as if I had no idea. He coughed. 'Ah, you'll never guess the answer, my child. Oh no. Isn't there a cup of coffee for me, Krystyna?' he asked, and his daughter, who couldn't find a place for herself to sit at the little table now, since it had only four chairs, set off to find him a cup. As soon as she was through the door he took a dark red cigarette packet out of the pocket of his pyjama top, and lit himself one of the unfiltered cigarettes in it, coughing. 'She used to be a cellist,' he said, looking at the doorway, 'but that's all over now, thank God. We sold the cello to get our papers. She was no good at it anyway. She taught at the Conservatory, wasn't good enough to get any further.' The old man ran his fingers through his sparse hair; he seemed to feel bitter about his daughter's lack of talent and success. 'Can you think what it was like, having to put up with that squealing all day long? She really got on my nerves.' He whispered these last words as the door opened, and his daughter reappeared.

'There are children present, Father.' Frau Jabłonovska flapped her hand vigorously, put the coffee down in front of him, and spooned sugar into his cup too. Music came from the radio again. Vładisłav Jabłonovski stood up, turned the little wheel, and drew me up from the table by my hand.

'Children, ah yes, I already had children. But that didn't bother a girl like Cilly Auerbach. You know, I was the best dancer for miles around.' He stopped by the table for a moment as we danced past, and gulped his coffee. 'I once won the big Stettin prize for dancing. Everyone was there. Everyone.' He made a sweeping gesture.

'Father, perhaps the lady is in a hurry. She wanted to leave the children here, am I right?' Frau Jabłonovska was stepping restlessly from one foot to the other.

I was about to say yes, she was right, but Vładisłav Jabłonovski was going on again.

'Only girls, girls everywhere far and wide, Ah, the number of men had gone down in the war, you see, and the chances of young fellows like me at the time weren't so bad. You've no idea how many of the women were tired of waiting for their menfolk. And a few of those men never came back at all, did they? But I could dance in those days, let me tell you.'

'Gypsies!' The voice from the room next door was as loud as if the speaker were standing here with us. 'Bloody Polacks! Gypsy rabble!' Something thudded against the wall; it sounded more like a heavy object than a human fist.

'Father, she has to go, didn't you hear me? She has to go now.' Frau Jabłonovska took my hand and pulled me away from him. 'Be good!' I called to my children as old Jabłonovski went on with his stories.

At the door of the apartment Frau Jabłonovska gave me her soft hand. 'Please forgive us, my father is usually perfectly calm. He's been lying in bed for weeks. And then he sees a young woman and gets all worked up, telling the same stories over and over again, how he was a hero, there's no stopping him. And what a hero!'

'Well, thank you anyway. The children didn't want to be left upstairs on their own. I'll certainly be back about one o'clock. You will look after them, won't you?'

'Of course. I like looking after children.' She looked at me half pleased, half expectantly. Perhaps she was glad that I didn't say anything about her father but just needed her. Perhaps, too, she was hoping I'd tell her where I had to go so urgently on a Sunday morning, and why I couldn't take the children with me. But I simply thanked her and left.

Hans Pischke, queuing up, has very few wishes

It was drizzling outside. The leaves of the birch trees looked heavy with rain and colourless. No wind moved them, the rainy drizzle weighed down so heavily. Two children were sitting eating sweets on the iron climbing frame which had once been red, but the red paint was splitting and peeling off most of it. The paper bag into which they were dipping in turn was softened by the moist weather, so that they could hardly get their hands into it and out again.

Three women were queuing outside the centre where groceries were distributed. I joined them. The second woman in line, a substantial lady in a yellow rain cape, was scolding those in front of her, announcing that she was about to lose patience, she didn't have the time to spend an hour queuing for nourishment, there were five hungry mouths upstairs to be fed, but the first woman in the queue, thin and conscientious, was not to be distracted, and told the lady in charge of the centre, slowly and in carefully correct High German, that she didn't like sausage, nor did she feel like beginning a discussion now of whether or not sausage was a basic foodstuff, she simply did not like it, certainly not the sausage they had here, she would rather have more cheese, she didn't understand why, instead of her ration of sausage, she couldn't have the cheese they stocked here, which was certainly no more expensive. If you left aside the processed cheese also available, it was strong-smelling Tilsit of the simplest kind.

The lady at the food rations centre said in friendly tones that she had her instructions and must follow them, she couldn't give anyone cheese in return for a sausage coupon. However, the first in the queue wasn't giving up until the substantial second, scarlet in the face, turned to us, and appealed to me and the young woman between us for support. 'I don't believe it. Asking for special requirements! Did you ever hear of anything like it? She's been standing there for ten minutes and I've been here for nine, well, roughly nine, anyway.'

The young woman between us shifted from foot to foot. She was wearing a pale yellow summer dress with a pattern of large flowers, and obviously hadn't been expecting the rain. The dress was clinging to her calves. She bit her lip and looked embarrassed, so I suspected that she might come from Russia or Poland and didn't understand what was being said.

The thin woman also turned round, holding up her sausage coupon. 'Maybe someone would like to swap?'

'Swap?'

'Sausage for cheese.' Her punctiliously correct High German was confined to the bare essentials.

'You could have asked that earlier, right? We like sausage, my five hungry mouths and me. Sausage spread and sausage with bits of ham, oh, we like all kinds of sausage. So there we go.' And before anyone else could get a word in, the substantial lady in the yellow rain cape snatched the coupon from the hand of the malefactor in front of her.

They both ordered their groceries and went on their way, at a safe distance of five metres from one another.

'As if we didn't have enough to do,' remarked the woman in charge of the rations centre, nodding at the couple as they moved away, and said to herself, but loud enough for us to hear her, 'Five hungry mouths, I ask you! There've been almost four thousand here in the last year, if you count the Polacks. Almost four thousand in this camp alone.'

The woman in the summer dress ahead of me went up to the counter.

'Good morning,' she said, placing a small stack of coupons through the hatch to the woman behind the counter. 'Maybe you can help me. What do I get for a coupon like this?' She took the top coupon off the stack. Her voice was free of any provincial dialect; she spoke with a melodious East Berlin accent. When she stood on tiptoe and leaned forward, the wet hem of the flowered summer dress rode up and stuck to the backs of her knees.

'T, that's for a ration of tea. Here, M, that's for milk. B is bread. You can choose between wheat-and-rye bread or crispbread.'

'Oh, then I'll take – isn't there some of both available?' She put a strand of hair back behind her ear. The rain had left little droplets in her hair, like a shimmering hair ornament, and glancing at her sideways I saw her fine profile. She looked like a Czech fairy-tale princess.

'If you have two coupons. One coupon equals one ration.'

The woman behind the counter helped her to look through her coupons and sort them out.

'This is for jam, no choice, we only have strawberry. This is for butter or margarine, and this one is for coffee, that's only once a week. You have children, do you?'

'How do you know?' She ran her hand over her hair and wiped the fine raindrops away. Now her hair was just wet and no longer a princess's hair. A princess didn't have children.

'It's the milk rations. One adult alone doesn't get that much milk.' The woman behind the counter snorted with satisfaction, turned round and packed up the young woman's rations. 'Sausage spread or sausage with bits of ham?'

III

'Sausage spread, please.'

'Do you need sugar and salt?'

'Yes, please, we have nothing at all up there.'

'Oil?'

'Yes.'

'Can you carry it all?'

'Yes, I'm sure I can.'

'If not I expect this young man will help you.' The eyes of the woman handing out rations twinkled at me, and the young woman turned round. A smile flitted over her face. 'Oh no, you don't have to do that, I'm sure there's no need.'

'Here, I've packed it all in a carton. That will make it easier for you to carry.' The woman in the food rations centre pushed a carton over the counter, and the young woman took it, thanking her several times, as perhaps I had done myself the first time I was here. As she walked away I saw how her summer dress, heavy with rain, was sticking to her calves, keeping her legs together in a curious way so that she could take only very small steps. Myself, I left out the thanks this time. After all, it wasn't the lady handing out food who gave it to us; I assumed she was paid for her work. At least she did have work, and the superior, triumphant smile of an employee who combined usefulness with kindness, getting not only her monthly salary but the repeated thanks of new arrivals. I handed her my coupons.

'Any special wishes?'

'No, thank you.'

'Would you like wheat-and-rye bread or crispbread?'

'Whichever you have more of.'

'Do you really want two butter rations? You have two coupons here.' The woman held up the coupons concerned.

'Must be a mistake, no idea how that happened. No, I don't.'

'Cheese instead of one of them?'

'No thanks.'

'Sausage?'

'No, no, just keep them.' Her questions were too much for me. What I liked about the food rationing system was that it told you on the coupons what you got for them, and there were no major decisions to be made. I took my rations and said I didn't want the canned lentils that were available today.

'I still have some green beans,' the lady called after me, but I didn't turn back and refrained from thanking her. I didn't feel like heightening her sense of self-importance; there was far too much of it in her voice anyway.

The woman in the summer dress was standing in front of the two children on the climbing frame. They must have either finished their sweets or put them away. The young woman put her carton down on the frame between the children and showed them her loot: crispbread, sausage spread, sugar, and the rest. She lit a cigarette and watched as they took out packet after packet, examined all the things as they turned them this way and that, saying something about them.

I tried to catch the eye of the woman in the summer dress; I wanted to smile at her and see her own smile, but she wasn't looking my way, so I walked past her, hesitating at every step, going slowly and turning my head several times, just in case she was looking round after all. Then I opened the door to my staircase.

The baby had stopped bawling; presumably it had gone to sleep, or been taken out by its parents for some fresh air. At least, the door to the room next to mine was closed. The hair was no longer jammed in the frame of my own door, but a sign like that wasn't clear enough. After all, a draught of air could make the door rattle and blow hairs away. And even if the hair had still been there, who was to say that other people hadn't had the same idea, and could be clever enough to examine a locked door for hairs jammed in it? It would be easy for them to put the hair back in the door just where it was before. I spread butter on my crispbread and went over to the window. The new young woman was sitting at the foot of the climbing frame and smoking. She looked up at her children and said something. Her children laughed. She rubbed her bare calves; she must be freezing. I passed the palms of my hands over my pullover and whispered something. The woman in the summer dress stood up, and took a small object out of her coat pocket, holding it out to the boy, who wore glasses. The boy shook his head, but his sister made a grab for it. Then the boy pushed off from the climbing frame and jumped on his mother's back.

The rhythmic creak of metal springs, accompanied by a whimpering sound, made me suspect that my neighbour was now pursuing different tactics, probably hoping to pacify himself rather than his wife in that way. I folded the open side of the packet of crispbread, taking care that the fold coincided exactly with the top edge of the written words on the pack. That way, it ought to be possible to see whether someone had taken an interest in my crispbread while I was out. After I had swept the crumbs into one hand with the other, I fetched the dishcloth from the kitchen and wiped the table down. The dishcloth smelled mouldy, and I had to wash my hands with soap to get the smell right off my fingers. If there was one thing I hated it was crumbs lying around, crumbs of any kind. I took the crispbread into the kitchen and put it away in my side of the kitchen cupboard, leaving it at a distance of one centimetre between the pack and the front of the cupboard as well as the right-hand side of my compartment, and I put the rest of the rations away just as carefully.

When I turned round, my neighbour was standing there stark naked, looking at me, taken aback. 'Oh, I didn't know you were there.' He put his hands to his head.

'Sorry.'

His prick was still slightly erect, and he quickly covered it with his hand, but it was probably meant just as a gesture indicating that he was aware of his nudity rather than ashamed of it.

'I'm parched.' He clapped me on the shoulder in a comradely manner and turned the tap over the sink on. I stepped back, and he leaned forward to drink water from the mains in deep draughts. Then he opened the fridge and took out a bottle of beer. The young family's side of the fridge contained nothing but beer. I wondered what the baby's mother lived on. I wondered whether she was still breastfeeding her child. Probably not; the baby was crying with hunger. Perhaps the young family didn't trust me, so they kept their food in their room. When my former room-mate, who used to masturbate loudly when he was drunk, moved out he left about forty-five empty bottles in his locker. He had stacked them on their sides, along with several packets of crispbread and a small pack of mouldy cheese.

I got out of the kitchen. The baby was crying again, and I heard its mother tell her husband, 'This is hell, please leave me . . . or I'll have to . . . ay.' I wondered what she'd been saying in the parts I couldn't hear. *Please leave me in peace. Please leave me alone. Or I'll have to . . . ay. Run away? Get away?* What would she have said? However hard I listened for her husband's answer I couldn't hear it. Sitting on my bed, I spent about an hour suppressing my urge to have a pee. The baby cried. I suppressed the urge to pee for fear of meeting my neighbour again at the door to the toilet, or his wife. The bottle for emergency use was full. Only when I couldn't wait any longer, and could see no other receptacle in my room to offer temporary relief, after I had listened to the noises from the next room for a while and had decided they were harmless, did I venture out of my room. The bolt had been taken off the toilet door. The holes for the screws were still full of fine, pale sawdust. And however hard I concentrated I couldn't pee, it didn't work. At the ration distribution centre I had heard someone say that in the fifties there had been notices on the walls. You were not to talk to your room-mates or anyone else in the building. They could have been spies from State Security or some other organisation, infiltrated to find out about the opinions and habits of the refugees. There were no such notices today. They had been removed; the authorities probably thought that their unsettling effect was worse than the security they were meant to promote. But I knew that the spies were still there, not as many of them as in the fifties, of course, but still enough to have one of them watching our apartment, slinking in, taking the lock off the door, inspecting letters or notebooks or using small cameras to make a photographic record.

I still couldn't pee. Maybe the bolt was defective, and the block warden had had to fit a new one. The baby stopped bawling for a moment. The silence was almost unnatural. There was only the rushing in the water pipes of the toilet to show that anyone else lived in the building. A creaking in the corridor made me close my flies in alarm. But there was no one outside. Alternatively the neighbour wouldn't let his wife have a moment to herself on the toilet, couldn't stand her lamentations any longer, and had simply kicked the door in, breaking the lock. Except that then the holes for the screws wouldn't be intact. The baby was crying itself hoarse. I didn't see any empty beer bottles in the rubbish bucket; presumably the young family didn't know that bottles were returnable. I took a bottle out and slunk into my room. A glance out of the window. The new young woman and her children had disappeared. I had failed to notice which building she had gone to, and which door she had gone through. At last I was able to have a pee.

Weariness overcame me. I've let myself be driven away once

already, I thought, it won't happen a second time. Then, in spite of the baby's bawling, my eyes closed.

I dreamed of the woman in the summer dress. She shook her hair, soft, thick hair, until the raindrops sprayed off it, fell on my skin, cooled and then warmed it, naked as I was. I wanted to tell her that I couldn't and wouldn't touch a woman, but my mouth formed no sounds, however hard I tried I brought out only air, my vocal cords seemed to have disappeared, I wanted to give her a sign by way of communication, but she put out her hand, I retreated, and the glance in the air between us was a single glance, not mine, not hers, a glance that made me feel longing and of which at the same time I was ashamed, a weak, a strong glance, a glance that understood and demanded no touch, and was gone when I recognised my mother in a wicker beach chair, her sun hat so low over her face that I couldn't see it, I only knew that it was her. Finally she stood up and walked away, I followed her until even her shadow was lost from sight, and when I looked for her footprints in the sand I found nothing but bird tracks the size of side plates.

That afternoon I had to go to Room 201 in the block where the offices were. I had an appointment at the employment agency. The fifteenth or twentieth, I'd stopped counting. If a summons came I went. As usual, the corridor was full of people waiting. The air was moist and heavy, as if it were full of stress and patience. The men and women waiting were clutching the few magazines. When the man next to me was called in, he handed me his magazine, an old number dating back to last August. They never once missed the chance to publish an article about the country I had come from in these magazines. This time I read: *Prisoners: psycho-shock drives jail inmates to right-wing radicalism*. The article under that heading had been torn out. I closed the magazine and passed it on to the woman on my left. She thanked me several times.

'Pischke!'

I stood up.

'Well, how are you doing?' Lüttich tapped his leather waistcoat with his right hand, exploring it, reached into it with his left hand and produced a small packet of tobacco.

I closed the door behind me. 'I'm all right. How about you?'

'Well . . . to be honest, I hate this job, but who's giving up a civil service post in a hurry? Considering the labour market at present?' I couldn't decide whether his wink was meant for me, or was due to a crumb of tobacco or something like that in his eye. 'Ah well, we can't all have it easy.' He took out a cigarette paper and pressed the tobacco down firmly.

'We can't?'

'Nope.' He rolled the cigarette, licked the paper, stuck it together and put it behind his ear, then knocked tobacco crumbs off his newspaper over the waste-paper basket. 'Sit down, won't you?' Crumbs of tobacco fell to the floor and lay around the basket. He folded his newspaper, stood up and turned to the coffee machine. 'Would you like a coffee too?'

I nodded. He held a cup out to me and pushed the card index over the table. As he did so, some coffee slopped out of the cup, not on the table but on my trouser leg. I took the cup from him.

'Thank you,' I said, before he could say anything, and opened the card index box.

'You don't really need to look. They're still not in search of actors. And to tell you the truth, in all my ten years here there's only been a single vacancy for an actor, and that was to play a concentration camp inmate.'

Lüttich always told the story of this one case, the only job in ten years for people of my profession, and in the end none of the actors looking for work had been able to accept it because the offer was withdrawn – the right candidate had been found through some other agency, or the authorities' own film society, and he didn't want to consider any of the countless unknown and unemployed actors, allegedly so as not to raise their hopes only to dash them again, but really, as I had already told Lüttich months ago when he first told me the story, because you could assume that there was a good reason for an unemployed actor being out of work, for instance that he was downright un-talented and unsuccessful, which made him impossible to place, not worth looking at. Lüttich had obviously forgotten my own reason after he first heard it, because he kept telling me his story again, although clearly without remembering either that he had told it already or what I had told him in return. I didn't think the worse of Lüttich for that; after all, he must have seen other unemployed actors in his office from time to time. He probably just wanted to be sure that he had told them all his story, so that folk like us wouldn't look at him again, every time, with humiliating hope in our eyes. To spare him, I kept my eyes down when I greeted him and avoided any direct glance at first – I didn't want him to think me stupid or presumptuous, or hopelessly hopeful, and this way I could go on being hope-lessly hopeful undisturbed.

Lüttich lit the cigarette he had rolled for himself and inhaled. I waited for him to breathe out again, but as so often he didn't seem to do so. I could neither hear him exhaling nor see the smoke that must have come out of his mouth or nose sooner or later. I tried to watch him inconspicuously; I didn't want actual eye contact. But there was nothing to be seen. Lüttich appeared to have swallowed the smoke along with his own breath. The smoke might be dispersing inside him or, for all I knew, leaving his body through some aperture out of my field of vision. Lüttich took his time before inhaling again.

'Suppose you tried your first profession again? I'm always

getting asked for electricians. There's a post on offer here, for instance.' With his cigarette, he pointed to a card.

'Yes.' Hesitantly, I picked the card up.

'What about that last job? You were going to apply for it too, weren't you?'

I made a throwaway gesture to spare Lüttich and myself the word *rejection*. But Lüttich went on looking at me expectantly.

'They already had someone' was the phrase that occurred to me. I felt that I was gritting my teeth far too hard, and saw, from Lüttich's sympathetic glance, that he felt sorrier for me than I did for myself. I put the card down between us, and he picked it up.

'You must keep going, man. Don't lose heart.' With the card in his hand, Lüttich scrutinised me. Then, still holding it, he stroked his beard. I could positively sense his eyes resting on my face with a mixture of pity and misunderstanding, until they fell on his neat and tidy desk again. Casually, as if you didn't need air for it or as if he always had enough air to be able to speak, he said, 'Don't you think we might start thinking what else you could do?'

I looked up, thought about it, and glanced out of the window as I wondered what ideas he might have for me today.

'For instance, they want people to carry out artificial insemination on cattle in Schleswig-Holstein. I'm not joking, there's a big farm with jobs for two men.'

'And requests for that kind of thing go to Berlin?'

'Sometimes they go all over the Federal Republic. Everyone must have equal opportunities.'

'Equal opportunities.' I nodded indecisively.

'What about it? Will you give it a try?'

'I don't know that I'm suitable for carrying out artificial insemination. Look, I'm only one metre sixty, and that's if I stretch.' I avoided standing up and just straightened my back where I was sitting.

Lüttich laughed. 'It's nothing to do with height, Pischke, they have syringes and heaven knows what. Anyway, it doesn't say anything here about size being a condition.'

'You grew up in Berlin, I expect, Herr Lüttich?'

'Sure, lived in Berlin South all my life, grew up there, went to school, worked, loved, got engaged, split up – all of it in Berlin.' He laughed, satisfied.

I shook my head. 'People carrying out artificial insemination must at least be large enough to get an outstretched arm up inside the cow.'

'You're an expert on the subject, are you?'

I shook my head again. 'Worked on a collective farm.'

'What? Well, then you use a stool or a ladder or something.' Lüttich could hardly keep from grinning.

'I'd rather not. I don't have any head for heights and I'm inclined to hypothermia. I'm sure I'd die of cold in Schleswig-Holstein.'

Lüttich drew the card index box back to his side of the table and leafed through the cards. 'Admit it, the real reason for your flight from the East was sheer horror, bestial horror.' He laughed, and coughed on the smoke that was obviously still caught in the finely branching structure of his lungs. 'Flight from work on the collective farm, eh?' Ash fell from Lüttich's cigarette into the card index box, but he didn't seem to notice.

I shook my head. The mere idea of giving Lüttich a more accurate notion of the advantages and disadvantages of helping with the harvest made me feel exhausted, just as much as the idea of revealing my motives for flight accurately. My eyes were closing.

'Don't go to sleep, Pischke. Look, here's something for you. How about retraining as a U-Bahn driver? Hey, that would mean a good safe civil service job, don't you see? Once in the Berlin transport service you can't be fired.'

'U-Bahn driver?'

'Don't look so taken aback.' Lüttich stubbed out his cigarette and clapped me on the shoulder. 'My brother-in-law keeps his whole family on his pay as a ticket-office clerk, a good secure pension, they've even begun building.'

'Building?'

'A house. You understand the word? *House.*' He made an expansive gesture in the air, no doubt to give me an idea of the size of the house.

'You want me to build a house?' Astonished, I looked at Lüttich. I had never in my life thought of building myself a house.

'Ah, well, I can see that's not for you. Well, you need a whole family for a house. And where would you get a whole family?' He drew on his cigarette; what I'd assumed was sympathy had become comfortable self-satisfaction. 'Yes, well, it's not so easy. And not everyone likes the idea.' Lüttich went on looking through his card index, obviously running out of suitable conversational subjects, but true to his activity as a fixer he didn't give up. 'But as a train driver on the U-Bahn you'd get credit.'

'I don't want credit. I've never run up any debts.'

'Very high-minded of you.' There was a cutting edge to Lüttich's encouraging tone. 'But I wonder if you'll go on that way, Pischke. To be serious for once, almost everyone needs credit sometime or other. We're not in the East here. And if you ask me, you'd be stupid to carry on like that. Stop and think, you don't want to stay in the camp for ever, do you? This is no kind of life, sleeping in iron bunk beds, living with a huge great fence around the place, sharing an apartment with strangers.'

With an air of determination, Lüttich closed the card index

box. 'Tell me, is it true that you're none of you allowed out for the first week? That you live in a special building for that week?'

I looked around uncertainly, and shrugged my shoulders. Was he talking about his employment agency here? The camp? The city?

'I'd have thought you must know that.'

'My first week here is quite some time ago. I don't like remembering everything,' I claimed, but all the same I couldn't help thinking of the medical examinations, getting undressed, getting dressed, putting out my tongue, having my stools tested, raising and lowering my arms, the interview room where I had to spend several days, because the questions about my person and my political views, as well as my sketches of the ground plans of prisons, simply had not gone out for checking to the three Allied secret services, to the CIA in the green parkland of Berlin, to the allocation office and the office for admission to the Federal Republic. Then there was the application form that I had had to fill in twice, because the first form got lost, the preliminary examination, and finally the issuing of the admission certificate – a permit, a ticket allowing me to move around the camp but not out of it, only further in, the right to claim a roof over my head, the right to look for work, the right to financial support and food coupons in the middle of a transit camp for refugees and people who wanted to cross the border. And yet as long as I sat there wondering why I was here, I could come up with no answer. I had once had an answer, I even knew how it went. I had wanted to be free and think and do as I liked. But I no longer knew what I did like, and I had also lost my sense of the meaning of freedom, of what thinking and doing as I liked signified in concrete terms. The answer had become so pointless that it wasn't an answer any more. Suddenly I thought of warm hands, strong hands. Those large hands were on my skin, and I clung to them as they clung to me. Those hands could feel comfortable, but I wasn't sure of myself there.

'All right, Pischke.' Lüttich dismissed the subject. He probably thought he was sparing me embarrassment. Then he laughed. 'I've just thought of something, Pischke. Never mind job-seeking for now. It's not that I need it myself, but the subject has come to my ears: do you hear anything in here about women going on the game?'

Surprised, I looked at the calendar on his wall. He asked questions like a Secret Service man or a police officer.

'On the game – know what I mean? Prostitution. I mean, it does go on in the camps.' Lüttich hastily rolled himself a cigarette with one hand, laughed nervously, licked the paper, swallowed, lit the cigarette and drew on it deeply. 'Women are short of money, an opportunity turns up and so on, well, it's understandable.'

I puffed out my cheeks and raised my eyebrows.

'Doesn't ring a bell, eh? I was only asking.' Lüttich was fighting with the saliva in his mouth, swallowed and stood up. He clapped me on the shoulder with unexpected vigour. 'Wouldn't you like to buy yourself Wrangler's too?'

'Wrangler's?'

'Well, proper jeans. Like these.' He patted his own trousers. 'You go around the whole time in those – well, I don't want to hurt your feelings, but in those shabby old cords. You see, I'm not here just to find people jobs. I can act as – let's say an adviser, too. With cords like those, looking the way you do, it's not so easy for employers to imagine what a splendid fellow you really are.'

'They don't have to. I'm not a splendid fellow. I like cords. It doesn't bother me that they're worn and shabby.'

'You just don't want to cooperate, Pischke. Here I've been for months, talking till I'm blue in the face, and the fact is you just don't want to cooperate. You're probably laughing at me the moment you're out in the street, go on, admit it, Pischke. You don't want a job. Maybe you feel you're too good for that kind of thing.'

Gradually, Lüttich's friendliness was disappearing from his voice and his attitude. Relieved, I looked him straight in the face for the first time.

'A total refusenik.' Lüttich nodded at me. 'What are you waiting for?'

'What am I waiting for?' I asked him, to gain time, and then I said, before I could even think about it, 'For a bit of luck.' And I smiled, because the answer suddenly seemed right and obvious, more so than just about anything else in these last few months.

Lüttich fixed me with a probing gaze that tried to comprehend and acknowledge everything. He shook his head.

'I just don't get it,' he said quietly, in a deliberately gentle tone. 'Here you all are, you arrive without anything, without winter shoes, without a washing machine, without even clothes to put in the washing machine, without a roof over your heads, without a penny in your pockets, let alone a mark, you hold up your hands, you take what you want and turn down what you don't, you make claims. That's what you do.'

Lüttich's words echoed in my mind, every one of them. I weighed them up, singly and together, put the winter shoes on one side, the idea of nothing on the other, put the washing machine on one side and nothing on the other, discovered a trace of mockery in Lüttich's eyes, which had been staring at me through his enumeration of all the gifts we'd been given and the lack of explanations, and lowered my own eyes. Here again I thought: nothing. I couldn't dredge up a single word I might have used to answer him. I pulled the zip of my anorak halfway up – it wouldn't go any further because it was jammed – and as I stood up I tapped Lüttich's desk in embarrassment and got myself out of the door.

'Bringing nothing with you,' I heard him going on behind me. Maybe there was bafflement in his voice, bafflement that kept missing its mark and left him with an uncomfortable and upsetting feeling similar to rage, a feeling that was too large and thus didn't want to be understood, and so he called after me, 'Those who want nothing won't get anything.'

There wasn't room for everyone waiting out in the corridor. I had to make my way past the people waiting, clambering over feet and outstretched legs. Out of the corner of my eye, I saw the woman in the summer dress who, for the fraction of a second, had been a Czech fairy-tale princess. She was standing between two crowded benches and studying a notice on a cork pinboard. *Caution, firearms!* I read it in passing. The small black-and-white pictures showed young faces, terrorists. I quickly turned away, I didn't want to meet her here. I clenched my hands into fists behind my back and made my way through the crowd. When I reached the staircase, I heard Lüttich's voice shouting down the corridor, 'Your stamp, Pischke!' He was standing in the open doorway of his office. Light fell on the scarves and fabrics from inside the office. I turned to the staircase again, and told myself that Lüttich's voice and appearance depended on imagination. Even when I heard him shout for a second time I wasn't going to turn back, not for Lüttich, who was waving the paper with its official stamp over the heads of those waiting to ask about work, not for the stamped document that I was to give the authorities in charge of the camp. Not for me myself. I was going to wait for luck, that was all. The sun had briefly broken through the clouds, and disappeared again. Sleet was driving between the blocks of buildings and blowing into my half-open anorak. I enjoyed going out under the cloudy sky and feeling sleet on my face, never mind the consequences.

Krystyna Jabłonovska does not take care

I scooped warm water out of the bowl with a cup and let it run over my father's hair. I rubbed soap over the back of his head. He did not make a sound, but pressed his lips together, and I was careful not to let any of the soap get into the wound behind his hairline.

'Take care.' He hit out at me with the palm of his hand, but it connected only with the hem of my apron. Delicate soap bubbles floated in the air. When I was drying his hair and he raised his head, the water in the bowl was red. I carefully rubbed his bare, rather hairy shoulder; the whole of his torso was covered with red spots.

'What are you doing?' The palm of his hand hit out at me again.

'Nothing.'

'That hurts, stop it. Why are you so awkward? Your mother was never like that. Ouch, that was clumsy! You're rough, Krystyna, don't do it.'

But I went on rubbing the ointment that the lady in First Aid had given me into his back.

'Go and look after your brother and leave me alone,' he said angrily. I didn't tell him that Jerzy didn't recognise me any more. All the same, the doctors were saying he would be discharged at Christmas. Discharged to go home, they said, meaning the camp, which he would recognise as home even less than I did.

I fetched more water from the bathroom and took the last clean corner of the towel, dipped it in the water, carefully cleaned the wounds with it and mopped up the blood and dirt that had come out of them.

'Open your mouth,' I said, but he pressed his lips together, waiting for the moment when I turned away to rinse out the towel.

'Fat and clumsy.'

'Why did you have to climb out of the bed?'

'Fat and clumsy.'

'No wonder they beat you up.'

'I'm a dancer – and what a dancer!'

'But you can't make the woman dance.'

'She wanted to.'

'Oh, did she?'

'Yes, she did. I didn't want to, not at all. Ouch!'

'So that's why her husband beat you?'

'That's why, yes. I wanted to stay up on the bed.'

'You must speak more clearly, Father, I can hardly make out what you're saying. You're mumbling more and more. If you don't keep still, soap will get into those sore places.'

'Huh! It was no such thing. He dragged me out of my bed. He took it as an insult that I didn't want to dance with his wife.'

'Yes, an insult.' I didn't believe a word of what my father was saying, of course, but he didn't have to know that.

'No one refuses his wife what she wants, he says.'

'Oh, Father.'

'She was too old for me. Why would I dance with an old bag like that?'

'She must be twenty years younger than you, if not thirty.'

'Huh, twenty years younger! How old is she, then? In her mid-fifties? Even if she were twenty I wouldn't dance with a woman like her. That Nelly, now, I'd like to dance with her. Won't she be coming to visit us again sometime?'

'She didn't come to visit us, Father. She wanted to go out and left her children with me.'

'I'll dance with her, I won't dance with anyone else.'

'I see.'

'Ah, that feels good, scratch me again down there. Yes, there.' I scratched my father's coccyx until he cried 'Ouch!' again, and I fetched the towel to dry him.

I mopped his face. 'What's the matter with your mouth? Why are you pressing your lips together like that? No wonder I can't understand every other word you say. You must open your mouth wider.'

My father didn't answer.

'What is it?' I stuck my finger in the corner of his mouth and pushed until it gave way.

'Ouch!'

One incisor was missing, the other was broken. 'Father?'

'I didn't want to dance with her.'

'He's knocked your teeth out.'

'No such thing.'

'Yes, he has. He's knocked them out.'

'Because I didn't want to dance with her.'

'He knocked your teeth out because you didn't want to dance with his wife?' Incredible. The older my father got the more he invented his own world.

My father did not reply, but pressed his lips together again as if that would change anything.

The door was opened, and our new room-mate came in. He was carrying a black plastic bag with red lettering on it, saying *Beate Uhse*. He looked at my father in surprise; maybe this was the first time he had seen him out of bed. The man had been carrying the same plastic bag around as long as he had been living with us. He put his cigarette down on the side of the ashtray standing beside the basin with the water stained red in it. The smoke stung my eyes. He was German. His footwear left wet traces of reddish ash; obviously they had finally got round to sprinkling it on the roads. With slush on his cowboy boots, the German climbed up on the lower bunk bed in order to look for something on his own upper bunk. I was getting tired of pointing out that the lower bunk was my brother's bed and shouldn't have footprints left on it, even if my brother hadn't used it for months and probably wouldn't be using it until Christmas. He swung himself athletically up on the bed. The black bag crackled, and paper rustled. A small transistor radio came into view. He switched it on and searched for a station. English voices were heard first, RIAS Berlin, then he found a music channel. *Let the words of our mouth and the meditation of our heart be acceptable in thy sight here tonight.* I could sing along with every word, without understanding any of it. Never mind where I was, in the canteen, the laundry, the song rang out several times a day from the big loudspeakers set up at intervals between the blocks, probably for broadcasting instructions. They seemed to be waiting for orders to evacuate the camp. The song itself appeared to be trying in vain to promote a good mood. The German took a carrier of beer out of his bag. He opened a bottle and drank from it. He tapped his knee in time to the music, and sang along with the refrain. My father, still pressing his lips together, asked whether I had said something. I shook my head.

'The radio is on.' I pointed upwards.

'What?'

'The radio.'

'Ah.' My father put his head on one side. 'Music, eh?'

'Yes.' The cigarette smoke stung my eyes. My father nodded his head as if he could suddenly hear the music.

'Your cigarette,' I said to the man in German. But the music was too loud for him to hear me. The cigarette glowed, a long caterpillar of ash curled over the rim of the ashtray and finally fell into it. My father wagged his head in three-four time instead of four-four time. The glowing stub fell out on the tabletop on the other side of the ashtray, where it charred, smoking only slightly. There was a smell of burning plastic.

'Where are your teeth?'

My father looked at me expressionlessly. I wasn't even sure whether he had heard what I said. His three-four time made his head wag back and forth.

Moscow – strange and mysterious, towers of red gold, cold as ice, sang the transistor radio. Our room-mate bellowed, 'Moscow, Moscow, Moscow.' He bellowed that one name and nothing else, drowning out the music, until a new catchphrase caught his attention and he switched to 'Hey, hey, hey, raise your glasses!' His cigarette fell in the beer bottle, and he stretched his arm and the bottle towards the ceiling light. 'Hey, hey, hey, here's to love.' He opened another bottle with his teeth.

'You must tell me, do you hear?' I tugged at my father's ear. He pressed his lips together. 'Where are they, your hair and your teeth, you know where they are, Father, your hair and your teeth.' I ran my hand over his hair, inadvertently touched the wound and felt him flinch. 'Hair and teeth,' I said quietly.

'Why do you keep shouting at me like that, Krystyna?' My father, indignant and evidently with his feelings hurt, looked at me and then, shaking his head, turned to the German, who was taking no notice of us as he sat on the top bunk, leafing through a magazine and singing along to songs on the radio.

'I'm not hard of hearing,' said my father, without turning round.

'Oh yes, you are.'

My father rocked his head in time to the music and didn't hear me, or at least pretended not to hear me.

'You have to keep your hair and teeth for ever,' I told his back view. But my father sat there like a statue as if I were shaming and pestering him not just with my questions but with the superstition that he could usually laugh off so easily. It meant bad luck for your hair or teeth to fall into the wrong hands. Even a bird carrying a hair over half the world in its beak was asking for misfortune from all quarters of the globe, and I remembered how I had tried, as a child, to picture what *misfortune* meant, and repeated the word to myself several times, so that I could grasp its meaning at least in one of my different tones of voice. I didn't succeed. However, I couldn't help thinking of the bird that would decide between good luck and bad luck if I carelessly let even a single hair blow away on the wind.

My rubber boots were under the bed. They were much too cold for me at this time of year. In the old-clothes room of the laundry building people tried to make helpful suggestions week after week. Didn't I have family members who could send me something, the lady presiding over it had asked, and how about the other sources of second-hand clothing, wouldn't it be a good idea to enquire elsewhere? She was sure there would be something next time, but footwear in my size, which was 2, simply didn't come in so often. Yet I had already seen, twice, the lady in the old-clothes room handing out boots that were very probably size 2 to mothers with children. Of course I hadn't kicked up a fuss; after all, the others were Germans – from East Germany, yes, but still Germans. Last time, the lady in the old-clothes room had put a pair of size 3½ rubber boots in front of me. The inside of one of the boots was discoloured and yellowish; they had a strong, unusual smell. But with two pairs of socks and a thick layer of newspaper I could walk reasonably well in them, although they made an unpleasant sound as I went along. But I didn't want to wear the rubber boots with my fur coat, even if my father never looked closely at me. The mere idea of someone in the street, in the bus or on the U-Bahn seeing me dressed in a fur coat and rubber boots made me blush.

It was not for the sake of my father's teeth but for my own peace of mind that I set off to find them. Had he said something about the employment agency just now? Why would he have gone so far? The employment agency was in the last block on the south side of the camp. Although there was still a light on there, no one answered when I rang the bell. I saw a dark patch on some gravel outside the entrance, and then another. I followed the bloodstains leading away from the path, and in the light of the lantern I could just make out something dark. The few dried-up blades of grass were surrounded by ice, and the blood was frozen too. I took my gloves off so that I could feel better in the twilight, and ran my bare hands over the ground. Snow drove into my face. I put out my tongue and caught a snowflake on it. My legs had gone to sleep with all that crouching down, so I got down on my knees and crawled on.

I searched the ground metre by metre. I found cigarette ends, crown corks that shone like coins, embedded in the icy ground. Sweet papers. Luckily no pets were allowed in the camp, or I'd have had to watch out for cat shit and dog shit. I crawled over to a bush with drops of ice instead of leaves on its branches. The frozen remains of the foliage rustled and crackled under my knees. Something cut me, I felt broken shards of glass or china, put them to one side and was careful where I put my knees. My hand felt something soft, a piece of rubber, something dirty white and drawn out at length like a balloon with all the air gone out of it. I let it drop and turned to the broken shards on my right.

I found something there that looked like traces of blood, but I couldn't be sure in the dim light. It might be my own blood, seeping through my tights from the knees that I had scuffed. All the broken shards made me crouch down again. There was a quiet crunching and creaking sound under my rubber boots. In spite of the cold, I thought I could smell the acrid odour that came from the boots. A packet of cigarettes lay in front of me. I could clearly see traces of red on the white packaging. The packet was still half full; I put it back and went on groping around. The teeth, I thought, and tried not to feel or see anything else, just the teeth that I wanted to find. I heard laughter behind me and turned round. Two small children were standing in the beam of light from the lantern, and at least one of them was laughing.

'Aren't you going to help me?' I called to them in German. My voice sounded like the cawing of a crow.

'What?'

'I asked if you weren't going to help me.'

The children came closer. The girl was giggling. The boy pushed the glasses on his nose back in place with his finger and bent down to me. 'What are you looking for?'

'Oh, it's you two. I didn't recognise you from a distance.'

Nelly's daughter put her small hand out to me. 'Why are you crawling around on the ground?'

'Teeth. My father has lost his teeth.'

'Lost them?' Katya giggled.

'Does he have false teeth?' Aleksei looked down at me curiously.

Supporting myself with one hand, I rose to my feet.

'There were some men fighting just now.' The little girl bent down and picked up a sweet paper.

'It looked horrible.'

Only now did I notice that the thick and surely heavy frame of Aleksei's glasses had no earpiece on the left. A rubber band stretched between the frame and his ear.

'Yes, and some people kept calling out *stop it, stop it*, but they didn't stop it.' Katya dug her hands into her jacket pockets.

'Yes.' I couldn't think of anything else to say. I took small steps to keep from freezing, and before I knew it the two children were accompanying me. We went along the path with the girl on my left, the boy on my right.

'One of them was your father,' said Aleksei, and I felt him avoiding my eyes, perhaps in embarrassment, perhaps out of consideration. Perhaps he had said the same thing to his sister. 'One of them was her father.'

'Are you from the Soviet Union?' the girl asked me.

'No, from Poland.'

'Oh, Poland.' There was disappointment in the girl's voice.

'Because our father is from the Soviet Union. And Poland is in between them, between us and the Soviet Union, isn't that right?' Aleksei stumbled.

It struck me that for him at least that was how it must have been once. 'Then you two speak Russian?'

'No.' They said it in chorus.

I opened the door to our staircase.

'Did you say you were looking for a tooth?' Aleksei took his hand out of his jacket pocket.

'Ah,' I said. What would the children think of me, so persistently looking for my father's teeth?

'Well, never mind. You can have it.' The boy put his hand out to me. 'Here you are.'

'Oh.' The tooth looked clean in his hand, white and shining as a pearl. I took it and held it up to the light. 'Where did you find it?'

Aleksei pushed his glasses back on his nose and shrugged his shoulders. 'Can't remember exactly. Somewhere on the stairs here.'

'I found money,' said Katya. 'Three marks twenty-four in all.'

'Really?'

'Yes, but I think I'd better keep it. I don't know who lost it.'

'I found some too, but only a groschen. I'll give you the tooth to keep. Maybe your father did lose it after all, and you just don't know.'

The little boy spoke like a grown man. It was comical. But I gravely shrugged my shoulders and thanked him for his present. We had reached the second floor.

As if rooted to the spot, the children stood in front of me, scrutinising me.

'I live here,' I said.

'We know,' said the girl. 'We've been in your apartment already.'

'Would you like to have something in return for the tooth?'

'Have something? Oh no. No, no.'

'Well, then,' I said, unlocking the door of the apartment. 'Thank you very much.'

'Hmm,' said the two children, standing as if rooted to the spot.

'Sleep well,' I said, closing the door in their faces.

Everything was the same as before in the room. My father was lying on his bed, the German on the other bed, both asleep. I put the light on and inspected the tooth. The longer I looked at it the more uneasy I felt. It seemed to be simply too white and unmarked for a tooth more than seventy years old. What kind of misfortune befell someone holding a stranger's tooth in her hands? I opened the window and threw it high and far out into the night.

'It's draughty, damn it, who's opening the window?' My father pulled the blanket over his head and grunted.

'Lights out! Let's have peace and quiet!' shouted the German from his bed.

I put out the light. Quickly, I took my skirt and blouse off, pulled my nightdress over my head and removed my underclothes only under the blanket and with some difficulty. The blankets were thin but warm, and felt slightly scratchy through the bedlinen. I imagined that the misfortune lying in wait could be death. But how could death be a misfortune if you didn't feel it yourself? Before I fell asleep I thought of all the misfortunes that could be making their way towards my father and me.

Nelly Senff hears what she would rather not

I was woken by a nibbling sound. It was still dark. The children were sleeping quietly in the opposite bed. Katya had squeezed herself into the lower bunk with Aleksei, something she had done quite often since we came here. She said it was cold up in the top bunk, and the air was too stale. The nibbling, rustling noises above me sounded as if they were made by some small rodent. It was so dark that I could hardly make out the white stripes of the mattress cover above me. The springs squealed, and I guessed that something was lying on its side so that it could nibble better. Once I had spent several weeks with Vassily in a house by the Kreidesee near Hemmoor. We heard rustling and nibbling in the evening and early-morning twilight above our bed. Vassily said it was the martens nibbling to survive like all other creatures: they nibbled legs of mice day in, day out. All the same, I wished to heaven it would stop.

As if by accident, I hit the bedpost. It was quiet, but only for a moment. Next came the sound of what was probably the mouse's backbone, as whatever was eating it crunched on, undeterred.

I often woke up when Susanne came home early in the morning. She tried to be quiet, but I heard her as soon as she turned her key in the lock, and sometimes I could see her shadow as she came in and took her boots off before anything else, removing something from one of them: a bundle of notes that she counted and then put away in her part of the cupboard. Only then did she take off her quilted jacket, and finally peeled off layer after layer of clothing until her naked body shone in the darkness and I could see how she had done her hair. My eyes had got used to the darkness. Usually she wore her hair in a ponytail. She never came home before five, and seldom later than six thirty. Then she climbed up on her bed and started gnawing as if she were gnawing for dear life.

When the alarm clock went off, I heard loud rustling and crackling, and then the crunching noises stopped. She had probably hidden mouse skulls and anything else edible in a hurry. The metal springs squealed again, and I was sure she was turning to the wall. I slipped into my sandals and went to the lavatory.

When I came back I switched on the little reading lamp that I had bought with the money they gave to welcome you to the camp. Susanne's clothes lay on one of the four chairs standing round our table between the two bunk beds. They smelled of smoke and sweat. Her underclothes were over the back of the chair, an almost transparent pair of bright pink panties, a matching bra with lace and little sequins on the top rim of the cups. Below her underclothes I saw a pair of nylon tights and some kind of top trimmed with fake fur. She had left her pale blue imitation-leather miniskirt on the seat of the chair. Her boots stood under the chair in the little puddle that had formed round them. As I did every morning, I took my towel and spread it over the chair. I took it off again, unnoticed, as soon as the children had left.

'Get up.' Katya had her arm firmly round Aleksei, and they had both turned their backs to me. 'Hey, you must get up,' I whispered to them, so as not to wake Susanne.

'Don't want to.'

'Can't.'

'Oh yes, you can. You must. Come on,' I said. I picked Katya up, took her out of bed and carried her to the chair. She didn't weigh much, she was as thin as a boy. Her hair had left its imprint on a cheek that was rosy with sleep. Her eyes were streaming, their rims were red. She coughed, sniffed and stared blankly at the table. To avoid saying, 'Put your hand in front of your mouth,' I put my own in front of it when she yawned.

'Here are your things, Katya. You too, Aleksei. I'll make breakfast for you.'

'I'm not hungry.' Katya wiped a tear out of the corner of her eye, sniffed again and put one finger up her nose. Her exercise book was lying on the table. I opened it and leafed through it. A great many red lines and flourishes showed how poorly she had mastered Western handwriting so far.

'You must have something to eat,' I said, and read what the teacher had said in red under her sentences. *We write capital L with a curlicue, and the same with S and V. Capital Z is different from little z because of the little line through the middle. Write the three sentences out twenty times by tomorrow.* Katya had not complied with this order. I saw only empty lines.

'No.' Katya shook herself.

'Then I'll pack something for you to take with you. Come on, get dressed, no wonder you've caught a cold.' I looked to the front of her exercise book. Every word, however tidily written, had red corrections above and below and in all the margins.

Katya groaned. 'They put little curly bits on everything over here.'

'Over here?'

'Well, here. In school here,' she said, yawning widely. I put my hand in front of her mouth again. She batted it away. 'Don't, your hand smells funny.'

'It doesn't matter if you get a 3 or a 4 now.'

'No, but the lines are all different, look, we had printed lines, and the curvy bit of the B pointed up here and not there. Look.'

'It's not all that important, Katya.' I closed the exercise book.

'Of course it's important. You're not looking properly.' Katya snatched her exercise book and crammed it into her school bag.

The empty bottles left by our neighbours in the other apartment were standing on the surfaces of the shared kitchen, and the floor was sticky under my feet. Cigarettes had been stubbed out in the lid of a preserving jar, the sink was full of a murky liquid, and cigarette ends with the unsmoked tobacco coming loose were also swimming in the liquid. I fished little paper bags labelled *Glühwein Spice Mixture* out of the sink. The kitchen was as dirty as if I hadn't cleaned it from top to bottom yesterday.

'Mama, my shoes don't fit any more.' Katya had come into the kitchen after me, and was holding one leg up in the air. 'Here, feel.'

'All of a sudden they don't fit?'

'Well, I'm growing.'

'But we were given those shoes only two weeks ago.'

'At least three weeks ago. And they've got holes in the sides, here, the whole sole is coming loose. Look. My feet are cold and wet all day.'

'You're forgetting to stuff them with newspaper in the evening.' I caressed Katya's head. She hadn't combed her hair yet. 'I showed you how to do it. No wonder they're still wet in the morning.'

'Meh-meh-meh,' she complained, and added, as she went out of the kitchen, 'The other kids have kind of snow boots, you know, with nice thick soles, and red or pale blue for girls.'

'Hmm. Plastic boots.'

'Yes, they match the school bags.'

'We've discussed this already.'

'But if,' said Katya, pretending to be thinking up a new idea, 'if, I mean, couldn't you buy some, and then we'd do without pocket money for a long, long time.'

Aleksei came into the kitchen. 'Mama, hey, Mama?'

'You get fifty pfennigs. I can't buy you shoes for that amount of money.'

The question of her school bag was lurking in Katya's eyes, and I wanted to get in first. 'All brightly coloured and made of plastic. Bright red plastic shoes, bright yellow plastic school bags, sky-blue polyester jackets. For heaven's sake, why would you want bags like that? They look so silly. All the children have the same. It looks ridiculous.' Alarmed by my own attempts to preach a sermon, I added. 'Whereas you two have something special, really genuine . . .' Here I stopped, feeling ashamed of myself.

' . . . genuine old school bags from the East.' Aleksei looked at me sympathetically. 'Anyone can tell you're not a kid any more, Mama.'

At such moments I wondered where Aleksei's calm attitude to me came from. His sympathy seemed almost supercilious. Katya and Aleksei both avoided my eyes.

'Do the other children laugh at you?'

Aleksei bent down to tie his shoes. Katya rolled her eyes as if asking such a question were particularly unseemly of me. If the other children laughed at them, they weren't going to say so, for the sake of their own pride. For a moment I wasn't sure whether my assumption was correct or whether their hints were pure invention to convince me of the necessity of countless new things. Katya had asked about shoes, that was all. Their other wishes stood between us only in my memory, and made my children seem strange to me. I hated this alienation between us, but the more I hated it, the stranger they seemed. I didn't like them when they were begging for school bags or fashionable soft toys. I couldn't give them any of the things they craved, and I no longer wanted to. I disliked their greed. 'If your shoes don't fit then we'll go over to the old-clothes store and take them back, and see if they have a pair that do.'

Aleksei sat down on the kitchen floor and tied the torn-off end of his shoelace to the end already in the shoe. His glasses slipped off his nose and fell on the floor.

'We have an appointment with the optician this afternoon.' I picked the glasses up. It was a good thing the lenses were so thick that they didn't break easily. I put the frame back on his nose and tugged the rubber band. It was so worn and limp that it would hardly stay in place. 'Then you'll get new glasses.'

'Do I have to go to the optician?'

'Yes, you do.'

A door slammed. The neighbour with the beer belly appeared in the doorway. His undershirt covered the top half of his paunch. I preferred not to look at his underpants and what was sticking out of them. I helped Aleksei. The neighbour stood in the doorway, shaking his head as if baffled. 'Good lord, all this racket every morning. Can't you lot keep quiet for once? We can't get a wink of sleep.' Grumbling, he went to the toilet. I could hear his loud farts and constant cursing from where I was in the kitchen.

At the door I hugged both children. 'You'll take Aleksei right to the classroom door, won't you?'

'Of course.'

I watched them going to the stairs. The window on the staircase was still dark. Aleksei turned back and waved to me. He looked as if he knew how I felt about the strangeness, and my hatred, and the shame his watchfulness made me feel, too. He waved and smiled as if he were sorry for me.

'Goodbye, both of you.'

'Mama?' he whispered.

'Yes?'

'What's an Eastpox?'

'Well, not an illness, anyway. There's smallpox and chickenpox, but no Northpox or Southpox.' I couldn't help laughing.

'But Eastpox, though?' he said, and Katya hauled him downstairs with her.

My step back into the apartment took my breath away. The air here was musty, as if not ten but a hundred people slept in the place, and as if it were not only winter but there were no windows to open. It stank of alcohol and other people's sweat. A human fug. Yet our own smell was part of its dense atmosphere, hard to distinguish from the rest, but present.

So as not to disturb Susanne while she slept, I tried to keep busy, occupying myself with housework and going to ask the porter if any post had come for us.

Later, it began to snow. The snow danced upwards in the air. A thin white layer settled on everything. On days like this, light came from the earth instead of the sky. I was in the laundry, taking the wet washing out of the machine and putting it into the spin dryer, when the door flew open and Katya burst in. I must come with her, she said, come quickly, Aleksei felt sick.

'Why aren't you two at school?' I asked. It was eleven o'clock, and lessons didn't end until twelve thirty.

'Quick, Mama, hurry, never mind the washing.'

I followed Katya through the snow. Aleksei was sitting outside the door of our building, throwing up on the icy rust of the shoe-scraper.

'The teacher said he'd better lie down for an hour, and she fetched me to sit with him in the sickroom and look after him, but he was feeling so bad, Mama. So we ran away.'

'Ran away? You simply left the school sickroom . . . ?'

'Mama, they pushed him over in the long break, and then

they stamped all over him.' Katya was out of breath; she sat down beside her little brother and put an arm round him. 'Mama, do something, can't you see how bad he's feeling?'

'Where are his glasses?'

'No idea. They must still be in the schoolyard.'

Aleksei wiped his mouth on his sleeve. He was white-faced. 'A bicycle on his face.'

'What?' He obviously wasn't thinking clearly.

'A bicycle, and they were laughing like anything, the Eastpox has a bicycle on his face.'

'Come along.' I picked Aleksei up and carried him up the steps. He retched again over my shoulder, but only a little fluid came out.

'Here, you must lie down for a bit.'

'No, Mama, I don't want to, everything's going round in circles, no, Mama, don't go away.'

'I'm going to call a doctor, little one, Katya will stay with you.'

I ran out of the apartment and along the path to the porter's lodge.

'Yes, what is it?'

'A doctor, please, call a doctor, my son has had an accident.'

'An accident?'

'He must have concussion. Quick.'

'What kind of accident? Where was it?'

'Please, just call a doctor. Block B, entrance 2, second floor on the left.'

'Want a tissue?' He handed me one through the window, and I went back along the path, searching the snow to left and right. My eyes stung with the bright white of it. Perhaps he hadn't lost his glasses until he was back in the camp. I wiped the tears from my eyes. *There we sat down, yea, we wept, when we remembered Zion.* The music rang in my ears. A woman was standing behind an open window upstairs, cleaning the glass. No wonder the local children were on the defensive, I thought, there've been kids coming into their class all along who leave again within the foreseeable future, sometimes they stay two weeks, sometimes four months, and there were some who stayed for two years. No one knew how long they'd be here. But one thing was certain, they'd be leaving again. Why wouldn't they turn against these intruders, this constant invasion from outside, the strangers who spoke differently and used different expressions, didn't wear snowsuits, had different boots and school bags from the rest of the class? People were annoyed, and guess what, annoyance won the day; within a short time the strangers would have been ousted, they wouldn't come back. Away with them. That was what the children in this school went through, day after day, year after year. The woman upstairs leaned far out over the windowsill to clean the end of it with a brush. You had to take care that there were no more than three children from the camp in any one class at the same time, the headmistress had told me when I gave her my children's old files and school reports. It had been all right these last few years, she added, after all, there hadn't been quite so many from the Eastern bloc coming over recently. But it was difficult enough, what with the Poles and the Russians. I'd find out what she meant, she told me, we'd see how it turned out. At the time I thought no more of it, and I still didn't entirely understand. Unlike my children I didn't have much to do with people from outside the camp. Perhaps I'd come to know the salespeople in the shop opposite. The sales assistants in the furniture stores through which I wandered on many afternoons in search of nothing in particular. I had noticed some time ago that neither of my children made new friends or was even invited to a birthday party. Katya claimed it was because of the little fair-haired doll she didn't have, just as she didn't have the right clothes, and didn't go to recorder lessons in the nearby evangelical church, like several other girls in the class, because she didn't own a recorder, let alone believe in God. Aleksei, however, had once come home and mentioned in passing that Olivier, the boy who sat next to him in class, had told him two reasons why he couldn't ask him to his birthday party: for one thing, the camp children never brought proper presents with them, and for another, since those children had no money at all, the others would wonder why he, Olivier, was inviting a boy like Aleksei to his party. By way of consolation he had given Aleksei two jelly babies. But I wouldn't have gone to his birthday party anyway, Aleksei had said, although he wouldn't tell me why not.

Up in our room Katya sat on Aleksei's bed humming a hit song. Aleksei had gone to sleep.

'Did you see him being pushed?' I knelt down beside the bed and stroked my son's small shoulder.

Katya went on humming; she didn't look at me, but she shook her head.

'Then maybe he just fell over.'

She hummed and shrugged her shoulders.

'Please keep quiet, Katya. Stop humming that tune, I'm sick of it. Wherever we go they're playing that song.'

'It's so catchy, Mama.'

'Couldn't he just have fallen over?'

'Don't think so, the kids were yelling and shouting, standing round in a circle, and when I wriggled my way through I saw them standing on him.'

'Standing on him?'

'Well, they were stamping all over him.'

'You say it like that – as coolly as if it was perfectly normal. Stamping all over him, did you say?'

'Goodness, Mama, don't go on like that. It's not going to do any good now.' My ten-year-old daughter was acting as if she faced this situation every day, and it was nothing to worry about if several children – as it seemed – were stamping on Aleksei. Instinctively I thought of Aleksei's sympathetic expression, and caught myself imagining that his classmates found it provocative. An eight-year-old who read the newspaper and spent half the day with his head in a book must seem strange to other kids. Aleksei knew more than most of those around him. He wasn't proud of that, but he made no secret of it, and he corrected other people, not distinguishing, I felt sure, between adults and children, family members and strangers. Sometimes I called him know-all and clever clogs, but then he just smiled indulgently and mildly. He didn't correct anyone's opinions.

'I'm thirsty.' Aleksei opened his eyes.

'There's only tap water, we've finished the tea. Get him a glass of water, please, Katya.' I bent over him and felt to see if he had a temperature, but my hands were so cold that even the metal of the bedstead seemed warm.

'No, Mama, not water.'

'All right. Katya, just for once, go and buy some fizzy drink.'

'No, I don't want to.'

'You don't want any fizzy drink?'

'I don't want to buy it, Mama, I don't want to go into the shop.'

'Here we go again – Katya, please don't make such a fuss. Can't you see that Aleksei's not feeling well? The doctor will be here in a minute, so go and buy some fizzy drink. My purse is on the table. Take a mark out of it.'

'No.'

'Can you tell me why you've been dead set against going to the shop these last few days?'

'Don't want to.'

A siren was approaching, getting louder and louder. I stood up and looked out. There were no roads between the blocks of apartments, only pathways. The ambulance had simply driven across the snow on the grass and stopped outside our door. Susanne sat up in bed, rubbing her eyes.

'Has something happened?'

'No, nothing,' I said, and I went to the door of the apartment before the sound of the doorbell alarmed everyone. The two paramedics came in and got Katya and me to tell them what we thought might have happened to Aleksei.

'Fine sort of accident,' said one of them, before stealing a glance at Susanne's bare legs and then laying my son on the stretcher, which was far too big for him. Susanne watched in silence from the top bunk. We were welcome to follow them, they told us, but there wasn't enough room for the two of us in the ambulance. They told me the address, and carried my child out of the apartment. I saw them pushing him into the ambulance outside the door. Then I packed his things, his pyjamas, his toothbrush and slippers. They all fitted into a single bag. Katya took the soft toy donkey I had put in his school bag two years ago under her arm. It had come all the way to the camp with us.

'Do you think he'd like to do some drawing?' Katya wanted to pack his coloured crayons.

'I don't know. He may be feeling too ill for that.'

'We could buy him felt pens.'

'Katya, we don't have to keep buying things, please don't make me crazy just now.'

'Do you think it's bad?'

'He's certainly not in a good way. Concussion, probably. Then you have to rest quietly for a few days.'

'Aren't you cold?' asked Katya, watching Susanne put her miniskirt on.

'Not really.' She rolled up the stockings that for weeks I'd mistaken for a pair of tights, and fastened them under her miniskirt.

'Are they spoilt?'

'What?' Susanne looked down at her.

'Your tights.'

'Nonsense, they're not tights.'

'Then what?'

'Suspenders.' Susanne giggled and zipped up her boots.

'I'd be cold myself.' Katya looked sympathetically at Susanne's legs. 'Do you smoke?'

'Not really. Well, not often.'

'You smell of cigarettes so much.'

'That's just my clothes.' Susanne laughed again and stroked Katya's head. 'Off you go, see about your brother.'

We were told to sit in a waiting room on the ground floor of the hospital. They wanted to find out what tests in which department Aleksei was having at the moment. A woman in late middle age was sitting on a bench by the window reading a magazine. She looked familiar. Leaning forward, I recognised her as Frau Jabłonovska, the Polish lady from our building, who insisted on striking up a conversation about my delightful children whenever I met her on the stairs or in the laundry room. She looked up.

'Hello.'

'Oh, hello.' She let the magazine drop to the lap of her fur coat and looked at us in surprise, then opened the magazine again and went on reading it, or looking at the black-and-white illustrations. Her father was the man who was mad about dancing; maybe he had had some kind of misadventure and she was waiting for him. I had cut her short the last few times we met.

'Aleksei gave that lady a tooth,' Katya whispered to me. She pointed to one side with her finger, and her whisper was so loud that I felt sure the Polish woman could hear what she was saying.

'A tooth?' Without looking the way she was pointing, I took the donkey from Katya's other hand and put it on the bench between us. The woman was breathing heavily. Katya stood up and went to look at the books standing on a low shelf. She chose a book and brought it over to me.

'Will you read me something?'

'Not just now. Read it for yourself.' I looked at the big clock; it was just after twelve thirty. Katya took the book back from me and held it on her lap for a moment. 'They've always been borrowed from the library van,' she said quietly. Then she stood up and took it back to the bookshelf. With cautious sideways glances, Frau Jabłonovska surreptitiously tried to keep us in her line of vision.

'Can't you borrow a book like that from one of the girls in your class?'

Katya shrugged. 'Yes, sure,' she said, just as I realised that she must be lying. I put one arm round her thin shoulders and looked at the clock again, jiggling my foot up and down. I heard that song again coming from somewhere or other. It echoed back from the pale beige walls. The sound was strange. First the voices moved like a skipping rope, almost mocking the lethargy I felt in defence against the song that defied melancholy, cheerful and carefree, but the more often the melody of the song was repeated the more strongly the rhythm of the voices rolled on, like a wave, as if we were all feeling the same thing and sitting somewhere by the rivers of Babylon. Part of the refrain was hummed by a large chorus, a swarm of voices over a sea, a backdrop of incredible breadth and freedom and love. I swallowed, suddenly feeling sick.

'What are you doing here?'

I leaned forward, but Frau Jabłonovska in her fur coat didn't seem to notice that I was talking to her.

'Excuse me, please.' I got up and sat down again beside her. 'We met not so long ago in the laundry. I cut you short as we were talking and left the laundry.'

'Oh?' A news magazine showing a picture of the Kremlin in winter lay on her lap. The red-framed picture looked curiously colourless, as if the snow or the coarse-grained print had drained all the sharpness and colour from it. The caption, in yellow, asked: *What is going on in the Eastern bloc?* She didn't seem to want to read the magazine.

'Yes, I'm sure of it. What brings you to the hospital?'

Frau Jabłonovska looked at me for a long time, breathing hard; the fur coat seemed too tight for her heavy breath.

'I'm waiting for my brother. They said they're getting him ready.'

'So he's been ill and now they're discharging him?' I smiled, to show that I wasn't going to be so abrupt with her this time.

'Well, I mean they're getting him ready, yes, because my brother died last night.'

'Oh.' I looked at her blotched hand, which was shaking, and the handkerchief clutched in it. 'I'm so sorry.'

'No, no. You can't do anything to help. That's all right. He was very ill.'

'Have you been nursing him?'

'No, he's had to be here for the last few months. They didn't call me, you see. I came here this morning. I've been waiting four days for them to phone, every night, and coming every morning or afternoon to see if he was still breathing. Today his room was empty.' A pungent aroma of mingled cooking fat and perfume surrounded her. The smell of her sweat came through the fur coat, although its hook-like fastenings were done up all the way to her throat. She opened her mouth so as to breathe out more easily.

'I wanted to be with him. Do you understand that? And then he just dies.' She took a breath, paused. 'Simply dies behind my back.' Frau Jabłonovska stroked the fur coat and pulled out a few single hairs. 'They promised to call me.'

'In the camp? But we don't have telephones in our rooms there.'

'Well, at least they said they'd call the switchboard. But I expect they forgot. Perhaps because they had so much to do.'

'How about this one?' Katya held up a book close to my face. 'Would you rather read me this one?' she asked, rolling her eyes.

'Come here.' I pulled her down on the bench beside me again. 'Sit next to me here and read to yourself for a little while, all right?' Then I turned back to Frau Jabłonovska. 'And now they're . . . they're getting your brother – ready?'

'They'll have to fold his hands over his chest and bind up his chin. Yes, they do that before the relations can come and look.'

'Bind up his chin?'

'Otherwise it will drop and his mouth will be wide open when rigor mortis sets in and then his jaw would stay open.' Frau Jabłonovska opened her own mouth wide. 'Like that.' She had some gold teeth.

'I see.' I pictured a dead man with his mouth gaping wide.

She closed her own mouth. 'Why are you here?'

I was about to tell her when the door opened. The nurse looked first at me, then at Frau Jabłonovska, and finally her eyes fell on Katya, who was kneeling in front of the bookshelf again. 'Jabłonovska?'

She stood up. Beneath the fur coat, her legs looked thin and spindly by comparison with her massive body. Her feet were shod in clumping rubber boots, and dragged as if the boots were much too big. She left the magazine behind her on the bench.

'Come this way, please.'

'Yes, just a moment. May I go to the toilet again first?'

'If you're quick, of course.'

Frau Jabłonovska followed the nurse out into the corridor.

Katya had found a new book and was sitting motionless, reading, with the book on her knees. I looked over her shoulder. 'I'm sure that's no better than the others.'

'Mama, you don't have to read it. And our father read this book.'

'What makes you think that?'

'I remember the cover.'

'After – how many years is it? – you think you remember the cover? Why would he have thought of reading a book like that?'

Katya closed the book. There was a brownish picture on the cover. Why would Vassily have read a children's book, and one from the West at that? I seemed to catch Katya out lying more and more often.

'I wasn't quick enough,' said Aleksei, as we reached his room. I went over to his bed and drew up a chair.

'You see, Mama, if he at least had trainers.' Katya leaned over her brother from the other side and laid her hand on his forehead, as if she were his mother. 'Guess who's here.' She opened the zip of her anorak and let the toy donkey out.

'Do you think I ought to be dead like our father?'

'No, my dear, certainly not.' I thought of the report the doctor had given me out in the corridor. I was to sign it. It said that I took responsibility for the consequences of the examinations, the medical staff assumed that there was no danger, but certain side effects of the X-ray process could not be excluded. Yet they had done all the examinations by now, and there was nothing for me to do but add my signature. Aleksei had concussion, a bruised skull, several other bruises and a broken rib. In addition, and the doctor pointed this out to me separately, they had established that he was suffering from malnutrition. At his height, he ought to weigh at least twenty-six kilos, and he was several pounds underweight. The doctor wouldn't even discuss the matter at any length with me; he had looked at me sternly, as if I were starving or neglecting my children.

'You know, Mama, I keep thinking our father wants to be here again, living inside me.' Aleksei's cheeks were red and rough-skinned. His eyes looked glazed.

'Inside you?'

'Yes, now that he's dead and doesn't have a live body any more I think maybe he'd like to live inside me. In my tummy.'

'What makes you think a thing like that?'

'Grandmother once said he lives on in us.'

'She didn't mean it that way. Grandmother thinks he'll live on in us if we remember him.'

'I know what Grandmother meant. But that's not enough, Mama. A soul wants more.'

So now Aleksei thought he knew what souls wanted. I shook my head and touched his lips. In spite of his internal injuries his lips felt unnaturally healthy.

The doctor came in and asked me to come outside with him. In his consulting room, he told me to sit down in the orange armchair, and offered me mandarin syrup diluted with water.

'Do all your patients have single rooms?' I crossed my legs, and was about to thank him.

'Single rooms? No, that will be only for the first three days because of the danger of infection.'

'Danger of infection?'

'Don't look so shocked!' He smiled magnanimously and relished the effect of his remarks for a moment, then leaned forward, folded his hands on top of his desk, and said, 'Your son has lice, surely you must have noticed that? His head is full of them. We must get rid of those first.'

'Oh.' I suddenly stopped and took my hand away from my head. If it started itching I'd bear it.

'You read the report?'

I nodded.

'Your son claims he was beaten up in school.'

He scrutinised me, obviously expecting an answer.

'Yes?'

'Well, we're wondering whether that's true. He seems to be in a very confused state. The school ought not to have sent him home like that. What I mean is, perhaps he wasn't there at all?'

'No? Where else would he have been?'

'Please don't upset yourself. Conversations of this kind aren't easy for us either. We see more and more such cases. Abuse – well, it happens in the best of families.'

'What?'

'Was he at home with you?'

'No, he wasn't in the camp. Not that I know of.'

'Frau Senff, our paramedics fetched him from – wait a moment – Block B in the transit camp. You do live there, don't you?'

'We live there, yes. But –'

'Take it easy, Frau Senff. I'm not the police. We have a duty of silence here too. It's just that it strikes us as very improbable, you see, the severity of his injuries, bruises of that kind, a broken rib, those injuries like pricking on his arms and back, obviously made by some sharp instrument. Needles – especially hot needles – are a favourite method.' While the doctor spoke, he sucked in air noisily through his teeth, as if he thought it both delightful and painful to talk about such things. 'Concussion with a bruised skull – it takes a lot of strength to inflict that.

He needs glasses and doesn't have any. In addition there's the undernourishment.'

'I never even noticed that . . .' I wondered whether what I was about to say was wrong. I lit a cigarette.

'You never noticed that your son is too thin, doesn't weigh enough? Everyone has access to a pair of scales these days.'

'No, Herr . . . what's your name?'

'Dr Bender. Would you please put that cigarette out?'

'Herr Bender, there are no scales in the camp except in the paediatrician's surgery, and who would think of getting their child weighed? I mean, except when they go to see the paediatrician. Yes, and last time he was examined everything was all right, at least no one talked about undernourishment then.'

'In that case we must accept what you say, and pass it on to the health insurance company. No doubt they will enquire further, because either you neglected your duty of care or the school did.'

'My children eat. They don't eat a lot, but none of us do. If you had your food handed out in portions every day perhaps you'd lose your own appetite.'

'There's no need to get personal, Frau Senff.'

'You were getting personal yourself.'

'You think I'd lose my appetite? Well, as I said, the insurance will see about that. It's not my business to decide on the cause of the injuries. I can only make my assumptions.'

'Oh, your assumptions?'

'Frau Senff, let's be objective. This certainly can't be easy for you.'

'No, it isn't,' I said, standing up, 'but I don't go meddling with *your* family life.'

'Meddling is sometimes important, Frau Senff.' He sucked in air through his teeth again and swallowed. Dr Bender acted as if it no longer interested him whether I stayed in the room or not. He made notes on his form, poured himself some mandarin syrup, which he drank neat, and finally picked up the telephone receiver to whisper something into it.

'Important, important,' I said, but he didn't even raise his head to look at me. Obviously I could go on talking, he wasn't going to be disturbed while he was putting his forms in order. 'Just keep on playing your part, right? How happy you all are playing your parts. Playing parts all your lives. Is there somewhere you can buy them?' I left the door wide open and went down the corridor.

Katya was lying on Aleksei's bed, right across him with her legs dangling down, and she was singing the song I was sick and tired of.

'Bastard.' Katya sat up.

'Bastard?'

'Yes, bastard, that's what a couple of the boys were shouting while they trampled all over Aleksei, bastard, bastard. And Eastpox too, of course.'

'Why bastard?'

'I don't know.' She shrugged. 'Maybe because they know we don't have a father, and our father and you weren't married.'

'Oh, come on, how would they know a thing like that?'

'Well, the teacher is always asking what jobs people's mothers and fathers do.'

'And how does marriage come into it?'

'I told her my father was dead.'

'And?'

'And then the teacher said: *So your mother is a widow. Widow*, it somehow sounded so nasty. But I know what a widow is. She's the old wife of an old man who dies. So I just told her you aren't a widow, because you weren't married to him and you're still quite young and not a widow at all.'

'So what? It's not so unusual to be born out of wedlock these days. I was born out of wedlock myself. Do you think my mother could get married just like that?'

'Why didn't Grandmother get married, then?'

'It wasn't allowed.'

'Why not?'

'I've already told you.'

'Tell me again, Mama, please, please.'

'They couldn't get married because she was Jewish and he wasn't.'

'Tell me how they met each other again.'

'No, not now.' I pushed Katya ungently aside. 'You'll hurt him, lying on top of him like that.'

'I wasn't lying on him any more.'

'Come here.' Cautiously, I raised Aleksei's arm. Of course it was light, Aleksei's arms were always light, but no one had said he was undernourished before. First I stroked his arm, then I pushed up his sleeve. 'What's that?' I ran one finger over the tiny blue-black prick marks. Two of the places were inflamed and looked like little craters, with tiny rings of dried pus round the open centre containing transparent fluid.

'Don't.' Aleksei tried to push my hand away.

'What's that?'

Katya bent over Aleksei's arms and stroked him.

'Why won't you tell me?' I was almost screaming at him.

Aleksei, weary and exhausted, looked past me, turned on his side and stared at the pillow in front of him.

'Mama, don't go interrogating him like that.' Katya looked at me sternly, as if I'd asked an improper question. 'They do that to a boy in my class too. They prick him with a fountain pen in lessons.'

'Prick him with a fountain pen?'

'Or something like that. With pencils. Once a boy did it with a pair of compasses, but the teacher saw him. You have to keep quiet in lessons, so the boy in my class doesn't dare to scream or they'll laugh at him in break and call him a softie or a sissy.'

'A softie?' Why do you cry so easily, Vassily had once asked me, and I didn't know what to say. I couldn't cry any more after I'd been given his death certificate. Even when I felt like crying, and it seemed the right thing to do. I stroked the little marks, some of which seemed to form circles and patterns. 'Those are tattoos.' I shook my head.

'They do other things too,' said Katya. 'For instance, the other day the boys peed in his shoes after sports.' She giggled. 'They were all wet.'

I closed my eyes and felt how the little craters were raised above his smooth, childish skin. 'Branding him,' I said quietly, and I thought of animals being branded.

'And then, just imagine, Mama, just imagine, that boy – I think he's adopted, they always say he comes from a home, he was the only child except me not to have a big pencil case. He comes to school with a zip-up bag instead, and they put dog shit in it.' Katya shook herself and stopped giggling. 'Disgusting, wasn't it, Mama?'

'Can't you stop talking all the time?' My eyes were heavy. Katya seemed to be on top of the world.

'And one more thing, Mama, just one more thing, once they wrote I Am Stupid in ballpoint pen on that boy's jacket. I Am Stupid. And then they were going to write something on my jacket too, but I ran away fast, and not even the boys could run as fast as me.' Katya giggled and giggled.

'Do you think that's funny?'

'No. Not at all.'

There were moments when I couldn't stand Katya's insistence

on sharing her childish cheerfulness with me. She did seem to me childish in the way it burst out in situations when I could have fallen asleep on the spot with exhaustion, and wanted nothing more than to be alone for ten minutes, maybe even moments when I felt like shedding tears and didn't, because there were no more tears to shed. When I rejected her I was ashamed of myself, particularly because it was not by chance that she persisted in laughing more and more the more desperate I felt.

'Hey, Mama, shall I tell you a joke?'

'No, no jokes.' I stood up, took the things I had brought with me out of my bag and put them in the empty locker. The donkey was lying beside the bed. My legs felt so tired that I sat down on the bed again. Aleksei must have lost his glasses in the school playground; it was good that he was asleep now. I wouldn't wake him up to ask him about that, but I'd have to put off the optician appointment. If that man Bender who called himself a doctor didn't live in another world entirely, I might have asked him if Aleksei couldn't have a new pair of glasses fitted here in the hospital. But I felt sure that the eye tests on someone with concussion would be tricky.

'I only want to cheer you up,' said Katya, flinging her thin arms round my neck.

At first I felt like a dead rock, gigantic in my daughter's arms. But then something inside me tingled, I felt shame spreading through me, lava crawled into my face and went cold on my hands. I sat there motionless in her embrace. I simply wanted to think of something sensible I could do. Even words seemed no more than useless sounds.

Frau Jabłonovska was sitting at the bus stop in her fur coat. She waved when she saw us coming.

'I think we're going the same way,' I said to her. Her fur

had lost its lustre. Instinctively, I wondered whether lice lived in a fur coat like that; after all, it was warmed from the inside every day.

'I'm sorry, no, I'm on the way to work. The midday shift.'

'Where do you work?'

'In a fast-food restaurant, cooking. I may be able to move to the cash desk from next week.' Proudly, she arranged the fur coat over her knees and held both edges so that it wouldn't fall open. Her smile might have been taken for the calm, robust smile of a peasant woman. I remembered what her father had told me behind her back; he had said she was a cellist, and not a good one. The cello that the family had sold in order to bury her brother here must once have stood between those plump knees. Frau Jabłonovska's proud look alarmed me.

'It must be tiring, spending all day without fresh air and daylight.'

'Without daylight? I never thought of that. Without daylight.' Frau Jabłonovska stroked her dull fur. 'But I like it. It's not all that tiring.'

Her robust attitude seemed to me deliberate. She wiped out one eye with her little finger. She was silent, and it seemed to me the silence of a woman at rest with herself, very different from me, and certainly not a woman who had to fight off tormenting thoughts. I was sure that peasant women led carefree lives. I didn't know much about women cellists. She wiped out her other eye with her ring finger. Her brother had died last night. Now he was lying with his mouth gaping open if they hadn't made him ready to be seen yet. The moments when I imagined Vassily dead were few and far between now. His limbs were distorted, his dark eyes now saw nothing, and something pulled at my insides. The children compelled me to go on living. At first I'd felt reluctant to live on, then ashamed of my own survival. At last one day I felt, for the first time, secret joy at a moment of forgetfulness. Frau Jabłonovska's description of her brother's open jaws had made my mind go to Vassily. But I could let it do that for a moment without dwelling on him. Arrogance felt strange, strange to me, not natural to me. You needed a cloak of invisibility. Polish gypsies, that was the term used in the camp for all Poles. It must be because of their delight in celebrating, because they often met each other inside the camp and could be so outrageously cheerful. They sang all night. The man in the laundry had told me that he often couldn't sleep because the Poles in his shared apartment celebrated all night. It insults our serious German sensitivity, the little man had told me, looking up at me. I didn't know whether or not to laugh.

The bus came, and we got in. Gypsies not only had no apartments, they were landless and practised no profession. People with no ties to anyone and anything outside their tribe, free people, Vassily had thought, lawless people, I had replied. Only no one wanted to be like them, except for Vassily, who used to claim at particularly childish moments that he had always wished he'd been born a gypsy – unfortunately, that wish had not been granted, and as you couldn't *become* a gypsy, he must remain unfree all his life. That idea of his had seemed to me a little foolish, foolish in linking his own existence solely to his birth, as if he believed in fate – and that belief had struck me as so unwontedly childish in him that I had liked him for it.

Only a few days ago, in the employment agency, I had been offered a job as an assistant in a drinks market. I had turned it down. I was a qualified chemist, and had worked at various other jobs, at least they had let me work at the cemetery when the Academy of Sciences informed me that they had no further use for me. That at least gave me fresh air and daylight. The

Weissensee cemetery was hardly used. What Jew died these days in East Berlin? The place had ivy and large rhododendrons. Damp shade. Tree trunks of sandstone with lichen living on them. Names and inscriptions. In addition, only my own whispering in my head, no chatter and no orders. The man at the employment agency said he would like to believe I was a qualified chemist, and as he said that he looked deep into my eyes and stared hard at my breasts, but according to his files I was unemployable in that field. Where was I going to leave my children all day? And it was so long since I had worked as a chemist, not to mention the different state of research in the two countries, *and then there's your status as a refugee, with a B pass – weren't you in any real predicament, didn't you have any real crisis of conscience?* His glance positively slunk along my neckline. Well, whatever I might have been, and his hand fidgeted under the desktop, he certainly couldn't get me a position as a chemist. No, I answered him back, I wasn't going to work in a drinks market even for one thousand two hundred marks gross a month, whatever that might be net. I stuck to my point however much the man assured me that it wasn't bad pay, in fact with the special Berlin bonus it was even good, and I heard him swallowing his own saliva. What was Western liberty for, if not for making decisions? So I slip into old shoes and a shared room with my two children, into the beds of countless predecessors and between the camp's sheets, but I don't slip into a strange way of life, not for a second time, or for a third or a fourth time. By comparison, Frau Jabłonovska, proudly hoisting up the skirts of her fur coat on her way to work to make room for me beside her, seemed so whole and at one with herself that I was suddenly sure, even if I didn't believe in the word *gypsy*, that there couldn't have been any fast-food restaurants in Poland. Frau Jabłonovska seemed to me curiously silent. *She's listening to music inside her head*, Aleksei had told me as I fetched the children on that first Sunday in the camp from her apartment that smelled of cabbage and lard, and they resisted because they didn't want to leave their glasses, still half full of cola. I would briefly have liked to stop her talking in the laundry. *What a tiny little dress*, she had said with moist eyes, taking one of Katya's dresses in her hands as if it were made of precious silk. She talked about my two children's good manners, and said nothing about her crazy father and her own past as a cellist, which could have been just her father's invention, entirely unknown to herself. Her chatter had worn me out to such an extent that I saw no other way of escape but to pick up my washing in the middle of one of her never-ending sentences and leave the laundry without a word of farewell. She obviously didn't bear me a grudge for that last meeting, and yet all her warmth and liking had disappeared today. She left me alone with my speculations about her life. Krystyna Jabłonovska said goodbye, she must change to another bus now, and Katya hurried to occupy the seat beside me.

Back in the camp I went along the path to our block until suddenly there was a bottle dangling in front of us. We stopped and looked up. The little man was crouching in his open window.

'It's for you. Take it, go on.' He drew on his cigarette and flicked it high in the air and away. The bottle danced up and down. Katya wrenched herself away from my hand and investigated the bottle.

'Don't do that. Come on,' I whispered to Katya, hoping she might forget her curiosity.

'It's all right. Wait a minute.' She tugged and pulled until the knot round the neck of the bottle came away. When Katya put her head back I couldn't cut it any more, and I looked up as well.

'Go on, take it.' He made a gesture indicating clearly that I was to take the note in the bottle. 'Why aren't you wearing your summer dress any more?'

'In winter?'

'You were wearing it in autumn.'

This little man was pursuing me. His appearances were getting more frequent and more urgent, as if his entire aim was never to take his eyes off me for a second. For days I had seen him everywhere, either following me, crossing my path as if by chance, or sitting in the laundry when I went there. Katya held the bottle out to me, and I positively snatched it from her hand. Sometimes I saw him walking up and down outside our block, as if he were waiting for me to come out of the building. The rolled-up paper fell out of the opening easily.

'What does it say?' Katya wanted to take the roll of paper from me. I gave her the empty bottle.

'Never mind, come on.' Holding the paper firmly, I put my hand in the pocket of my jacket.

'I bet he's an admirer, Mama.'

'Could be.' We climbed the stairs. I put the little roll of paper on top of the wardrobe and decided not to open it. Whoever lived in this room after us and used the wardrobe could find out what the dwarf had written. I wasn't about to read it myself.

Once I had been to ask the porter if there was any post. I was sure that a letter from my mother was bound to arrive saying when my uncle would come from Paris. After all, he had said he was coming to visit, and I still didn't know when that would be. It was raining in torrents. The little man was standing in the porter's lodge, leafing through a thick telephone book and apparently not noticing that there was someone standing behind him, waiting for her turn and freezing. He lit cigarette after cigarette, and only when I tapped him on the shoulder did he step aside. I asked the porter about post, but there were no letters for me. Disappointed, I set out to return to our room, passing the first block of apartments, then the second, and I had already noticed him going along beside me. He struck up a conversation, saying he'd had his eye on me for some time, although that wasn't usually a thing he would do, he thought nothing of women, nothing at all. I was the only one who had caught his eye, I mustn't laugh, he said, but he would like to get to know me because I wore such a pretty dress, it didn't go with the rain at all. But his words were so pressing, his hope so obdurate, that I didn't feel at all like laughing. I thought his story of the dress was just an excuse to bring him closer to me. That was what I feared, and I did not meet what I felt sure was his imploring gaze. He kept walking a step in front of me, almost stumbling as if it were difficult to keep up with me, and now and then his shoulder collided with my breast. That too, so it seemed to me, was nothing but a guileless attempt to get closer. He was a loser, he told me, a weakling, he hadn't even succeeded in fleeing from the East. But then, as if miraculously, he did get away, although he didn't believe that the state had hit upon the idea of buying his freedom of its own accord. Presumably they'd had to take him as a free gift thrown in when it was someone else they wanted. I nodded, but that didn't satisfy him. I too, he said, had seemed to him improbable at first, a fairy-tale princess. His eyes were shining. *Three Wishes for Cinderella* – surely I knew that film. Once again, and as if accidentally, he nudged my breast. Now he saw me differently, as more human, but I wasn't to worry, he couldn't do anything with women, he'd tried and it was no good. I didn't believe that he'd tried, although I thought it probable that it hadn't worked.

Even the story of a woman who had left him was not something I wanted to hear about. I lacked the patience to listen to this driven man. But he needed no sign of any attention to go on talking. I heard him telling me how they were together on the beach, and assumed it was about that woman. I didn't want to ask questions because I was afraid he would go on talking even longer. How she had sat in her seaside basket chair all alone, she had been looking out to sea and didn't want to be disturbed. While he had been rolling in the sand in front of her like a dog, and getting only a contemptuous glance from her, if that. Perhaps it had been the fear, he said, the deep horror, that made that his one pictorial memory of those seven years. Could I imagine that, he asked, after seven years she had simply left!

I didn't want to imagine anything, I had walked away from him in the middle of his sentence, I had left him in the middle of exclamation marks, indeed question marks, I had said this was where I lived, and I had disappeared into the entrance of my building.

After a week in hospital, Aleksei had lost two pounds in weight and was in a room with four other boys.

'Have we come to the right place? Is Aleksei Senff here?'

The three of us looked up, and saw a tall, slender figure in the doorway. The woman looked anxiously around, dwelling on every face, until she stopped at ours. She had a small boy in tow.

'This is my son Olivier. He wants to say he's sorry. Olivier, go on, say sorry.' Olivier was dragged forward from behind his mother's back, and inspected the ceiling with interest. 'Listen, Olivier. Do you want your father to come and . . . ?' Olivier tried stamping his foot, and accidentally kicked the leg of my chair with his boot.

'Excuse our riding things. We're in such a hurry today.' The mother did not offer me her hand. Mother and son were both in jodhpurs. The woman took off a thin leather glove. 'We had no idea, my God, if his teacher hadn't phoned on Friday! We had visitors at the weekend, and now this. Olivier, say you're sorry. Here.' Olivier raised his hand a little way, no doubt expecting me to take it. All I could feel were his cool fingertips which he hastily withdrew, as if afraid of catching something. A case of Eastpox, I thought. He put his hands in the pockets of his jacket and turned away from us. His mother took something wrapped in shiny paper with a big silvery bow out of her bag. She pressed it into her son's hand. He threw it on Aleksei's bed as if it were a bomb with the safety catch off, turned on his heel, and marched towards the door with short, firm footsteps. The woman shook her head; she was wearing glasses with large tinted lenses, and her eyes were smiling through them. At the same time, she avoided looking straight at me. She turned to Aleksei and Katya without a word. She smiled at her knee. 'Oh, children! You can do what you like – top of the class so recently, and he has to go attracting attention.' She looked lovingly at her son, who was just closing the door behind him. 'But what can you do?' She put her glove back on. 'As I said, Frau Senff, Olivier is very sorry. Such a terrible thing, when the phone rings and you go to answer it without suspecting a thing.' The woman did not waste a glance on Aleksei and Katya, but picked up the package from Aleksei's bed and pulled the ends of the silver bow. 'The teacher said Olivier wasn't the only one. Maybe not, but it's worrying all the same.' Relieved, the woman heaved a sigh and put the package back on the blanket. She lifted her hair, all cut to the same length, from below, and dabbed the corner of her mouth with her fingertip to left and right, as if afraid that her glossy

172

lipstick was smeared. 'Luckily it was no worse. You see, Olivier has assured us several times that it wasn't his fault, and another boy was the ringleader. But I said he had to say sorry all the same.' An expression approaching sadness came over her face, and she dabbed the corners of her mouth again. 'After all, he's been well brought up.' She laughed, and adjusted the silk scarf round her neck. 'At least we try to do our best.' And with a wave, she went towards the door.

Hans Pischke meets Nelly Senff in the laundry

There was still a dark piece of fabric stuck on the bottom of the drum. I reached into the machine to get at the sock and wrung it out before adding it to the other things in the basket and taking it over to the spin dryer. First I cleared the fluff out of the spin dryer. The air in the laundry building was stagnant; I almost felt as if I were breathing in fluff, warm, dense, moist fluff. Item by item, I put my washing in the dryer. When I glanced up, I was looking into black eyes, and the blood shot to my face. I watched as she went to the washbasin, almost dancing, and turned on the tap. She was squeezing and wringing out a small pair of trousers, rubbing washing powder on their knees. Then she turned off the tap. My mouth felt dry; I pushed my tongue back and forth. Her hair looked silky, but it was only its lustre, and lustre was nothing. People like her were well off; they could wash small pairs of trousers and didn't have to wonder why.

'What is it?' she asked out loud, suddenly turning to me.

I looked over my shoulder in alarm, but there was no one except the two of us in the laundry.

'Nothing – excuse me.'

'Why nothing? You're watching me.'

'No, really I'm not, I only looked your way.'

There was a thin chain round her neck with an oval pendant, reminiscent of an amulet, dangling from it. Her round, silver-framed glasses were misted up. The woman who had still been wearing a summer dress a few weeks ago, and whom I had accompanied on her way home in a fit of longing in order to confide in her, shrugged her shoulders and rubbed the fabric of the small pair of trousers.

I put garment after garment into the spin dryer. By chance, I happened to have heard two women talking about her. They were saying she had no husband, so they had to hide their own husbands from her. All the same, she looked perfectly harmless. Perhaps she had run away from her husband. A tear was running down her cheek, leaving a trail behind it before it fell.

'Excuse me.'

'Yes?' She was kneading the fabric, and didn't seem to want to be distracted. 'What is it?' Now she did look up, and her black eyes were gleaming.

'Why are you crying?'

'What makes you think you can ask me a question like that? We don't know each other at all.' Holding the bundle of fabric, she passed her forearm over her face and wiped away the trace of the tear.

'We sometimes see each other in passing,' I said, and realised that must sound like a justification to her but couldn't be good enough. 'I'm only asking because you had a tear on your cheek.'

'I'm not crying. I'm washing clothes and the washing powder stings my eyes.'

I closed the lid of the dryer. It began rotating slowly, jolting on the spot.

'Do you happen to have a different kind of washing powder?' The woman was smiling at me.

'Different kind of washing powder? Sorry, no. I use the same as you.' I pointed to the carton. The washing powder was given out in the camp, and if you wanted to use a different kind you had to go out of the camp to the shop on the other side of the street, passing the porter and his red-and-white barrier. Disappointed, she nodded.

'Shall we have a cigarette?' She put the trousers on the washboard. 'You don't often talk to people, do you?' She passed her tongue over her lips.

'Why do you say that?'

'Because you ask such abrupt questions. Most people don't ask the sort of thing you do.' She laughed; her laughter was like a way of forgiving me. 'Even if I really had been crying. Least of all then.'

'Hmm.' I inhaled the cigarette smoke and tasted its sweetness on my gums, a pleasantly tart aftertaste that only Western cigarettes had.

I can say anything now, I thought, and I said, 'You don't have a husband.'

'Why do you ask that?' She narrowed her eyes and examined me from above.

'I'm not asking, I know. People talk to each other about things.'

'What people?'

'People here in the camp.'

'Oh, that.' She turned her back to me again and rinsed the trousers out under the tap, her cigarette in the corner of her mouth. 'I'm Nelly,' she said, looking at me over her shoulder and offering me her wet hand.

'You've got another tear on your eyelid.'

'It's the smoke,' she laughed, putting her finger under her glasses and running it over the eye.

'Yes, so I see. There are any number of reasons.' She kept her hand held out expectantly. I was afraid to take it, yet at the same time I could hardly wait to do so. I didn't want to hurt her feelings. 'I'm Hans.'

'What sort of handshake is that?' I saw repulsion in her eyes.

'What do you mean, what sort?'

'Exactly. Not a handshake at all.' She blinked, and fanned the smoke away with her hand.

'Did you open my message-in-a-bottle?'

'Your message-in-a-bottle?' She looked at me in surprise; then her face brightened, as if it had now occurred to her that I had let a bottle down out of the window a few days ago, and first her daughter and then she had been fishing for it. 'Oh, that?'

'Well?'

'No, I haven't read it, not yet.' She laughed. 'The perfume was you too, am I right?'

'What perfume?'

'You left some perfume with the porter for me. And the flowers hanging from the door of my room a few days ago, they were from you. Am I right? Just don't go falling in love.'

'Don't worry, I'm incapable of love.'

She looked at me with a question in her eyes.

'Don't worry, I'm incapable of love!' I repeated it in a loud voice to drown out the spinning of the dryer. But her glance was still sure of love and correspondingly incredulous. I pressed the button to open the dryer, the lid sprang open, and with a few more jolts the machine came to a halt.

'As bad as that?' She didn't seem to take me seriously.

'No.' I couldn't repress a smile as I leaned forward and reached into the dryer. 'You're wrong. It's not bad.'

'If you whisper into the drum of the dryer like that I can't hear a word.'

'It's not bad,' I repeated, straightening up and taking out my shirt.

'The way you handle your washing anyone would think you were holding something fragile.' She pointed at my hands, making fun of me.

'Is that so?'

'Yes.'

'Well, aren't clothes valuable?' I bent down and put the washing in the basket.

'Depends how you look at it.' She shrugged and sat down on the bench. 'Come on, sit here beside me.' Although my washing was done now, and I could go, I sat down beside her, and as she said nothing, and I didn't know what to say myself, I said, 'Imagine if I had to buy new clothes just because I hadn't handled my washing carefully enough.'

'So what? You'd just have to buy them.'

'I'd have to go past the porter to do that.'

'You would indeed have to go past the porter to do that.' Nelly gave me a sly glance.

'I haven't done that for about thirteen months.' I laughed, and it occurred to me that this didn't fit the image of someone who left flowers. After all, there was no shop inside the camp, and where would whoever left the flowers have got them if not from outside?

'You're crazy.'

I laughed to prove her doubts correct, although it sounded hollow, but she wouldn't notice that. All the same, I said, 'Sorry, the perfume wasn't me and nor were the flowers.' I shook my head, amazed by the certainty with which she had suspected me. The more I denied it, the surer she seemed to be. I was a little pleased by her certainty; it flattered me.

Nelly laughed as if she had caught me out lying. 'Well, thank you anyway. But take my warning seriously. You'd be spending your money for nothing.'

'The things people are ready to believe of me,' I said quietly, and still incredulously. In fact she couldn't have opened my bottle post, and immediately I wished for nothing more fervently than that she never would open it, and I had never put the blank note in the bottle, or at least still had it in my possession. I liked the idea of loving her, and the fact that she thought I might made me feel happy for this one moment. What flowers had been left on her door? And how did you decide what flowers to give a woman? I envied her admirer. He was even capable of choosing a perfume, while here was I smoking her cigarettes and strutting in borrowed plumes.

'Not long ago I shared a cell with a man who wanted me to love him,' I said.

Nelly offered me a second cigarette, which I accepted as if I were someone else, a man in the prime of life who talked to a woman like Nelly every day, gave her flowers and laughed with her.

'You were in prison?'

'But I couldn't, do you understand? Although he was really nice, not like the people I have to live with here in the camp.'

'Loving a man may call for a different approach,' she said, smiling.

'Why?'

'I'd have thought so. To a man, I mean. Why were you in prison?'

'Not for any exciting reason.'

'Once, when you were following me home, you said something about an unsuccessful flight.'

'A ridiculous story.'

'A long one?'

'I don't remember.'

She looked at me incredulously.

'Four years, maybe.'

She was silent for a moment, perhaps thinking what four years meant. 'You'd like to touch me, wouldn't you?'

'Because I was in prison?' I asked faster than I intended, and won time for my shock and the image of her that was falling apart before my eyes, as if she were made of ashes. She seemed to me grey and calculating. A grey little heap, tasted and burnt to ashes long ago.

'I'm sorry. Since we started talking to each other . . .' I stopped, and wondered whether I would hurt her unnecessarily if I confessed that not for a second had I thought of touching her.

'That's all right,' she said, as if she knew what I wanted to say. She wound a strand of hair round her finger, and pushed off from her washing machine with her foot. Our bench tipped slightly backwards. 'My children's father disappeared a good three years ago. You didn't by any chance meet him?'

'Disappeared?'

'Some say dead. Others don't believe them. I can imagine him either dead or alive.' She reached for the little oval pendant on her chain and let it slip through her fingers.

'What's his name?'

'Vassily. But what does a name mean? Batalov, Vassily Batalov.'

'Russian?'

'Probably.'

'You seem to have known him really well.'

She pretended not to notice my irony. 'Well enough.' She opened the old-fashioned locket and showed me a photo.

I cast a fleeting glance at the tiny black-and-white picture lying in her hand, right in front of her breasts. My sensation of lightness ebbed away, as well as any idea that I could love her. I nodded appreciatively. 'He was tall, am I right?'

'Fairly tall.' Nelly was still holding the photo out to me, but I did not take it. 'What is it? Do you know him?'

'How could I know him?'

'Well, maybe from prison.'

'I was alone most of the time there.' I took another look at the photo. 'He does look to me familiar now.'

Nelly closed the locket and let it slip back into her neckline, between her breasts. 'Oh, you're crazy. Look a third time and you'll be sure, a fourth time and he was your cellmate, right?'

'Could be,' I nodded, caught in the act. It's a fact that if you look at a photo several times your feeling that you know the person it shows is reinforced, because there is no movement in a photograph, and in the observer's mind the person photographed seems to have moved, even if you only looked away and lost sight of him for seconds. Whenever the Stasi or a Western secret service put photos in front of me, a time always came when the people in them looked familiar. 'Do you miss him?'

She looked intently at the washing machine, her lips moved in search of the right word, a beginning, then she cast her eyes down and looked up. 'You've finished your washing, haven't you?' She glanced at my full laundry basket standing beside our bench. 'Then I won't keep you.'

You're not keeping me, I could have said, but it felt too difficult for me, and the cheerfulness I had derived from her certainty that I'd fallen in love with her had evaporated. I stood up too, and picked up my basket. She did not detain me, said not a word that I could have answered in any way, and so I pushed the door open.

'See you,' I said, going out, but she probably hadn't heard me. The cold air met my face.

A siren was howling over the terrain of the camp, and a fire engine came towards me from the porter's lodge. There was already an ambulance standing outside my apartment block, its unsteady blue light falling on the people nearby. In the twilight their faces were almost unrecognisable. The blue light flickered on the walls of the buildings. I walked faster, passing the first two entrances. People formed groups, looking up. I did not follow their eyes. Holding my basket of washing in front of me, I forced my way through the crowd of spectators standing close together. I recognised Nelly's children holding hands. 'Make way, make way, please,' came a voice through a megaphone. 'Careful, step aside.' The people moved, but hardly left the spot. I heard a woman's high laughter behind me. 'She owed me another ten marks.' 'Then you can forget it,' I heard a man reply.

A fire-engine ladder was extended. Between the dusk and the blue light, images seemed to be coming apart into small pieces. I could hardly fit a single whole picture together. Suddenly a hand reached for mine; I pushed it away. When I turned, I saw fear in Nelly's face. She had followed me with her laundry basket under her arm. Close as she was standing, she seemed to me a good head taller. Her breath was close to my face.

'Your children are standing over there,' I told her, pointing over the heads of the crowd to where I thought they would be. Nelly nodded and turned round, trying to make a way through to the children.

Down in the entrance to my building, its inhabitants were crowding so closely together that I had difficulty getting in. The staircase leading up was clear; I took a deep breath. Even before I switched on the light in my room, I looked through the window and saw the firefighter who was standing on his ladder only a few metres away, gesticulating wildly to his colleagues below as he tried to convey something to them. I stood in the doorway of the room, not venturing either to turn on the light or to go to the window and draw the curtains. A piece of fabric was hanging in a tree, something white, a nightdress. The wearer's head emerged from its neck. Blue light flickered over the walls of the room. At eye level with the firefighter, I saw him put the white nightdress over his shoulder, struggling with the rope that she must have knotted tightly, and then he cautiously climbed down the ladder. I waited until his helmet and the piece of white fabric had disappeared. Even without looking closely, I knew it was the old woman who had occupied the room in the apartment just above mine ever since I had been in the camp. She too, it seemed, had not succeeded in leaping out of the camp to find freedom. Or then, perhaps she had. I envied her.

Krystyna Jabłonovska changes her mind

I tipped portion after portion of *pommes frites* into the chip pan, watched them dancing and the fat sizzling, throwing up bubbles until the chips turned brown and the next portion went into the pan. My eyes were sticky with the fat. Time refused to pass. Once I tried pushing my hair back under the cap I wore, and the chips turned black before I could lift the strainer out.

'Faster,' called the cashier. 'You must go faster.' She drummed impatiently on the cash register. Her forehead was shiny. Sometimes I wondered why she seemed so driven; after all, we didn't have to work to the same rhythm. Perhaps she got a bonus based on the turnover. A few days ago it had occurred to me that perhaps her own money, not someone else's, was topped up if I cooked more chips in a shorter time. I badly needed to go to the toilet but dared not ask.

'Faster – hey, didn't you hear what I said?'

I turned and nodded to her. However hard I tried, and however fast I worked, her time was running away and mine was moving sluggishly.

'Not crisp enough,' she said, tipping a portion of chips back into the pan of fat. 'Listen, the customers are complaining. Don't you know what work means?' The cashier asked questions without waiting for any answers. Anyway, she thought I hardly understood any German, just as she herself didn't want to understand the German I spoke. I had stopped answering her.

'May I go to the toilet?'

'What did you say?' She looked blankly at me and cupped a hand behind her ear. 'Speak clearly when you're talking to me, and speak German.'

'The toilet. May I go there?'

'Do you have to go now?' The cashier pointed to the queue in front of her counter, and I tipped more chips into the pan of fat, turned the sausages, added more of them, took my handkerchief out of my apron pocket and tried to blow my nose. It was swollen, and seemed to be stuffed up with the fatty vapours. I pressed my thighs together to avoid an accident. My face was burning. The heat couldn't be turned down, the air was heavy, the people around me seemed to be moving in slow motion, as if the heat were so intense that they were flickering before my eyes. The hands of the clock seemed to have been slowed down by the fat as well.

'Sausages with skins,' called the cashier, as if she was repeating it for the tenth time, which indeed she might be. 'With skins, don't you get that?'

I looked at the sausages. None of them had skins. I had to go to the freezer, although I could hardly walk, four steps back, sausages with skins, four steps forward, five without skins, ten with, all of them curry-flavoured. The curry powder made my nose itch. It was even more difficult to deal with the itching of my lower back, where my hands couldn't reach properly to scratch and make it feel better. The sausages burst one by one. My father had a scar on his arm, long and open like that as if an injury had never healed. When he shouted at me he claimed it was my fault, I had given him that scar. When I was twelve, he said, I had crossed the street with my cello on our way to the Warsaw Conservatory. Playing chicken, he said, he supposed I hadn't seen the tram. As he was only a little way behind me, he had given the cello a good kick to keep it from getting under the wheels of the tram, and that was what came of it: he had an arm that wouldn't heal up. I turned the sausages and ran the tongs over their skin to make them burst more quickly. If you started at the top and moved the tongs to the other end at a certain speed, you could score a more or less straight line down the sausages in only one go.

'Two shashliks.' The cashier looked over my shoulder. 'Look, haven't you put any shashliks on?' She sighed and reached over my arms, picked up two shashlik skewers with her red hands to put them on the grill, and a piece of meat fell off and landed in the chip pan. Sizzling fat spat on my arm. The cashier groaned. Sonata for cello and piano in G minor, on the day when Jerzy died, and I got there too late because no one had been able to let me know in the camp. I had got out a stop too soon on my way to work, and went into a record shop. I'd listened to it. I would never be able to play like that Jacqueline du Pré. But for the first time I understood why Jerzy had been so enthusiastic about it.

Suddenly the fast-food restaurant seemed to have been swept empty; only a single customer was standing at the cash register waiting for his two shashlik skewers. 'You Easterners are all the same, never mind which part you come from. That's a fact. Along comes one of you saying she's experienced. Tell me another.' The cashier had lit a cigarette, and waved it in my direction. I was standing slightly bent forward with my legs crossed, to avoid having an accident, turning the skewers. The man drank from his beer bottle. The cashier wasn't even trying to complain quietly; she probably thought I didn't understand her. 'They just don't know what work means, no. You can tell them a hundred times, they don't get it.' The man said something that I didn't catch. She laughed and agreed with him.

The skewers were ready; paprika, curry and ketchup. I was pushing the cardboard plate over to her as the swing door opened and Petra came in.

'Change of shift. Go and change your clothes,' the cashier told me. I hurried to the toilet door, taking small steps. As soon as I was sitting on the toilet the door handle was pushed down. Through the thin door I heard something from outside that sounded like 'Oh no!' and 'hours'; I was working out in my head how much I had saved up so far, and decided that from now on I would save not just fifteen marks but the whole thirty-two marks of my day's wages. Then I'd be able to get my cello back from the antiques dealer in two weeks' time.

In the little broom cupboard, Petra pulled a T-shirt over her head. Her breasts were as round as the breasts of the young girls in underwear catalogues. She turned to me in alarm. 'I didn't hear you.'

The cashier came over to us. 'There's money missing again,' she told Petra, speaking over my head.

'Much?'

'Well, almost twelve marks. On a day like this, too.' She was spitting with anger as she spoke. She counted out the notes again, fanning them on the narrow little cupboard before our eyes as if to prove her point. Now and then she licked her fingertips. Then she took the change and stacked up the coins in towers beside the notes as she counted them. 'There we are, ten marks twenty-three,' she told Petra, and then looked at me. 'Not nicking anything, are you?'

I shook my head, wondering what I could say.

'I'm not having anyone nick money from me, get it? I always take the key with me if I have to go out for a minute.' She looked from me to Petra and back to me again. Then she looked at Petra. 'I'll have to deduct it from her pay. I can't be forking out the extra on a day like this. She needn't think she can get away with it. Can't even turn round for a moment, the way they go behind your back.'

'Maybe you gave the wrong change.' Petra said that quietly, as if in passing.

'Me?'

'It can happen.'

'Not to me, love, not after twenty-five years, you bet.' The cashier gave me another reproachful glance, and went out without another word to the cash register in the front part of the restaurant, where she greeted Herta, come to take over her shift.

'Don't think too much of it,' Petra told me as she buttoned up her overall. Her left eye winked at me, and I wasn't sure whether she did that on purpose. I could never be sure whether it was a nervous tic around that eye or was meant for me. She took a little folding mirror out of her bag and refreshed her lipstick, pressing her lips together and rolling one over the other. 'If you ask me she always pockets the missing money herself.' Petra had thin lips, and overpainted the top lip in a heart shape. Now she chose a rather darker lipstick and used it only on her lower lip. 'That's what I'd do if I was cashier.' Petra dabbed white eyeshadow on her eyelids and took another look in her little mirror before closing it. 'I'm leaving this job.

'What are you going to be?'

'A sales rep. See this lipstick? You can't get it in ordinary shops, it's exclusive. I invite my girlfriends home to my place, put out a few salty nibbles and offer them Coca-Cola. I get that on account, of course.' She put a piece of chewing gum in her mouth and offered me the pack. I took a piece myself, although I didn't like chewing gum.

'Pretty colour,' I said, nodding to her.

'I bet you could do the same.' Petra took out a little cosmetic case and powdered her nose, forehead and chin.

'Oh no. Thanks, but our apartment's too small.' I thought of my father lying on his bed in the camp, hoping that someone like Nelly would come along one of these days, or another miracle would happen. When I came back from work in the evening, he would tell me he was going to waste away here, all because of me. Because of my stupid idea of getting treatment for my brother in the West, where he'd died in any case. Yesterday evening he had said, for the first time, that Jerzy had died because of me, the move had simply been too much for him. I hadn't said anything in reply to that. *If we'd stayed in Stettin he'd still be alive.* Over the last few weeks I'd stopped answering my father; I let him talk, and it all came out of its own accord. I was going to have him on my conscience too, he was sure of that now. I chewed the gum cautiously in case my fillings fell out. The chewing gum was strawberry-flavoured, and such a large piece that I felt I was choking on it.

'That's what I thought at first myself – I thought I couldn't do a thing like that in my apartment. But then the boss told me no apartment is too small. Except in the clink,' she added, laughing. 'If we're a bit cramped for space, well, it's comfy, and the wares look extra good. So long as there's a nice atmosphere.'

'Are you two going to have a coffee or what? Get a move on, can't you?' The cashier looked back at us with an admonishing expression, and went on talking to Herta. Get a move on. I imagined Petra's nice atmosphere, and rather wished I could sit here longer listening to her. Every day I felt less inclined to go back to my father in the camp. Was that going to be my home now? Petra lived in the north of the city, in one of the new housing estates. The apartments there were affordable, and equipped with everything: hot water, central heating, fitted kitchens. A lift in every building. There were carpets on the floors of the apartments, and the rubbish went straight down a chute from the kitchen to the cellar. I'd heard there were even doorbell intercoms for talking to your visitors. Why not a little apartment like Petra's? Then I wouldn't have to take the cello to the camp first and expose it to my father's gaze, I would take it straight to the little apartment and get a job teaching at a music college.

'And I can take care of the atmosphere, honest.' Petra closed her powder compact. I took my cap off. Petra held my arm. 'But don't pass any of this on, will you?'

I nodded.

'They don't have to know about it here. I'm not giving notice until I've signed the contract.'

'Don't worry,' I said, taking off my overall.

'And another thing.' She reached for my arm again. I hung my overall on the hook and put on my fur coat, which I kept in a large plastic bag so that it wouldn't absorb too much of the smell of frying fat.

'Yes?'

'Maybe it's a teeny bit embarrassing, but seeing that we're good friends, Jabłonovska, don't you use any deo?'

'Any what?'

'Deo. Deodorant.' She pronounced the final T sharply and distinctly. 'Haven't you come across it? Kind of a spray so that you don't smell of sweat. You know – working all day like this, in such a small space. Well, I only wanted to say, if you see what I mean.'

She opened the slide in her hair, stood in front of the little mirror fitted beside the cupboard, and shook out her hair. She saw me watching her and winked. She had pretty hair, strawberry blonde, you could only see the dark roots at her hairline. She took a can out of her bag and sprayed something on her hair. I couldn't say if it had a fragrance or not, my nose was numb from all the cooking oil.

'What's the matter? Close your mouth or a fly will get in.' She laughed at me, and I closed my mouth. 'You're not cross, are you, Jabłonovska?' She tied her hair back in a ponytail, which didn't suit her age.

'No.'

'You two going to be much longer back there?' Herta had taken over the cash register.

'This is all in confidence, right?' Petra slipped neatly into a thick pink snow jacket, with a white collar of artificial fur snuggling round her neck. 'Bought it yesterday. How do I look?'

I thought of Russian children, but I said, 'Like the Christ Child, a mixture of the Christ Child and an Eskimo.'

Petra nodded, satisfied, took the jacket off again and hung it on a hook. 'See you, then.' She pushed me ahead of her, past the frying equipment, the cash register and the counter.

'Goodbye.'

Except for Petra, who just looked up briefly and winked, no one answered me.

When two meet outside

'What a coincidence! Aren't you Frau Senff?' The woman thus addressed turned round. A bag hung limp and empty over her shoulder. She narrowed her eyes and scrutinised me to find out who I was.

'You're living at Marienfelde, aren't you? In the camp.' I propped myself against my car with one hand and smiled at her.

'Who are you?' There were tiny drops of water on the lenses of her glasses.

'John. John Bird. I work with the American assessment authority; we had a conversation about two months ago.'

'You what?'

'We. I said we had a conversation, don't you remember? About your reasons for wanting to leave the GDR.'

'Sorry.' She adjusted her empty shoulder bag and prepared to go on walking through the drizzle.

'Wait a moment, I'm not about to attack you. Can I walk a little way with you?'

'No, thanks.' Her cough sounded dry and rough.

'Come along, let's have a coffee. There's a cafe just ahead here.'

To my surprise she smiled, and said, 'Why not?'

We went in, she sat down on one of the red velour benches, and I could see the interior of the cafe, which was almost empty in the morning, in the large, dim mirror behind her head. A few men smoking pipes and reading the newspaper sat over coffee, served on little silver trays with tiny glasses of water that no one drank. There was never more than one customer at each table, some of them smoking not pipes but unfiltered French cigarettes. Nelly wound a strand of her hair round her finger and waited for me to sit down opposite her.

'Wouldn't you like to take your jacket off?'

Still seated, she awkwardly took off her jacket, which was thin and drenched with rain. Under it she was wearing a full blouse of some filmy material; you couldn't help noticing that she didn't have a bra on. I took her jacket to the coat stand – the damp fabric gave off an almost familiar smell – and came back as she was sitting down on the bench again with a box of matches. In the mirror I could see the friendly and persistent nodding of an elderly gentleman behind me; he had clearly given her the matches.

'Have you started smoking?'

'Why do you say started?' She waved the match in the air until it went out and dropped it in the ashtray.

'When we were talking two months ago you said you didn't smoke.'

'I don't remember that. But yes, I've only just started.' She didn't even try to suppress her yawn. 'Maybe I don't necessarily smoke in front of my children; the room fills up with smoke so quickly.' Her cigarette was glowing, and I could see her breath in its red light.

'You're young.' It was a statement, not a question.

I still wasn't sure whether to tell her that just now in the street I had taken her for a child prostitute, couldn't help it because she had been going along the pavement with a hop and a skip, and was even better at it than the girl ahead of her whom I had often seen in Kurfürstenstrasse. There was a strength in her step that, contrary to my expectations, suggested a girl who liked to have fun, and not just for a little packet of heroin, or because of the big fellow in the fur jacket who would be keeping track of her business deals from the car round the corner, with a mastiff on the back seat opening its jaws and letting its tongue loll out. She seemed to like my noticing her youth. Three of her fingers toyed with the matchbox, and I could sense a fleeting smile in her eyes.

'You think I'm young?'

'No, I know you are. Not exactly how young, but you can't be thirty yet.'

'Who knows?' Her smile drew a narrow line between us, not so much a wall as a skipping rope challenging me to jump over it. The matches in the box she was holding made a slight sound. Then she kept her fingers still as if waiting for my next question.

'What are your two children doing – going to school, I expect?'

'At the moment, yes. My son was in hospital for ten days. But he's been back at school for two weeks now.'

'Was it anything serious?'

'Don't you have children?'

'I'm afraid not.'

'But you're married?'

'Are you interrogating *me* now?'

'Who said anything about an interrogation? I see your ring, and I tell myself you look like a married man.'

I heard the rattle of the matches falling against each other again. If I asked her whether she was earning a little extra money here in Kurfürstenstrasse, I felt sure she would respond by asking me if I came to this part of Marienfelde often. So I hesitated, and asked, 'What does a married man look like, then?'

'There are some married men who go stalking. You can easily tell them by the way they walk and how they look at women.'

'And how do such married men look at women?'

'Curiously, with a certain self-confidence and a very natural sense of superiority. Hungry and at the same time used to being satisfied all their lives. Greedy but not looking as if they are really taking a risk. Like a king with a large appetite who slinks into the castle kitchen at night and takes the lids off all the pots and pans, dipping his finger into the food he's chosen, ordered for himself, to see what tastes good and to gulp it down, eating his way from pan to pan before they spread the table for him as usual next day.'

The coffee came. I put a sugar lump on my spoon, ran coffee into the spoon and watched the suger turn brown. I put the sugar in my mouth. 'You mean I'm that sort of man?'

She watched without trepidation as the sugar dissolved in my mouth, then her eyes went to the window, and I was already feeling afraid of the quick way she noticed things when she said, 'Cherry trees. How strange. Cherry trees in the middle of this town and the middle of winter.'

This time I didn't follow her eyes. I wanted to keep her where we had just been, so I looked at her expectantly. She still hadn't answered my question.

'And then you're a man with a remarkable profession. You work for your government in a crucial position, in the Secret Service, looking for the truth and getting as close as possible to your possible enemy. In a way you might well believe you're part of the government, that's evidence of a hunger for power and an unconditional will to subordinate yourself to a greater cause. The challenge is probably to keep the appetite for power under control every day, so that it doesn't get distracted from the cause.'

'You think I'm one of those kings in the castle kitchen?'

'A married man.'

'What would you say if I asked whether you'd come to a hotel near here with me?'

'Cherry trees are so old and black in winter that their blossom looks so pretty in spring mainly because of the contrast.' She was not looking at the cherry trees, she was looking at me.

'Will you come with me?'

'Why not?'

The coins clinked on the little silver tray that the waiter pushed towards me. He had her jacket and my coat over his arm.

The fine rain wasn't falling all the time. Her smell was sweet and sharp. I picked up my coat and held it over us like an umbrella until we had gone the few steps to my car.

The rooms in the hotel were tiny; you could hardly put one foot in front of another. Her ears were burning and she was breathing fast. Her skin was soft. Only afterwards did I undress her entirely and carry her the short distance to the bed. She lay there on her stomach, and didn't want the blanket I offered her. I had already wondered, back in October, if she wasn't freezing in her flower-patterned summer dress and light brown tights. Her throat stretched out long and white beneath her dark hair. I stroked her shoulders and my hand went on down her back, down to the hollow of her knee, where there was a black birthmark like the map of a country. I ran my fingertip along its borders until she drew up her knee, and the country disappeared into the hollow behind it.

'Why do you hide that bit of dark skin?'

'I don't like it.'

'See how much of it I have,' I said, taking her hand and carrying it to my shoulders.

'That's different.' Her hand lay in mine, cool, as if it didn't belong to her, and as if every touch and movement a few minutes before had been those of another woman.

'The differences aren't that great. Human being and human being. Skin and skin. Colour and colour.' Her own colour tasted salty. Her aroma, sweet and sharp, slightly sourish, attracted me; the coolness of her skin, the silver that couldn't be tasted but only seen, made me freeze and repelled me. She did not seem to mind that. I sat up and put my hand on her breast.

She was looking at me attentively. While her body was resting in the cool, her thoughts never seemed to be at rest. 'But all the same, your hand always comes from above. Aren't you afraid of boredom and surfeit?'

'Why does it come from above?' I put my hand under hers and drew it close to my chest.

'It's against us. You're the one who decides, or at least a part and thus a physical part of a state that decides whether we can stay, and if so what as.'

There was a delicate silver chain round her neck. I pulled at it with my forefinger, and was about to pick up the little locket that appeared against her throat, but she pushed my hand away.

'Is this *we* you mention a group?' I took her hand and made it feel my face, my cheekbones, my nose and my short hair.

'No, it's a *we* of individuals. Refugees, people moving west, emigrants. A hand comes down from above on each of them, picks them up or waves them on.' Her hand lay motionless in mine, then came to life and set off on a journey. I felt her small hand on my back, on my buttocks, it would always be too small to hold one of them. Her hands came from all sides, touching my scars, the numb places, sometimes they only stroked and didn't grasp, sometimes both her hands grasped.

'You come with certain qualities, and we look to see what they are. There's a difference, depending on whether you were being persecuted or not being persecuted.' Not for the first time since

I had met her in the street just now I thought of Batalov, whose presence I sensed as clearly as if he were hiding behind the curtain or was reflected in her eyes instead of me.

'We look. No, it isn't looking, more like testing to see if the qualities to be discovered are suitable.' Her voice was rough, and her eyes shone allowing me no view, however vague, of what was in them.

'And are they?'

Nelly didn't smile; her gaze fell somewhere between us.

The photographic wallpaper had a great deal of blue in it. Palm trees on a South Seas island. I was almost sure that there was nowhere in Knoxville with photographic paper on its walls; only in Germany did such a thing seem possible. Whenever I changed position my eyes fell on the narrow, slightly crooked window that would have shown a view into someone's backyard but for the pink frills hanging in front of it. The old bed creaked. You couldn't fall out of it so easily, not when it curved in like a bowl, holding us there. Not a soft, yielding nest. A nutshell in the ocean, on a course for an island in the South Seas. Nelly's aroma was not fading, but our hour in the room would soon be over. I caught myself hoping that the next guests would not arrive immediately after us, to bathe in that aroma, unauthorised.

'When I look at you like that I could forget where you live and where you come from.' Her cheek was warm, and I let my lips rest on it for a moment. She might think me driven, a king who could never be satisfied. King Insatiable. 'And who you are,' I said, completing my train of thought in a whisper.

I leaned back only briefly, so that I could get a better look at her and touch her, as she said, 'Not me.'

'You're not you?'

'No. Yes. No.' She rubbed her nose in the sweat on my

chest, and I thought I saw revulsion in her eyes. 'I can't forget myself.'

My arms wanted to answer her. The blue receded into the distance and the palm trees seemed close enough to touch. Batalov might be living on a South Seas island, keeping his head down and in his isolation uttering only noises like a character in a comic. *Krssssstzch* as he eats the flesh of a coconut, or *zchcht* when he bites into a banana, and he would wait until she came, which she would do by devious yet predictable ways, the right ways for a fairy tale, to set him free of his comic-character noises. But there was no sign of Batalov yet; instead, looking into the mirror, I saw my hands clasping her breasts and her mouth opening. I couldn't be sure whether it was pleasure or pain distorting it, and in the case of any doubt decided that it was the mirror's doing. My arms had earned no answer.

As I dressed her and first cleaned her glasses, then put them on her nose, she asked whether I would dress my wife too. And I asked, in return, why she wasn't living with friends but in the camp.

'Are you after names again?' Her voice sounded both sharp and soft. 'I don't have any real friends here in the West. Certainly not friends I could simply ask to let me and my two children stay with them.'

I sensed her eyes on my torso, on the scars she had just been touching. The tongue of my belt buckle fell on the softly carpeted floor with a slight, muted sound. When I bent down the wooden floor under the carpeting creaked. I picked up the tongue of the buckle, but there was no way to fasten it now.

'You know it's dangerous to make friends in the camp.'

She was sitting on the bed, watching my attempts to do up my belt with a faulty buckle.

'There are spies. State Security has been planting its people there for decades. There was an attempted abduction in the camp last year. What's so funny about that?'

Nelly had put her hand to her mouth and was chuckling into it.

'Even Russian organisations try to reach out to their lost sheep.'

She snorted with laughter into her hand. 'How seriously you take your job.'

'It *is* serious, I don't have to *take it* seriously.' Her laughter was beginning to annoy me. I made a loop in the end of my belt.

Her laughter, which had made me think of a young girl at the end of October, now sounded to me like the laughter of a child, and in the end it sounded more like a goblin than a human being.

'And who's to say I'm not a spy myself?' she asked.

'I'm counting on it.'

She looked up in surprise. Her face was smooth, as if she had never been laughing. 'You're counting on it?'

'As you're one of the unknown factors I have to count on it as well as other things. Otherwise I couldn't do my job at all.'

'Are you telling me you're working at this moment? We sleep together and that's your work?'

'No, but my work is part of my identity. I couldn't stop feeling responsible for a moment. So I have to count on an unknown factor like you at any time.'

The radio alarm clock came on. *Let the words of our mouth and the meditation of our heart be acceptable in thy sight here tonight.*

I did up my tie with a firm movement.

'Can't we turn this thing off?' Nelly hit the radio alarm with the flat of her hand. It didn't react. She hit it with her fist, and the radio alarm fell silent.

I went down the narrow staircase ahead of her and pressed a

tip into the landlady's hand. Her thanks were rough, barely audible, she turned her back to us, took clean sheets off a shelf and climbed the stairs.

Rainwater was thrown up by the passing cars, and I opened my car door for Nelly. 'That song is all wrong,' she said as I sat down beside her in the car.

'Why are you letting a song upset you so much?'

'I'm not upset. Which of them ever wept for Zion? A song like that makes fun of us.' Her breath was white vapour between us.

'Us? The group that isn't a group but consists of individuals?'

She didn't reply. During the drive she kept her hands in her jacket pockets.

'It's getting thicker,' I said at a crossroads. She pursed her lips and then drew them in until they were stretched over her teeth, so that it looked as if she had no mouth, and the pale fold of skin replacing it had just been clamped together on the inside.

As we drove under the S-Bahn bridges, I made another attempt to break her silence. 'The President's been enjoying unexpected popularity for the last few weeks. There was a change of mood among voters back in the past under Kennedy, and it looks like Camp David will save Carter's presidency for him. It's just a pity the electoral turnout is so small at home.'

Nelly was looking listlessly ahead and playing with a strand of her hair. She turned her head slightly. The gasometer was almost lost in the mist.

Only when we were passing the little sign saying *Marienfelde* did she take her hands out of the pockets of her jacket and say something. 'Your President always reminds me of a cat. Puss in Boots.'

'How do you come to know English?'

'I don't know English.' She dug her hands into her pockets again.

'Yes, you do. That seems to me unusual for someone from over there.'

'I don't.'

'You understood the words of that song.'

She said nothing, but kept her lips firmly closed.

'I thought so even when we were interviewing you.'

Nelly suddenly burst out laughing again. 'The spy who secretly speaks English,' she gurgled.

I patiently let her finish laughing, then braked and turned into a side street. 'Here we are.'

'Not quite.'

'We won't go past the porter together.'

'No, I don't expect that would do your reputation any good. Are you working now?' There was humour as well as gravity in her eyes. Perhaps the gravity was only pretence.

'I will be in half an hour's time, yes.' I switched off the engine and stayed in my seat.

'As scientists we got a basic knowledge of English, or at least we did in my department. Not all of us, but I was one of those who did. After all, we had to be able to read Western publications.' She nodded as if it were not just her own words she believed.

'You didn't work as a scientist for very long. Is a basic knowledge of your subject in English enough for you to understand the colloquial language?'

'You're looking at me very sceptically, John Bird. You don't believe it is?' Her eyes sparkled. No, she wasn't taking me seriously.

'I don't know.'

'Belief isn't the same as knowledge.' Nelly laughed, and I remembered the statements of faith with which she had entertained Harold and me in October.

'That's why I said I don't know,' I told her, thinking that I would have a conversation with the CIA in the evening, a conversation that I hoped would get me out of this camp and into a job that did justice to my work and my deployment here.

'What is it you want from me?'

Her question came abruptly, and I hesitated for a moment, wondering whether to answer it. She would be thinking that our investigations seldom went beyond the admission procedure. What did she think I wanted from her? We could have been useful to her in October, but by now it was December, her admission procedure was considered closed, and here she was living in the camp. She no longer depended on our goodwill. She was still looking at me, pale and cool, her big brown eyes were not veiled, in spite of her long lashes. Her chestnut-brown hair was not styled in any way but fell, strong and heavy, to her shoulders, with an auburn tinge to it as the sunlight broke through. Her eyes seemed to be frozen in expectation of my answer, not a lash flickered to interrupt her gaze.

'Don't you ever cry?'

'Am I supposed to cry? Is that what you want me to do?'

'I only wonder why you don't cry.'

'I don't wonder.'

Outside, a woman was walking past with a small white dog. The dog wore a red cape over its back and buckled under its belly, no doubt to protect it from the cold and the rain. I took my pack of cigarettes out of my shirt pocket and offered Nelly one. She got the matches out of her bag and lit one ahead of the offer of my lighter. Through the glow of the cigarette tip, she drew in air, its oxygen burning up before it could reach her mouth.

'Your tears are all used up – am I right?'

'If you like to put it that way.' Smoke poured from her mouth, her lips swelled gently. 'I don't think you're interested in tears. The only thing you want to get from me and see you're getting is humility.' She smiled.

The car windows were misting up, and when people passed outside you could only just see their vague outlines. I was going to tell the CIA: I'm ready, I was ready even before the first course of study, all through my training and the second course of study, at every moment of my life I've felt ready, I would be thinking, and I would say: I've been prepared for it and mature enough for a long time. What matters to me is our freedom, and I will preserve and create the conditions. Security. That's what's at stake. That was the great idea for which I had flown my Honey Bee six years ago for days on end over the fields without a break, accompanied by many comrades, although like them I had had to read the Pentagon Papers a year earlier; perhaps we flew because anything else would have been like giving up our identity even if for the first time in history that didn't lead to victory. Anyway, my flight left a trace behind, a scar on the landscape with dense, dirty clouds above it, but on Christmas Day I crashed near Haiphong. I would tell them that I was willing to go wherever they sent me, however hopeless the enterprise, and would not admit that I was burning to follow their instructions, and that I had had to shed tears when I saw the movie *The Deer Hunter* a few days ago, I wanted to say that I would defend my country. My wife would not represent any obstacle, she never had.

'Why do they carry out those examinations?' Nelly drew on her cigarette and blew the smoke down into her lap.

'What examinations?'

'The medical ones. In the first week. Why are the new arrivals quarantined, and what's the idea of keeping physical traces of them in little tubes – you have to give samples of your blood and stools. Why are their bodies examined and measured? What's the point of all those things if it isn't to humiliate them?' Whenever Nelly used the words *humility* and *humiliation* she seemed to be forced to smile.

'The medical examinations are done for reasons of security. Because the city is an island, politically speaking, it's feared that pathogens could be introduced, and then epidemics could spread through the camps and into the city as a whole.'

'You don't mean that seriously?' She laughed and swallowed, ground her cigarette out, swallowed and laughed.

'It's not as funny as all that. Somewhere in Russia they cultivate the smallpox virus and carry out experiments.' Suddenly the idea occurred to me that the public might not know about those experiments, and I could just have blurted out a small piece of secret information. 'Imagine someone arrived with TB. If we didn't take blood samples, and do an X-ray in cases of any doubt, keeping the new arrival in isolation meanwhile, he could infect the whole camp in no time. Children would take the pathogen to school with them, and the staff and others working in the schools would carry the disease into the city.'

She opened my coat, pushed the lapel of my jacket aside and placed her hand on my chest. Did she want to feel my skin, my heartbeat? Her hand wandered over to the left, where my heart still beat under that hand for freedom and security and independence, so far as I knew. And yet her cool hand aroused something else. Lust maybe, the wish to keep a danger under control, a desire to overpower her, to measure my strength against her. She took the cigarette pack out of my shirt pocket and smiled the way she smiled when she said *humility*. I held my lighter out to her. The flame was low. She took it from my hand and lit the cigarette for herself.

I ran my fingers through her hair and touched her throat which, white and warm, was only the outside of her innermost being, a piece of skin compared to the conviction that what I wanted from her was humility.

'What I want from you and everyone else is only humility in the presence of the independence and liberty that you should experience as soon as you're away from the Eastern bloc,' I said, and I said it with irony in my voice, hoping she would fail to hear its falsity, because I had only just invented the irony in that statement so as not to let her know anything definite about me, let alone true. But she looked at me without guessing that I was eager for the task I would be given after I had been considered worthy of it in conversation this evening and taken on. I thought I would do justice to that task here in this car, where the misted glass cutting off the view of the outside world changed nothing, any more than the outside world changed me and what I did, so that I was loyal if not devoted to the absolute aims of my government, and had internalised it so that I felt the fusing of liberty and security and independence like something burning. And the burning, the brief pain that her teeth caused when she bit, gave me an idea that I myself represented liberty. And she should show humility in the face of liberty, so I left her head in my lap and her mouth at liberty, I ran my fingers through her hair and down her throat, felt her backbone, thought of the Statue of Liberty and nothing else.

Not even when she looked up and smiled, or the way she smiled when she said *humility*, did I feel like returning that smile. Humility could only be seriously received, and I was ready for anything. Her smile became a mask that I wasn't going to take the trouble to remove. I was due to start work in seven minutes' time, if she would finally remove her hindquarters from my car and, for all I cared, go the last few metres to the camp on foot, then I could go in search of a parking space and be in the office on time. But instead of climbing out, she ran a finger over my forehead.

'Where did you get that?'

'Another time,' I said, leaning forward and reaching across to open the passenger door for her. If I told her that I had no idea, all I knew was that my Honey Bee had been shot down, but while the ejector seat had worked my memory, for some time, had not, she would probably reply scornfully: In 1972? We'd gone across the open borders to Poland then, the most revolutionary country of all after the great strike. She would tell me about American movies she had seen there, and how she had admired the sky over Masuria.

In fact she got out and said, turning to me once more, 'To each his own heroic deeds.'

Fine rivulets had formed patterns on the misted panes. It was possible that she hardly ever read the newspapers, and where she was living at the time there had been no information at all showing how little we had succeeded in featuring as heroes in that war. Finding nothing else, I used the sleeve of my coat to wipe the car windows. My vision was still slightly distorted, but it was good enough for me to start the engine. Although I was driving fast and found a parking space at once, I passed the porter just as she was asking about her post. She did not even turn to look at me, so I couldn't resist waiting for her a few metres from the entrance and saying, 'You claimed there was no safer place than a communist country with a wall around it. I'm afraid I have to tell you that you're wrong – you, or was it your mother who's supposed to have said so? A simple wall doesn't ensure your safety. Only the order to shoot does that.'

She looked at me, taken aback, and didn't seem to recognise me, then turned away as if I were a lunatic standing in the street talking to himself out loud, calling to passers-by without expecting any answer, and then went on her way with her hopping, skipping gait that had attracted my attention only two hours ago on Kurfürstenstrasse.

A heavy hand came down on my shoulder. 'Not talking to the women inmates of this camp, are you, John?' Rick was offering me his pack of cigarettes, and I took one. 'Do you know her?' His gas-fired lighter was empty.

'Should I?' I couldn't find my own lighter. Presumably Nelly had pocketed it.

'No. Pretty woman, I noticed her before.' He found some matches, and I cupped my hands around the cigarette to keep the wind from blowing out the flame.

'She's all right.' We were making for the gateway and crossing the parking lot to our office. 'I was asking for the time; my watch has stopped.' I tapped my Omega to reinforce my point. 'But no one around here seems to understand German.'

'Try English, then.' Laughing, Rick held the door open for me. It went through my mind to wonder whether his remark could be a hint; maybe he knew Nelly himself, and I wasn't the only one to be aware that she spoke English. But then I told myself that he could hardly know her, too many people lived here for one of us to get really well acquainted with any of them, I decided, and with a certain relish that felt almost forbidden or at least perverse, I breathed in the smell of the corridor in the building and felt a sense of relaxation spread through me. Every morning, and on days like this at midday when I arrived at the office, merely going through the doorway set off a comfortable and pleasantly numbing sensation. Part of its comfortable nature was the fug consisting only in the foreground of cold and fresh smoke, while underneath it lay a mixture of male urine, since obviously the toilets weren't well enough cleaned, and sweat, the sort that clings to the coats of people long dead as well as the underarm fabric of the modern polyester shirts we all wore. Although no one here changed his shoes or even unlaced them, there was a pungent, cheesy aroma of butyric acid on the second floor.

A woman of about forty was sitting on the chair in the interview room. Her hair was dyed with henna, her trousers of silvery artificial leather were flared. I could see from her files that she had fled from the GDR at great risk to herself. The questions I must ask her would be mainly the standard range.

'Your name?'

'Grit Mehring, born in Chemnitz. Until recently I lived at 64 Dimitroffstrasse, Berlin.' She crossed her legs and looked at me provocatively.

'Thanks. I can see when and where you were born in my file.' I leafed through it and found the sketch that this woman had made at our request of the place from which she had fled. Avoiding her eyes, I imagined her trying to get away under cover of darkness in that get-up – red hair like a beacon round her head, and silvery fabric shining in the beam of the searchlights.

'Can you give me a brief account of how and where you crossed the border?'

'Crossed it?' She uttered a scornful laugh. 'I didn't cross anything, I swam the Teltow Canal.'

'You knew there are orders to shoot on sight there?'

'You bet I knew, but I also had information on the place where the searchlights hardly reach and the bank allows you to dive in.'

'The whole place is mined.'

'You don't need to tell me that.' Her head raised, her eyes half closed, she looked straight at me.

'Your account of it here says that you were being persecuted in East Berlin. How are we to understand that?'

'You mean you don't know?'

'We want to know about it from you.'

She doubled up and buried her face in her hands. The CIA had asked for all my reports, and I was sure that they would make a good impression. At the same time, there could be someone in Argentinische Allee making final preparations for the interview with me. I signalled to Lynn to get up and give the refugee a handkerchief. It took her several minutes to blow her nose thoroughly.

'Ready now?' My patience left something to be desired; I was thinking of this evening when it suddenly occurred to me that tomorrow was Eunice's birthday.

'Why are you wrinkling your nose like that?' the woman asked. There was insecurity in her voice. Her expression, proud only just now, had changed to its opposite since she buried her face in the handkerchief. She was looking at me wide-eyed, almost obsequiously. Why did I have to keep wrinkling my nose now and then without noticing it? People had mentioned it to me a number of times, and seldom did I realise from the reactions of whoever I was talking to – whether they were clear, apologetic or injured – that I must have wrinkled it again. Eunice might have said something to me. Not that she had to warn me, and of course she wasn't obliged to remind me of her birthday, but I thought I recognised a certain malice that had recently shown more and more often in her persistent silence on the subject. The cigarette pack in my shirt pocket was squashed almost flat. I pinched the filter of the last cigarette with two fingers and took it out. No doubt it gave Eunice satisfaction to reproach me for my negligence, and while she herself neglected the house-keeping, smoked grass and ran up a phone bill of dizzy heights, the best means of doing that were the specially created holes in the air that seemed to follow my neglect of her. I blew small smoke rings.

'Could I have one, please?' The henna-red refugee pointed to my cigarettes. One advantage of this workplace was its inexhaust-ible supply of them. Lynn handed me a new pack of Camels, and I opened the silver paper, stood up and offered the woman her cigarette. She took it with a shaking hand, and bent it so much as she took it out that it threatened to break apart. I gave her a light.

'Thank you very much, thanks.' Her hair looked greasy, as if she hadn't washed it for weeks. Maybe the refugees weren't allowed to shower for the first few days after their arrival, or else she had simply forgotten about her hair.

'Right, then. You'd better describe these instances of persecu-tion.' I sat down at my desk again and tried to look attentive. The other day Eunice had told me that she had booked a flight, and would be opening the tattoo studio with her girlfriend in February. As soon as I said that was an excellent idea, even if I didn't consider Berlin-Zehlendorf a suitable place for it, Eunice had raised her voice. I had to listen to her, she said. Hadn't she just told me she'd booked a flight? She wasn't going to open a tattoo studio here, she was going to open it back home in the States. I had probably nodded, and caught myself thinking that the mere idea of not finding her in our house any more, not having to pay attention to her gutted animals and winged wolves or even see them every evening set off a great sense of relaxation in me. When I stood up to leave the room I had heard her, behind me, saying that I was one of those people who simply didn't want to see those nearest to them any more, a kind of age-related case of long-sightedness, and that long-sightedness led to the fact that I just didn't see the person closest to me, namely her, these days, and if I did she was sure it was only a blurred image. I had turned to her in the doorway. I thought that behind her facial expression, which was trying hard to simulate genuine indignation, I saw mischievous delight. Eunice became excited by these little things, as if we were competing to feature as the innocent party in the failure of our marriage.

'Harassment. It was more like harassment.' The red-haired woman inhaled smoke. I glanced at the file in front of me. Grit Mehring, that was her name.

'It was already beginning ten years ago. Oh, probably much earlier, but that was when I noticed it. That was when they set the Firm on me.'

'The firm?'

'I'm sure you know the expression. State Security, the Firm.' Grit Mehring propped her arm on her knee and her chin in the hand holding her cigarette. That meant she could draw comfortably on the cigarette without having to sit up straight in her chair.

'How did you notice that?'

'Well, it was perfectly obvious. An elderly married couple lived in the apartment next to mine. My letters were opened, and one day I caught the woman standing in front of my letter box crumpling up a letter in haste. I found it later in the dustbin.'

'Was that the only repressive measure taken against you?'

The red-haired woman sobbed, but went on bravely smoking her cigarette, wiped tears from her eyes and continued. 'Later I looked through the peephole and saw them standing outside my front door when I had visitors. Then I was refused permission to study law, and in spite of her good marks my daughter wasn't allowed to take her school-leaving exam.'

While the secretary taking the record typed away, I made notes with my ballpoint so as not to seem inattentive. There were dozens of cases like hers.

'And when I asked why all the answers I got were negative, the Firm asked questions of their own, how long I'd been friendly with whom – sometimes they could recite whole conversations I'd had word for word.'

'So you were living next door to that married couple in Dimitroffstrasse all this time.'

'No, they're not stupid. One day they switched the married couple for a young man living on his own. That was striking, I can tell you, because he had a four-room apartment all to himself. Enough to make anyone suspicious. The Communal Housing Authority tries to be fair to people applying for apartments.'

'You mean your new neighbour was another informer?'

'I'm sure of it. He made up to my daughter first, and then sounded her out.'

'How old was your daughter at the time?'

'It's not so long ago, maybe four years. She was fifteen then.'

'Where is your daughter now?'

'She wanted to stay over there. She'd found a boyfriend. You can imagine that a couple don't run for it just like that.'

'What did you mean when you said your neighbour made up to her?'

'Well, he began a relationship with her. She had an abortion. Underage. I don't suppose I need to tell you what that means to a mother. Yes, and then I found him going through my wardrobe. Don't ask me why my daughter ever let him into our apartment. But I had to work in the daytime, until one day I reported in sick, and there I was coming in through the front door at ten in the morning.'

'He could just have been curious about you.'

'No, he wasn't just curious. He was stupid too. When it was all over at last, she told me – my daughter, I mean – that he tried to recruit her.'

I looked at the red-haired woman enquiringly.

'For the Firm, of course.'

'And is that man still living there?'

'I've no idea where he is now. He moved away. And I'd recommended him to move, at that. Talk about disgraceful.'

I glanced at the file.

'Do you want to know his name?'

'Wait a moment, all in good time. Who moved into the apartment next door to you after that?'

'A family with three children. But I'll tell you something, they were in it too. I'm not quite sure, but almost.'

'When did you decide to get out?' So as not to interrupt the red-haired woman in full flow, I held out a cigarette and a light to her wordlessly. Miss Killeybegs brought in coffee, and Lynn handed the cups round.

'It was high time, but you'll know that it takes a while to come to a decision like that. And my daughter was still a minor. I had no prospects. I wasn't allowed to study, and no one was going to employ me as a technical draughtsman. Harassment, all of it. I know hundreds who got work at the time, and I can tell you they were no better at the job than me. I was the only one who was always rejected, without being told why. After a while they gave me a job as a postwoman. I ask you, what kind of life is that?' She drew on her cigarette and waited patiently until I had finished writing on the sheet of paper in front of me with my ballpoint. It wasn't that I didn't trust the girl typing up the record, but I mustn't lose the thread. I wrote down the basic information for myself, so that in any case of doubt I could ask more precise questions.

'Could I maybe have another?' She pointed to the cigarettes,

'Of course.' I stood up and gave her one. As I held out my lighter, she smiled uncertainly up at me.

'Don't worry,' I said, going back to my desk. 'The reception procedure is quickly dealt with in cases like yours.' I heard her breathe a sigh of relief behind my back.

'You can go in a minute, Frau . . .' I had to glance at my file again. 'Frau Mehring. First, could you perhaps name one or two of the employers who refused to give you a job in – you said technical draughtsmanship was your profession? – as a technical draughtsman at the time? You can tell me their names now. And I expect you also remember the names of the neighbours who were presumably working for State Security?'

'Presumably? Definitely. And I'm sure they're still doing the same. Well, the married couple were called Zimmermann. Dorle and Ernst Zimmermann. They lived next door to me until about '74. Then the young man arrived; that was in the summer. I only wish I could forget his name. He well and truly drove a wedge between me and my daughter at the time. They don't consider anything beneath them.'

'His name?'

'Pischke. Hans Pischke.'

'And what was the name of the family after them?'

'Maurer. He was Karl-Heinz, she was Gertrud, or was it Gerlind? No, Gertrud, I think. They moved in with their three kids about a year ago.'

I often registered great relief in the faces and bearing of the applicants I was questioning when they could say what they had suffered over the years, and what they had been condemned to keep quiet about until they felt they were safe with us and could finally pour it all out. Nonetheless, they were glad when the conversation was over and they had our official stamp on their permits. Grit Mehring wasn't one of that sort. She sat where she was, still tense, and did not seem interested in the end of the interrogation.

'But you don't have any evidence against this Maurer family?'

'No, I'm sorry, I just suspect them. And they were probably made to move next door for nothing, now that I've gone.' She ran her fingers through her red hair. A smile passed over her face, as if she liked to think of the useless efforts of State Security. Instinctively, and unintentionally, I returned her smile.

'How about the employers who rejected you?'

'That's quite some time ago. Must be six years. I haven't been able to work in my profession for six years, can you imagine that? Delivering letters!' she said, with a disparaging hiss between her teeth.

'If anything else occurs to you, will you let us know?' Her file was not a large one, there wasn't much more we needed to know. The names were enough, and there were always a few remaining question marks. I closed the folder and stood up.

'Are you going to stay in the camp for now, or do you have friends outside?' I asked, giving her my hand.

'I'll probably have to stay for a little while, but then I'm sure I can go to friends.' She followed me into the corridor, and Lynn closed the door behind us.

'Just one more question – your trousers. Did you escape wearing those?'

She looked down at herself in surprise. 'Why?'

'A colour like that, well, it's striking. The searchlights would pick it up right away.'

Her laughter was almost explosive. 'Oh, I see. No, we didn't get trousers like these over there anyway. Mine were in rags by the time I arrived yesterday. At first they wanted to take me to hospital in case I had hypothermia. Who goes for a swim in the Teltow Canal in December? But I'm fine, I really am. I feel better than ever before.'

'Then that's all right.' I turned round, but as she was holding her hand out to me I felt obliged to take her long, bony fingers again.

'The trousers are from your stock of second-hand clothes here. Take a look! They've probably been lying there for months and no one wanted them. Not bad, are they?'

As if the clothes were ours. I let go of her hand, nodded, and thought: Not bad, just unsuitable. And not a clever choice, because it gives her away. Looks as if she's trying to make up for her lost youth. Something in me tensed up at that thought, and I told myself that as a good man who wanted to see himself constantly on the side of what's good I ought not to think of these people in such terms. But maybe that's how it was with the unlived life, the lost years, that many refugees had in their baggage.

'Have a nice evening.' Lynn went past me with her coat on, giving me a thumbs-up sign. She had finished work for the day. I'd told her about the conversation ahead of me. As a rule such interviews entailed instructions, sometimes reprimands, rarely praise. But I said nothing about my hopes and the fact that I had already been able to send all my reports to the CIA. It was not a good idea to make your colleagues aware of such things, however well you knew them, and I went bowling with Lynn every Friday, while it was only a few months ago that she and her husband, who also worked for our intelligence service, had invited Eunice and me to an evening meal. I even went shooting with her sometimes. All the same, you never knew what kind of position colleagues might get you into, or whether the job didn't require the utmost secrecy by virtue of its very nature.

In winter the light stayed on in our department all round the clock. It was hardly ever full daylight out of doors, and at night lights were left on for the sake of security, although not all the offices were occupied by people on night duty. It was twilight outside now, and my watch said just before four. A poor observer, Rick, I thought, tapping my Omega, as if an Omega ever stopped. The light from the neon tubes was functional. Lynn claimed it was chilly, but to me it felt functional. I pushed the curtain a little way aside and watched two children trying to catch a big, black bird. It was clearly lame, and couldn't fly away. All the same, the children spread their arms out and kept trying to drive it into a corner – sometimes it hopped under a bush, or along beside a wall – and they were clearly afraid of grabbing it. It was larger than a crow, but I didn't see how a raven could have lost its way and ended up here. A woman joined the children, gesturing with her hands. She obviously didn't like her children chasing the bird. I recognised her by her jacket; she was wearing the same trousers as before. Only now did I remember that Nelly was the mother of two children. The thought of Vassily Batalov had kept going through my mind, but I hadn't dwelt so much on the fact that he must have touched her and made love to her as on the question of who he had been and perhaps still was, maybe without her knowledge, maybe with it but not to our knowledge and in spite of our suspicions. Maybe even without his own knowledge. In such cases you couldn't rule out any possibility. And those two children were presumably not just hers but his as well. Their mother was now talking to a small man while the children were shooing the lame bird away behind her back.

This case was one of my more inglorious, and I would certainly not be mentioning it this evening unless they brought it up. I could fall back on saying that Fleischman had been in charge of the interrogation, and he was one of their best men, but such references did not really carry much weight. If it hadn't been for Nelly's intriguing aroma maybe I would indeed have staged our meeting and considered it part of my job. Such things happened to me, just like other things that did not have such potential in them. Responsibility meant something else, responsibility meant always being a step ahead, always being a thought ahead. And yet I would never live up to my own standard of responsibility, that was my code of conduct, and my ambition sprang from it. Except that I realised, not without regret, that I myself always fixed the extent of the standard, and consequently there was no more precise assessment, no objective estimate; only the CIA could confirm my value with a new appointment or punish me by withholding it.

The door opened behind me, and a colleague whom I knew only slightly in this assessment department, for which I would not be working much longer, or at least not as a member of our intelligence service, looked at me with some alarm, but at the same time deferentially.

'What is it?'

'I hope you're well.' He obviously had something important on his mind, and was too agitated to control his tongue.

'What?'

'A phone call came just now.'

'And?' The CIA certainly wouldn't be phoning me, or only if they wanted to change or even cancel our appointment. But it was out of the question for the CIA to be calling me here, two hours before the time of our appointment at that, to clear up any point; I felt sure that all strands of the organisation worked too perfectly and smoothly for that. Rejecting that notion in the fraction of a second, I returned to reality, which certainly had me in its grasp. 'My wife, am I right? You've had the pleasure of speaking to my wife. And what seems so important to her that she'd call me here?'

'No, Mr Bird, it wasn't your wife. We passed on the names from your interview with Frau Grit Mehring, and we just had a call back from the camp administration. One of the Stasi people that she mentioned is in the West. And guess where!' My very young colleague here whom I knew only fleetingly was gasping for air.

Nelly Senff evades Dr Rothe

I had just turned a page when I suddenly heard creaking behind me. Susanne hadn't come back from her night out, so I turned, expecting to see her. It was much too early to be the children; they wouldn't be back from school for a good hour yet. Right behind me stood a tall man in a blue suit. He was carrying his coat and hat over his arm.

'Senff, is that right? Your name is Senff.' He stepped aside so that I could get a better look at him.

'You might have rung the bell.'

'Your doorbell doesn't seem to be working, and the door of your apartment wasn't locked. So as there was no answer when I knocked . . .' He looked at me, as if expecting me to end his sentence. 'Am I disturbing you?'

'That depends.' I put a finger between the pages of my book.

His chin was smoothly shaved, but he had a moustache with its ends turned slightly up. He spoke softly, bringing out his words as if it were a great strain for him to speak so slowly and quietly. The only lines on his face were fine ones, lines betraying neither age nor experience, more likely just a chance trace left by the passing years. His hair seemed to be prematurely grey, almost white, although I'd have guessed that he was no older than his mid-forties.

'May I?' He indicated the vacant chair with his hat.

'Yes, do.'

'These are for you.' He held out a box of chocolates to me. I hesitated to take them.

'Why chocolates?'

'My name is Rothe. Dr Rothe. I'm sure you've heard of me.' He held his hat and coat firmly on his lap, and put the chocolates on the table in front of him.

'Should I have?'

'Well, I come to the camp now and then. Someone or other here ought to know me.' His skilfully placed pause was presumably to give me time to remember, but I felt nothing but his expectation. 'I'm said to have a certain fame. The organisation of which I am a member, and on behalf of which I am here to see you, is called the Bears' Club. Perhaps you're thinking of the Berlin bears, but ours is an international organisation. We work in South Africa and Thailand, in South Korea, Germany and the United States.'

'Doing what?'

The smile at the corners of his mouth betrayed no pride. Just vanity cloaked by his mild manner. He was enjoying my ignorance of him personally, and putting off the moment of explanation. 'Do help yourself.' In no time at all he opened the box of chocolates and pushed it over the table. He was smiling a mocking, superior smile.

'Why chocolates?'

'Why chocolates? You must be wondering what these little attentions are for, and what you have done to earn them.' His smile was intolerable. 'Don't worry, they're not poisoned.'

'Ha, ha.'

'You can't take a joke?'

What made this man Rothe so keen to sound sympathetic, so generous and so sure of himself? What did he want? I looked at him and wondered whether I ought to know who he was, whether his face seemed familiar to me, and if maybe he was something to do with one of those secret services.

'Celebrating again, are they?' He pointed towards the door, obviously referring to the music coming from one of the neighbouring apartments. It almost seemed to me that someone else had said that – it just didn't fit with his distinguished appearance.

'Who?'

'Oh, never mind. You do have Poles in these apartments, don't you?' Dr Rothe leaned back, and the chair creaked under him. It seemed too small for this man. 'We know all about the conflicts that arise from living together here in the camp. Some have one kind of lifestyle, others have a different one. To us they're all alike. I'd be happy to explain separate aspects of the situation, if you're interested.' Clearing his throat, he bent down and fished for his hat, which had slipped off his knees. His head touched my leg. When he looked up again he was bright red in the face. 'Excuse me,' he said, passing a hand over his forehead. 'Well: we help people in need. People like you, victims of the inhuman and unworthy systems created by dictatorships. People who have been persecuted and, like you, are looking for refuge here in the West, sick people who, again like you, have a right to expect protecting arms but themselves want asylum in Germany.' He took a handkerchief out of his jacket pocket and mopped his gleaming brow. His fixed smile lent a touch of unreality to this recital, which sounded mechanical. Still red in the face, he had a white triangle only round his nose. 'Their origins and religious affiliations play no part at all so far as we're concerned, only repression and the suffering they have to bear. What matters is the need in which we find such people.'

'You think I'm sick?'

'No, you may not be, or I hope not yet. But perhaps you're not thinking only of yourself. There are sick people who get help thanks to our organisation. Do you know how many people there are, at this very moment, who are being tortured, are suffering from starvation, or are simply and unjustly deprived of their freedom? Think of the friends you had to leave behind in the East. Are they free? The Bears' Club will help. We've won awards and distinctions for our work.'

'You mean you do a flourishing trade in suffering? Other people's torments make you feel good?'

'Why so bitter? We don't feel good about other people's torments, only about our means of helping them.' This man Rothe looked smug and self-satisfied as he leaned back again, making the chair creak under him. He dabbed his temples with the handkerchief. So they formed clubs, did they? I couldn't help wondering where the people of this generation in Germany got the money they apparently used so generously and lavishly to decide who they'd help and who they wouldn't, making up their minds who was worthy of their kindness. Fine beads of sweat were caught in the man's moustache, quivering with every breath he took, and he was breathing heavily. I was on the point of saying: I suppose you were always on the right side, were you? when he abruptly rose from the chair.

'Could I have a glass of water, please?'

I looked for a clean glass in the kitchen. The water from the mains had been brownish since this morning. I thought of John Bird's warning about all the informers to be found in the camp. Why shouldn't he be playing a double part, the emissary of a club and at the same time working for State Security, turning up here with chocolates?

When I returned to the living room, he had his back to me and was leaning over the table. I put the glass of water down in front of him, and at the same moment I saw that he was holding a sharp object in his trembling hands.

'You must forgive me.' He straightened up and hastily left the room. I heard him shut the toilet door. Obviously he knew his way around this apartment; at least, he hadn't had to search for the toilet. The thing in his hands was pointed, and there had been a metallic gleam to it; the shape reminded me of a syringe, but I couldn't be sure because of the way his hands were holding it. The price ticket was still on the box of chocolates. A black leather case with the letters *V.B.* stamped on it in gold lay beside the box. The case looked to me familiar, but I couldn't place it. Clearly the man who called himself Dr Rothe kept the sharp object in the case. The newspapers here were full of stories about heroin and those addicted to it, people who couldn't be assigned to any particular class. I also thought of illnesses that could account for his sudden disappearance with the syringe. I looked at the time. It seemed to me as if he'd been in the toilet for ten minutes, and as I couldn't hear any sounds coming from there I wondered if it would be advisable to see how he was. The music from the apartment next door had stopped. There was no one but him and me in this apartment. His coat had slipped to the floor, his hat was on the chair. My eyes fell on a slim briefcase leaning against the leg of the table. Quietly, I got to my feet, bent down and snapped the catches open. There was a thin leather folder with a zip fastener in the briefcase. I still heard no noise in the corridor. I took the folder out and cautiously unzipped it. A sheet of paper slipped out and fell on the floor. Several names were written on it in ink. Jerzy Jabłonovski was crossed out, and there was a cross with a date on it above his name. An arrow then led from Jabłonovski to my own name. *Nelly Senff, single, two children, doctoral degree in chemistry, worked at the Academy of Sciences until April '76, applied for exit permit, then worked as unskilled labourer in the cemetery, suspected double agent.* There were several closely typewritten pages in the folder. Hearing a creaking sound in the corridor, I looked up, but all was quiet again and there was no one to be seen. I hastily skimmed the lines, reading individual words, *republic*, *Semite Association* and *constitution*, here I picked up *security* and there *false data*, and repeatedly the word *Fräulein*. I tried to make some kind of sense of it. The text was peppered with the abbreviations *LW*, *IM* and *VB*. *Elimination* and *object* were underlined. A metallic noise alarmed me, reminding me of the sharp item with which he had disappeared, and which perhaps wasn't for his own use after all but was intended for me – a small gun, a surveillance device – yet I couldn't take my eyes off the letter, and clutched the sheets of paper firmly as if they were my only clue to the identity of this Dr Rothe. Several names: *Ziegler*, *Mayer* and finally *Batalov*.

'Your name was recommended to me by a Frau Jabłonovska. Unfortunately her brother is dead already, and it looks as if she doesn't need our help now.' His voice was even softer than before, and the red had disappeared from his face. Startled, I let the folder slip back into the briefcase. His form entirely filled the doorway, and since the table stood between us I couldn't see whether the metal object was still in his hands. I hoped he hadn't spotted his folder in mine. His eyes were bright. 'There's not very much more we can do, but we would like to help you now.' He was bringing his words out slowly, one by one, and I thought I sensed a threat in his voice.

'I didn't hear you coming,' I stammered, getting to my feet.

'We would like to help you now,' he repeated with emphasis. He was looking down at me disparagingly and at the same time in a tone of insinuation.

'What kind of help do you have in mind? What for?'

I doubted whether this man was really a doctor of any kind. More likely, from the way he gave his name, he had bought the title like a title of nobility, something to be added to his name with its effect in mind rather than showing where he got it. He took a step towards me, and I abruptly took one back.

'Fräulein Senff, we know what a dreadful and unusual situation you are living in here, with your children. I assume that you feel your surroundings are not worthy of you, perhaps even hopeless.'

'No, I don't. Unusual, yes, but not dreadful and not unworthy of us.' I crossed my arms and felt the windowsill behind me. I couldn't retreat any further. 'Anyway, it was my own decision, freely made, to come here. What do you want?'

'Don't worry, Fräulein Senff. Please sit down again. No one can blame you for being suspicious, Fräulein. After all that you've been through.' His smile and his soft voice were sending me out of my mind.

'All that I've been through? Please don't be impertinent, Herr Rothe.'

'Dr Rothe, please, Dr. And I certainly didn't mean to be impertinent, Fräulein Senff.' He brought out the word *Fräulein* like a code or a cover name. Perhaps I'd been credited with the title Fräulein in the State Security files. I was breathing heavily; too much air had collected in my ribcage and I didn't know what to do with it. 'On the contrary, we want to help you.' He recited his sentence to the end, with relish.

For a moment I wondered whether to counter him by saying that he could call me Dr, too. But his insistence on the title rendered him ridiculous in my eyes, making him look, with his white hair and the hat that he passed over his knee now and then, and that imperturbable smile on his face, frank and distinguished at the same time, like a child dressed up as an old man. I wasn't going to set my doctorate against his or prolong this conversation by so much as a syllable.

'I have a cheque made out to you, a cheque for a considerable

229

sum of money.' He was fidgeting with his hands, and I tried to see if he was still holding the sharp object. Perhaps he had put it down in the toilet, or hidden it ready to use in his waistcoat pocket. 'And we would like to help you look for an apartment and furnish it, think of that. We want to help you get on your feet again. May I ask what profession you are practising?'

'None. Listen, I'm not working.'

'There, you see.' Triumph flickered in his small, bright eyes. *Degree in chemistry*, his file had said, *worked at the Academy of Sciences until April '76, applied for exit permit, then worked as unskilled labourer in the cemetery*. 'Perhaps we can help you there as well. But do sit down.'

'I don't want your help. Haven't I expressed myself clearly enough?'

'Calm down, Fräulein Senff. Think of your children and the clothes they wear, the food they eat, the address they give when they're asked where they live. I assume you take your maternal responsibility willingly and to the best of your ability.' He took another step towards me, and I slid slightly to one side with my back to the windowsill. 'Don't you think your children feel it's a humiliation to come home through a barrier and go out through it again?'

'Stop going on about my children. My children are none of your business.' My own shouting echoed in my ears, but the man didn't seem to be impressed by it. I said, quietly now, 'What do you know about humiliation?' took a step forward and sat down on the chair, exhausted.

'Fräulein Senff, it's nearly Christmas. Wouldn't you like to think of celebrating the festive season within your own four walls next year?'

'No thank you. Perhaps you could leave now? I'm busy.' The book was on the table in front of me. I felt as if years had passed

230

since I put it down there. I opened it and indicated that if he would only leave at last I was going on with reading it.

'It isn't always easy for people to accept help. There may be reasons for your refusal, Fräulein Senff, and for the pride that finds expression in it – yet I am afraid, Fräulein Senff, that you will not change your situation in that way.' He walked round behind me with slow steps. 'We mean well.' His hand suddenly shot out, and I flinched back. But then he pushed the box of chocolates even closer to me. 'Wouldn't you like one?'

I shook my head. With long fingers, he reached neatly for a chocolate and placed it on his tongue. It lay there for a fraction of a second, and finally disappeared into his mouth with a plop. He munched slowly and with relish, never taking his eyes off me. The wall and the porter guaranteed our security, they said. Yet there were rumours of abductions. Still, how was he going to anaesthetise me and then drag me out of the apartment, down the stairs and past the porter? He perched on the edge of the table as if it were the most natural thing in the world, and held the box of chocolates under my nose. The gold foil was dazzling. The bitter-sweet smell made me retch.

'Perhaps you'd like to work for us, think of that. We could get on well together, you and I,' he said, smiling. Maybe it was irony that made him smile like that. He took another chocolate from the box, put it on his tongue, and kept his eyes fixed on me.

'I'm not a victim, Dr Rothe. However keen you may be to dispose of your kindness, your helpfulness and your cheque.'

'You're mistaken – this isn't about me. Don't pretend to be stupid. We want to help you, Fräulein Senff. After all you have been through, perhaps you find it hard to recognise it when someone means you well.'

'What do you mean?'

'You don't believe what you hear, but we really do mean well. You are a very difficult case, and if I may say so also a case to arouse sympathy. On your own, two children, no apartment and no job. You are young – you still have prospects, Fräulein Senff.' He raised his voice slightly, as if he had learned that a rising note conveyed urgency and drama to what was said. 'And to us you are an interesting case. Your status as a refugee . . .'

'That's none of your business either.'

I was trying to decode the signs in my book. *White-hot*, I read, and arranged the letters in order, not for their author but for me, *not a hair of your head will be harmed, I am out of the worst of it where it was white-hot now*, not him, me, I'm not out of it yet, I thought, and if he hadn't had that silly smile on his face, stoical as an idiot, I'd long ago have gone for his throat, I'd have harmed all the hairs of his head, however short and white, until they were broken, and I wanted to say: You'd better look for another case, I'm not what you want.

As he rose to his feet he said, 'We've been looking for you and we've found you, Fräulein Senff, even if you don't give me what could be described as a friendly welcome. You're the woman for us.' He laid a hand on my shoulder – firmly, as if determined not to let me get away.

No, I'm not, I wanted to say, but hard as I was trying my lips only formed the words; my voice failed me.

'I know more about you than you think.' His fingertips were pressing down on my shoulder blade and collarbone. I heard him swallowing, saw his half-open mouth, and felt his thumbs rubbing my collarbone. His trousers were neatly pressed. Only now did I notice that the zip was open. Apparently he had forgotten to zip them up again when he was in the toilet.

As I was staring at his trousers, I thought of the word *Fräulein*, and the syringe and his intention of helping me.

'Come with me.' His fingertips were still digging into my shoulder blade and my collarbone. 'Come along.'

My doorbell rang. I jumped up and ran to the door. Frau Jabłonovska was standing outside, with a man I didn't know.

Were they supposed to be coming to Dr Rothe's aid? Without hesitation I pushed past them and ran down the stairs. I heard Frau Jabłonovska saying something, and as if to stop myself forgetting what it was I repeated it to myself over and over again. As I was running over the open space between the blocks of buildings I whispered, 'I just wanted to,' and then found that I had already forgotten the rest of her sentence.

I wandered aimlessly between the blocks, and came up against the wall that surrounded the camp. I turned, walked towards the wall between two other blocks, and turned again. Under no circumstances did I want to go to the porter's lodge. It would be only too easy to catch up with me there. Wherever my footsteps took me, I ended up again and again in a blind alley. Wherever there wasn't an apartment block there was the wall. Clouds hung heavily over the buildings. Single raindrops fell, heavy and thick. All the doors of Building P were closed. I wondered if this could be a holiday, perhaps one of those I didn't know about yet. But then my children wouldn't be at school. My children. The rain was falling more heavily, and I went back to our block.

'I'll put him in my bed,' I heard Aleksei saying as I reached the front door.

'No, I want him in mine,' Katya said.

There was no sign of Dr Rothe and Frau Jabłonovska.

'We must bring the raven up here, Mama. He'll freeze outside.'

'He doesn't look so pretty any more, his feathers are all dull and tangled. I think he feels sick down there.' Aleksei took his school bag off his back. 'Very sick.'

'Has someone been here?' I asked.

'Who would have been here, then?' asked Aleksei.

'Maybe her admirer.' Katya rolled her eyes and giggled.

'The raven will die of starvation before he freezes to death.' Aleksei was looking at me seriously. Any kind of pet was forbidden in the camp, or we could have brought the cat with us. *We want to help you now.* After all, a raven is not a pet, and it would die in our room if I let them bring it in. But Katya and Aleksei agreed with each other: they must help the raven. He could make a nest for it in his bed, suggested Aleksei. He didn't believe me when I said the bed would be far too warm for it. He'd be well hidden then if anyone came to check up on the rooms, replied Aleksei. I thought that was a mistake; at the latest, the sheets would give away the fact that we had had a strange guest in our apartment. *Fräulein.*

'Please, please, please,' said Katya, and she promised, unasked, that they would neither of them want anything for Christmas, nothing at all, I wouldn't even have to think about the stickers that featured at the top of their wish lists. In fact it was the stickers that I wouldn't have minded at all, because all the following wishes, up to and including the miniskirt, were far beyond what the money made available by the camp management would run to.

But no one, Aleksei explained, could forbid us to nurse and feed the raven on the outside windowsill. The raven and the food he was going to give it would be safe there from the greedy crows, who were faster.

You will not change your situation in that way.

As I had seen the difficulty that Katya and Aleksei were having in catching the raven, I made them a suggestion. They could try to lure the bird up to the outside windowsill, they could do anything in their power to do that, but they could not in any circumstances have it in the building. The two of them nodded

234

and clapped their hands, as if they had won something, but I was sure nothing would come of it, because the raven obviously had a broken wing and would certainly not be able to flutter the five metres up to our windowsill.

They both sat by the window, looking intently at the grains they had scattered on the sill. Now and then they pushed one of the grains over the edge of it, no doubt hoping that the black bird would notice that safety awaited it up here. A sparrow came down, and then another. The children flapped their hands and arms, but the greedy little birds were not going to be driven away. If the raven down on the ground hopped out of their field of vision, the children ran downstairs to see if it was all right and brought it grains, which it ignored, but which were pecked up by the crows.

After a little while Aleksei decided that they must try a different tack. He was going to borrow a book from the library van. *Think of your children.* I kept an eye on him from the window. He was standing patiently outside the closed door, waiting for the library lady, who must have gone to the toilet, to come back. I opened the window and waved to him, calling to him through the cold air: wasn't he freezing? *I assume you take your responsibility as a mother seriously.* But he turned as if he didn't hear me or know me. I put on my jacket, on the pretext of going shopping. *A case to arouse sympathy.* Katya, who was doing her homework, didn't look up but pushed her wish list across the table as if by chance. She did not say anything but just waited for me to take it.

'Where's Susanne?' she asked as I opened the door of the room.

'No idea. I've been wondering that myself.'

'She's usually asleep at this time of day. She's never been out as long as this before.'

'She'll have her reasons.'

235

'Is she allowed to be out so long?'

'If she has reasons. I'll be back soon.'

Outside, the ground crackled underfoot. I crossed the open space that was sparsely covered with blackened grass. Twilight was falling. I shook myself to keep from freezing. The door of the library van was open, and there was a light on inside. Aleksei would be asking the librarian for a book about ravens. The hell with being a case to arouse sympathy. *We mean you well.* As if anyone had to mean me well. Someone who meant me well would spare me such remarks, he wouldn't even think them. I turned right on the path and went over to Block D. At the second entrance I opened the door and went up the steps which I thought would lead to Hans.

A rather older man in his underwear opened the front door of the apartment. I asked whether Hans was in.

'No idea, want to go and see?' The beer bottle in his hand threatened to foam over. He held the door open to me, and I hesitated for a moment.

'Which is his room?'

'Right at the front here.' He was watching me as if he meant to wait until I had opened the door. A baby was crying.

He took a gulp of beer. 'Take no notice,' he said, 'just crying like kids do.' Under the baby's crying I heard a woman's, but he seemed not to hear that. I pressed the door handle, but the door stayed closed. *You will not change your situation in that way.* I tried the handle again, but it did not give way.

'Too bad, then.' He took a step towards me; a few more centimetres and his beer belly would be pressed against me. 'Anything else?'

'No.' I instinctively stepped back, and he came after me.

'You can come in.' His voice was slurred, and the bottle was almost touching my arm.

'No thanks, just tell him regards from Nelly.'

'Will do.' His voice was suddenly loud and compliant; he clicked his bare heels and held out the bottle to me as if swearing an oath on it.

People like you, victims of inhuman and unworthy systems.

Relief flooded through me as soon as I was in the stairway and going down the steps. On the next landing Hans was there in front of me. Every time I saw him, Hans looked smaller than I remembered him. I moved aside so that he wouldn't have to stand on the step below me. My glance went up to where the man in his underwear was standing in the doorway and raising his beer bottle in greeting.

Hans followed my eyes up. 'What are you doing here? Do you two know each other?'

'No, I was coming to see you, but you weren't in.'

'Come on, then.' He went ahead of me, not seeming at all surprised by my visit.

He passed the other inmate of the apartment without any greeting, and closed the door to his half of the room.

'Here, sit down beside me.' Hans patted the mattress. I did as he said, as if it were to be taken for granted that we would sit together on his bed, and liked the warmth and familiarity of his expression.

'Do you know a Dr Rothe?'

'Should I?'

'Or a Bears' Club?'

'Sorry.'

I looked at Hans. Although he had been living in the camp for so long, he too seemed never to have heard of the man with a certain degree of fame.

'I had a visit at midday today.'

'From this Dr Rothe?' Hans took his shoes off.

'Maybe. At least, he and his Bears' Club wanted to help me.'

'Help you?'

'Yes.' I laughed out loud with relief. 'But I really don't want any help.'

'Help with what?'

I shrugged. 'I just don't want to think about it any more.'

There seemed to be some uncertainty in his eyes, an uncertainty that might be because of my unexpected closeness to him, my body within reach. I put out my hand and stroked his cheek. It was rough. His lips were soft, and I stroked them only once. He reacted to the touch with strange composure. He didn't move.

We've been looking for you and we've found you, I thought, and said, 'You know something? There are times when I'm scared.' My hand followed his narrow shoulders, went down along his arm and took his hand, which was lying relaxed on his thigh. His hand was cold as ice. He didn't reply. I was reminded of the pressure of his hand, which was no pressure at all. 'I'm scared just like that, for no reason at all.'

As if of necessity, he removed his hand from mine. 'Would you like something to drink? Water or Nescafé?'

'Both.'

Hans came back with two cups, one containing water, the other coffee powder, and placed both on the floor in front of me. He plugged a mini-boiler into a socket and sat down on the bunk bed again beside me.

'Do you often get visitors?'

'From outside, you mean? Never. How about you?'

Hans shook his head.

'My uncle was in Berlin for a few days last week,' I said. 'He had business here, and wanted me to go and see him at his hotel. The Kempinski on the Kurfürstendamm. But my son was ill, and I couldn't get away.'

238

'Why didn't he come here?'

'Here?' I shrugged and thought about it. 'I didn't ask him. To be honest, I wanted to spare him the sight of it. He comes from Paris.'

'So what? Can't an uncle from Paris bear the sight of a transit camp?'

'Well, yes, maybe he could have done. But I couldn't. He went into exile, and he has his own idea of the Germans and their camps. I didn't want him to see me here.'

Hans nodded, as if he understood what I meant.

'I couldn't really have entertained him here, do you see? How could I have a guest here? I wouldn't even have been able to cook something.'

'Cook something?'

'I know it sounds silly, but when I think of it, it strikes me that I used to cook a lot, and I feel how much cooking means something like home to me. Of course, sometimes it's been a nuisance, you don't always do it just because you want to when you have children. But here, where there's only one hotplate that works and the other doesn't, where there's one large saucepan without a lid to fit it and a milk pan in the cupboard, I miss cooking.' I couldn't help thinking of Frau Jabłonovska and the smell of cabbage in her apartment when I first went to see her there. She obviously had less difficulty than me in cooking with a single pan. Or maybe she had been clever enough to buy saucepans with her arrival money or even bring some from Poland.

'Do you and the children eat in the canteen?'

'The children do sometimes. I sit with them and keep them company, but I can't. I can't eat there myself. It simply takes my appetite away. Maybe I don't feel really grown up in a canteen like that, where they prepare the food and serve it up. I feel totally useless and almost ashamed of myself in front of my children. It feels like a prison.'

'A prison?'

'When you eat only what's put in front of you, and you're just not in a position to decide what you'll cook and how, and your children aren't eating the food you've bought and prepared for them at your own table. It means you're not giving them a home any more – perhaps you are in your mind, but not in practice.'

'Don't the children sometimes eat in other places? At school or in the kindergarten?'

'Yes, but usually it's the parents who see to their breakfast and supper – and they almost always go out to work while the children are eating somewhere else. So they are seeing about their food, or at least indirectly.'

Hans scratched his face nervously. Apparently the ideas of children and cooking were more than alien to him.

'Prison, did you say?'

I nodded. It occurred to me that Hans had been putting up with this state of being reduced to infancy for about six years, first in prison and then in the camp. But he didn't let anything show unless by the scratching, which might be only a bad habit. He was listening to me almost unmoved, as if he didn't know the feeling I'd described at all, or had got over it long ago, as if one day you reconciled yourself to having no responsibility for the simplest things, and no possibility of making decisions.

'Don't you know anyone else in the West?'

'No.' I shook my head. I'd have liked to hold his hand to keep him from scratching himself. As I thought that, I caught myself wondering whether my answer was true. 'How about you?'

'What, me?' Hans scratched his face until his cheek was red. 'No. Well, yes. A distant cousin called Birgit. She once visited me. And my half-brother. My father went to the West as soon as the war was over and started a new family there. He died long ago. My half-brother lives in Munich. I called him once in my first few days here. He said he works very hard and next moment he asked what I wanted. I told him nothing in particular, I was just ringing to say hello, and maybe we could get to know each other. Then he said, very quickly, that he couldn't do anything for me.' Hans was scratching his cheek again, and a tiny drop of blood showed where his skin was raised. 'As if I'd asked him for something. Don't ask me why I phoned him in the first place.'

'Perhaps for the same reason that I miss cooking. If you call someone you're making a link. If you know someone, and the two of you had met, you'd have been a little more present here, you'd have got a little further.'

'Closer to home, you mean?' Hans looked at me sceptically. 'I don't know, that sounds very much like . . .'

'Like what?'

'Oh, when I hear the women in the laundry or read a newspaper that's been left lying around, I get the impression that everyone explains everything they can to themselves, as psychologically as possible, hoping that it will then be very profound or true. But it's neither. Those explanations are no good in real life.' Hans looked at me, and I wasn't sure whether he was being realistic or bitter or self-pitying. 'What's this story about the father of your children? Do you really think he was eliminated?'

'I'd rather not talk about that.' I leaned against the bedpost. He'd asked me questions once before. I thought I saw sympathy in his face. Maybe he thought it had just been an unusually difficult separation, and that was a more familiar idea to him. He could imagine what it was like to be a woman who'd been betrayed. He had stopped scratching himself. I saw in his eyes only the warmth of a human being who suddenly didn't seem to be a man so much as the recipient of my unhappiness, a listener to it. Why should I alarm him and make the tear that was about to drop from his eyelid, and arose from his sympathy for everything imaginable, look ridiculous with a story of death and uncertainty?

All the closeness and familiarity between us had suddenly disappeared.

What was my life and the loss of a man I loved supposed to mean to him? I'd met him only a few times, and his soulful look had left me cold more than once, or even repelled me.

His hand stayed calm and relaxed on his thigh, and he made no move at all to suggest that he wanted to embrace me.

There was a musty smell about him, as if of clothes that had been lying in a cupboard too long. All the same I wanted to touch him and bridge the distance between us. I didn't want to talk, just to forget, touch him and forget about it all. I wanted to forget the *Fräulein*, the initials *V.B.* stamped in gold, the possibility that a man claiming to be called Dr Rothe had in his possession a case that reminded me of one I'd seen years ago in Vassily's apartment, a case that was also empty, and by coincidence, or perhaps not by coincidence, could be placed on the table in front of me.

'Don't you want to tell anyone about it?'

The naivety I thought I saw in Hans's face touched me. I felt like crying. Then I felt like kissing him. I did neither.

Absolute attention could take up a lot of space between two people, so much space that they couldn't reach each other.

'Why do you ask? It wouldn't mean anything to any of you.'

'Any of us?' His fingers tensed, almost imperceptibly.

'Any of you people here who don't know about him, anyone in the West.'

'We're in this camp, now in the West.' Hans folded his arms.

'You may have left the East, I may have left prison there. But where have you ended up? Haven't you noticed that we're living in a camp surrounded by a wall, in the middle of a country surrounded by another wall? You think this place, here inside the wall, is the golden West? You think this is the great gift of freedom?'

Hans sounded bitter, not ironic. Only a man like Rothe had a sense of irony here. The water in the mini-boiler had been boiling for some time, but Hans didn't move. What was a lost love, what was death itself if they became a weapon and the reason for injuring a human being? Hans had turned his eyes away from me. I'd have liked to put my arm around him, but just as I didn't like what he was saying, he didn't seem to want physical contact with me.

'They want to send me a daughter.'

'A daughter?'

'They say she's mine.'

I looked enquiringly at Hans.

'I don't know her. They call it reuniting families.'

'By force?'

'The girl grew up with her grandmother. I suppose the grand-mother died last year, so that's why the girl's living in a home.'

'What about her mother?'

Hans made a dismissive gesture, or perhaps it was a sad one. 'The woman left her child with her mother ten years ago and never came back.'

'Never came back.' I shook my head, and tried to work out what that was supposed to mean.

'I know it sounds strange. No one's been able to find out what happened to her or where she's hiding now.'

'Was that possible with us in the East? To disappear?'

'Not officially. Of course not. But think of all the people who did disappear. Went on the run. Ended in prisons. Your Vassily disappeared too, didn't he, funeral or no funeral. I hardly knew the woman. And even here several people disappear every year. Without trace.'

'So how did they come upon you?'

'How? There must be an agreement for the girl's maintenance somewhere or other. They'd call it acknowledgement of paternity now. When I arrived here and was interviewed they asked me about children. I don't know who got this whole thing under way. There must have been an application.'

'Maybe they didn't want her in the home any more. Because of the expense.'

'I think it's more likely the governments agreed that the child still had a father. And maybe she said she wanted to go to the West.'

'Just like that?'

'She must be fourteen now, and at fourteen children can decide what they want to do.'

'So now she's coming?'

'Yes, she's coming.'

In the dimly lit room, it seemed to me that Hans was narrowing his eyes as if he had sand in one of them. But the tears I thought I'd seen just now, thinking they were for me and showed his sympathy, had vanished without trace. He was sitting up straight, leaning against the bedpost, and so we both sat there leaning on his bedpost, each occupied with our own thoughts.

'Do you know what people say? *She's a slut*, they say.' Hans was probably looking at me without blinking.

'A girl of fourteen? Who says so?'

'No, not the girl. They say it about you.'

'Why me?'

'Who knows?' It didn't seem to interest him. He stood up and asked if I'd still like a Nescafé, but I said no. He took the plug out of the socket.

'I thought you'd be younger.'

'Is that bad?'

'No, just odd.' The idea of a mother abandoning her four-year-old daughter and disappearing made me uneasy. To break the silence, I said, 'Perhaps she loved a man in the West, tried to escape and was shot.'

Hans sat down beside me again. He didn't say anything. Presumably every possible thought about it had gone through his mind countless times, until one day maybe he came round to not thinking about it any more, because you can't think about things you don't know. I was feeling incredibly tired.

'When is she coming?'

'At Christmas.' He laughed, but what I heard was a hiss through his teeth. 'A girl of fourteen, a total stranger to me. I suppose she's going to sleep in the bottom bunk here while I sleep in the top one.' Hans laughed, he laughed like a lunatic, breathing in as he laughed instead of out.

'Come on, let's lie down for a moment,' I said, thinking only of stretching out.

There was hardly room for two people side by side in such a narrow bed. Even though Hans was so thin, our arms lay on top of each other, and one of my legs kept falling off the bed. Rain pattered against the windowpane. Hans wasn't laughing any more. He lay beside me, probably thinking of his daughter. I was sure he'd never cooked or made a home for another person in his life. Perhaps he, too, was waiting. For the arrival of his daughter. For a word and a gesture from me. For something unforeseeable to happen. I listened to the rain. Hans was breathing deeply; it sounded like a sigh. His musty smell no longer suggested that of a secret lover but a good friend.

'Your hair tickles,' said Hans.

It was possible that the initials *V.B.* didn't stand for Vassily's name but were something to do with the organisation that Rothe worked for. 'The Bears' Club,' I said softly, and laughed. 'Victorious Bear Department.'

Hans was obviously beginning to feel uncomfortable; he turned over on his side to have more room. 'Bears' Club. Isn't that some kind of rich people's association?'

'I don't know.'

'Yes, I think someone told me about it before.' Hans propped himself on his elbow and looked into space over me as if I weren't a woman at all.

'I must be going.'

'Wait a moment.' Hans tried to hold my arm, but I stood up.

Hans had holes in his socks. I could see his white toes in the dim light. He stood up himself and took me to the door of the room.

'Five thirty and pitch dark.' His arm reached for the switch; the light made him look pale.

The words *a case to arouse sympathy* suddenly sounded quite different to me. I made a detour to the laundry to see if my washing from that morning was still there. The smell of ironed washing rose to my nostrils, a pleasant smell, almost like something burnt. Frau Jabłonovska was standing by one of the machines at the back, singing as she placed one ironed garment after another in a small leather case.

'You were in a great hurry just now,' she said as I went over to her.

'Didn't you once tell me you'd worked for a dry-cleaning firm?' I asked.

'Yes, I did, but not for long. I'm working in a fast-food place now. The dry-cleaning was better, if you ask me. You don't get orders shouted at you all the time there. I don't earn as much, but my head is my own.'

'Huh. That's what you think,' said a woman at the washstand, joining the conversation as she turned to us. She had her hair in a bun with a hairnet over it. 'My head is my own. My belly's my own. It'd be better if there wasn't all this women's work. Yup. Think how long they talked themselves blue in the face, saying they wanted to do away with work not worthy of a human being. Yes, and while some of them never stop talking we lot are working shifts.'

'May I?' A red-haired woman reached in front of me and picked up the washing powder.

The door opened, and Hans took a step inside. When he saw me he turned and disappeared again.

'Yup, and *he* mustn't miss anything,' the woman with her bun in a hairnet at the washstand went on. 'I wasn't a bit surprised to hear he's a Stasi informer. He seemed so odd from the first, slinking round corners and making lists.'

The blood shot into my face; I coughed and turned to the wall. My cough wouldn't stop, it convulsed my chest muscles, the lining of my ribcage seemed about to break, nothing seemed to be in its right place inside me. Frau Jabłonovska patted me on the back. 'I came along to see you just now because –' she began but my coughing interrupted her, and her patting turned to stroking, she was stroking me down my back.

'What was that you said – how long has he been making himself at home here? Two years?' The woman with the bun went over to the red-haired woman, who was standing in the corner holding a piece of fabric with a strange silvery gleam under the tap. 'What, two years, that little bug?'

The red-haired woman nodded.

'Did you hear that? Did you hear that, everyone? How much longer, huh? I can't wait to see!'

'Later,' I managed to tell Frau Jabłonovska in between coughing. Whatever she had wanted when she came to see me, her explanation would have to wait. I left Frau Jabłonovska with the other two women and stumbled out of the door.

I felt as if I were coughing my lungs out of my body. Hadn't Hans asked me what happened to the father of my children? Of course it could be true that he was working for the Stasi, and had been planted in the camp to sound out me and other inmates. That was why he seemed to be following me, why he was pretending to be interested in me personally with his letter in a bottle and his hesitant friendliness, whereas he was really interested only in my function. No wonder he claimed never to have heard anything about the Bears' Club, or at least anything to its discredit. After all, it was possible that he was hand in glove with Rothe. Passing the porter's lodge, I asked if there was any post for me. He held out a little present and smiled. He looked at me so long and so intently that I briefly thought he himself might be the admirer who sent me flowers and perfume. But then he looked at his papers again, made notes, drank a sip of coffee and acted like a porter going about his work, nothing else. I found it hard to imagine that Hans had made up the story about his daughter. Didn't he say that it was many months since he had left the camp? Hadn't that confession been as good as an alibi showing that he couldn't give me flowers or perfume? I thought of his cold hand and its limp pressure when I shook it, and how he had put his head round the laundry door just now, only to go off again as if he were afraid of something?

My shopping list was short. It was still two weeks before Christmas, and I had hardly anything to do in those two weeks but find a present for the children. I would ask Frau Jabłonovska about the dry-cleaning firm some other time. Herr Lüttich of the employment agency was ready to offer me any job in his card index. But so far there was nothing for a chemist who had studied in the East and hadn't worked in her profession for almost three years. I remembered how often his hand disappeared under the top of his desk, when I was sitting opposite him, and he hardly had time to glance at the box of index cards without taking his eyes off me, smoking the cigarettes he rolled himself, and then having to bring his hand out again. There couldn't be any shortage of dry-cleaning to be done. His hand was damp when he said goodbye to me, and he never neglected to say that I should look in again tomorrow or in the next few days, something for me might turn up at any time. I could get Katya's stickers from the newsagent's shop on the other side of the street. Drizzle was still falling from the densely clouded, dirty orange sky. When it was cloudy the city was never really dark, however moonless the night. The cars in Marienfelder Allee had built up into a jam. The street was being widened ahead of me, and temporary lights were holding up the traffic. I made my way through the cars and the exhaust fumes, their vapours glowing red among the rear lights, and saw the powerful figure of John Bird behind a brightly lit display window just in time. Presumably he had a break, or had finished work for the day and was buying a TV magazine. I turned round and made my way back over the street again among the bumpers and exhausts. The telephone kiosk smelled of cold smoke and urine.

'It's me. Nelly.'

'I thought you'd disappeared off the face of the earth.'

'Yes, well, I still owe you money. It's difficult for me to phone you.'

'You don't owe it to me.' His laughter sounded malicious.

'The organisation, then.'

'Ten thousand isn't chicken feed. That was a special price, do you realise?'

'You think I'd forget a thing like that?' How could he suppose I wasn't aware of my debt? I fidgeted with the cradle of the phone and was about to press it down when I heard a click and a slight hissing sound in the receiver. Gerd was breathing in deeply and no doubt keeping cigarette smoke in his lungs.

'What about it, then? Shall we meet?'

'I don't know. I'm run off my feet. Looking for an apartment,' I said untruthfully. 'And looking for work,' I added not quite so untruthfully, 'and taking the children to school and meeting them after school.' A bit untruthfully, all the same.

'Are you still in the camp?'

'I'm still here, yes.'

'Why not come and see me sometime? You still have the address, I suppose? I'll pay for a taxi and you can come here, how about that?'

'Thanks, Gerd, but I really only wanted to ask if you know a bookshop that sells second-hand books.'

'Oh, there are any number of them near here, on Winterfeld-platz and in the Hauptstrasse. Are you looking for anything in particular?'

'*Pippi Longstocking*.'

'Surely your children have a copy already.'

'What?'

'Well, every child knows that story.'

'We did have one. But now Aleksei wants another.' I could feel the smooth case of the cassette in my jacket pocket. How was Olivier's mother to know there was no cassette recorder in the camp to play it on? All the same, the cassette was Aleksei's pride and joy. Ever since she'd given it to him he had been looking forward to the third part of *Pippi Longstocking*, although he didn't even know the first part.

'I'd be happy to look. I can't do it today, I have to go to the group soon.' He drew on his cigarette. 'Might interest you, too. Nuclear power and all that. We meet every week for discussions.'

'What?'

'This is a bad line, isn't it? We meet for discussions, I said. On nuclear power. Although we sometimes spend the evening on problems with personal relationships, well, whatever comes up. Or unemployment. A million out of work, outrageous, don't you think? The Chancellor says if we go above five per cent the outlook is bad.'

'Does he?'

'And we discussed that, because in theory it affects us all. We're not against it, but at this point, if the working class is entertaining the idea of –'

'Gerd, excuse me, I can see my bus coming. See you some time.'

'– well, that doesn't make it any easier. Hang on a minute, Nelly. Hey, hang on.'

I rang off and came out of the phone box. My breath was a white cloud in the air. Slowly, I went to the bus stop. The timetable was almost illegible. If that last number was a five, the bus would be here in thirteen minutes' time. Or perhaps it would take longer in the traffic jam.

Four weeks ago, I had applied for a visa for Christmas. The children had been badgering me for weeks, saying how nice it would be to spend Christmas with my brother and my sister and their children. Even if my mother had refused to celebrate Christmas for years, not because the Christian customs hurt her feelings, just because she hated all the presents and the excess of everything that threatened to confront her at that time of the year. She talked crossly about the extravagance, and always spent Christmas Eve with her own mother, who employed a new cook every year and invited friends in, even now that she was ninety years old. The story went that these were feasts where we and our children would only be in the way. My visa application had been turned down, no precise reasons given. It was true that I'd heard of cases where visits had been permitted a month after you got an exit visa to the West here, but governmental decisions seemed to be arbitrarily made. Maybe the government feared I might just stay, and then they wouldn't have known where to send me. I waited for twenty-five minutes, and then decided that the bus just wasn't going to come this evening. The shops would have closed by now anyway. So I crossed the street and made for the red-and-white barrier.

I had burned the letter rejecting my visa application in the ashtray, and I didn't tell Aleksei and Katya about it. I thought that the pleasure of their anticipation was more important, even if I didn't know yet how and when I could turn their minds to something else.

When I got back to the apartment I felt a cold draught of air. The door to our living room was standing wide open. Fat brown and black worms were sticking to the wall above the radiator. On closer inspection, they turned out to be slugs, obviously looking for a way to the world outside between the windowsill and the radiator which was not available to them. I saw other, much smaller worms among them, creatures that looked like maggots, small white mealworms. There was a black bird standing on the table with its head tilted sideways to get a better look at me. The short end of a mealworm was sticking out of its beak, and its feathers looked tangled, not like the plumage of a raven, I thought. The light was on, so the children couldn't be far away. The room had chilled off, there were raisins on the windowsill, and a white substance that looked more like curd cheese than snow was sticking to a saucer. I closed the window.

I heard voices from the kitchen, Katya's giggles, and an impatient 'Oh, do stop that' from Aleksei. The children were sitting on the work surface in front of the window, and Aleksei was reading aloud from a book. "'Greatly feared by farmers. In Mecklenburg, even in the last century, ravens were observed in meadows where cows were giving birth. The birds not only fell on the afterbirth but when labour had come to a standstill pecked at the sexual organs of the cow, trying to eat the calf stuck in the birth canal.'" Susanne opened the kitchen cupboards and put various items of food on the stove in front of her. She laughed, and told him to go on reading aloud.

I crossed my arms and waited for the three of them to notice me.

'Are you taking your bed with you, too?' asked Katya.

'Of course not; your mother sleeps in the bed, so how could I take it with me? Anyway, it belongs to the camp.'

'Where are you going to sleep, then?'

'I'll wait and see. I bet it'll be in a four-poster bed with a great big canopy.'

"'At a length of sixty-four centimetres, the raven is our largest songbird. When the thermals are good, ravens can often be seen circling in pairs at great heights. The mating season begins in late winter, and the males perform aerial acrobatics in their courtship display.'" Aleksei was not going to let Katya and Susanne interrupt him.

Susanne put the food she had been looking for into a bag, turned round and saw me. 'Oh, there you are.'

'And where have you been all day?'

'Your children were wondering too. Well, Christmas shopping can take a lot of time.' Susanne helped Aleksei down from the work surface, and laughed almost hysterically. While the children went into the living room ahead of us to see how the raven was doing, she whispered to me, 'Had a final conversation with the management.' She laughed again, as if she were powered by an engine. 'They must have realised that I wasn't working in the bread-making factory at night.' She wiped tears of laughter from her eyes. I shook my head, at a loss.

'Imagine, it took them three months! *Your night pass was solely for that purpose*, one of them told me, and another said he didn't want to know where I went at night, but I had obviously found somewhere else to stay, and I'd better get back to it as soon as possible. Here was I living in the lap of luxury, he added, and the advantages of the camp were not intended for the likes of me. *You don't get away with this, my girl*, said the other one again and again, as if I were a naughty child being expelled from school. Honestly, they don't have all their marbles!' We'd reached the living room. Susanne took the travelling bag she had packed off the bed. '*Not a single night longer!*' she laughed, raising a threatening finger.

'Where are you going now?'

'To be honest, Nelly, there are more comfortable beds than these, don't you think?' I suddenly thought of what Hans had said. *She's a slut.* Susanne's laughter, explosive and free, her mockery of the authorities, was that of an ally.

'Good luck.' My voice sounded dry, almost resentful, so that I wanted to add something friendlier. I put my arms round her and gave her a hug.

'Never mind, that's all right,' she said, blowing her nose, and for a moment I wasn't sure whether she might not be crying after all. 'Think of me, will you?' she said.

'Of course,' said Katya, flinging her arms round Susanne's waist, until Susanne freed herself and opened the door. Perhaps Katya wanted a miniskirt because she adored Susanne. Aleksei was holding a slug in front of the raven's right and left eyes alternately, until it turned its head left and reluctantly snapped up the morsel it was being offered. 'Ravens are sacred birds,' said Aleksei, holding up a mealworm. 'It said that in the book too. In other cultures they were revered as bearers of good news. Birds of the gods.'

'And don't stay here too long,' said Susanne, closing the living-room door behind her.

Hans Pischke presses down his left hand

Her name, I discovered, was Doreen. She had been fourteen in September. They'd be bringing her on Monday, so we would be reunited on Tuesday, for our first Christmas together in the West.

The man in the camp management office had offered me his large, warm hand and congratulated me. He said he felt proud of this moment.

I couldn't wait to get out of his office, I was in a hurry to forget his expression. Back in my room, I paced up and down.

Human beings should be forbidden to increase and multiply. Sex clutched the globe of this earth like a kraken, leaving traces all over it, along with the sliminess of birth and decomposition, its tentacles scrambling on and on, attaching itself to everything by suction. Something might seem to disperse, but then it concentrated again, yet still it grew and grew and grew, inexorably and absolutely. Only the baby in the room next to mine didn't want to grow. It wanted to scream and that was all.

The old woman had done the right thing. She had thrown her rope into the tree and let herself drop. She probably hadn't wanted to think about the disposal of her body. Or perhaps she had liked the idea of making a last dramatic appearance. The kind of appearance that maybe people are after when they fall from the Golden Gate Bridge into the sea. Many of them came a long way just to kill themselves there. None of them fell facing west towards the setting sun, into the open Pacific Ocean, none of them turned their backs on the human race. They jumped exclusively into the bay surrounded by built-up areas where thousands of watchful eyes dwelt on its waves. Perhaps they had Alcatraz before their mind's eye, or perhaps the sky, or someone familiar to them. But into what water could the old woman have jumped, off what bridge, from what height? The camp offered nothing but the open ravines between the blocks of buildings, so it had to be a rope that offered her safety.

If I had any questions, I could ring this number, I'd been told. The man in the camp management office had said it was the number of the home where she was living. I didn't have any questions. I just wanted to say she didn't need to come, ought not to come, mustn't come. But who was I to say it to? I didn't know her. I twisted the note with the number on it in my hand. I plucked a hair from my head and tried to jam it in the door of the room.

However, it wouldn't stay put. Obviously the door had warped in the last few weeks. It couldn't stand up to the winter and the air of the central heating. I took a matchstick and split it in half, pressed it well into the crack in the doorway so that you could hardly see it, and set off.

I ran down the stairs.

The father of her children, Nelly said, had *disappeared*. The pain of that might be responsible for the fact that she looked so ageless and unmoved. Her cheerfulness put me off, only the corners of her mouth betrayed her pain. She was sad, not beautiful.

The mother of the girl who was supposed to be my daughter had seemed to me beautiful. She'd had nothing cheerful about her, nothing that had to hide pain. She'd always seemed rather sad, had looked out into the world and at me with melancholy eyes. The sadness of her eyes and her whole mouth was so mysterious and beautiful because she didn't let you know why. I asked her questions, but there was no sorrow in her life even if she looked as if there were. She wasn't in despair, let alone devastated, just melancholy. One day, and it wasn't long in coming, her melancholy no longer attracted but repelled me. Her melancholy came from the inner well-being that left nothing to be desired. When we parted I told her that melancholy is something that you have to be able to afford, and she obviously could. Was that fourteen years ago? No, it was fifteen years ago. She told me the child was mine in writing some months later. I had undertaken to pay maintenance and acknowledge paternity, although to this day I doubted that I was really the father.

On one of my first days in the West I had walked through the city, aimlessly going into every shop and looking at what there was to buy. In Budapester Strasse I found a shop selling pictures, unframed high-gloss pictures, Picasso and Mick Jagger, sunsets and kittens in baskets. The salesman said he had very different things that might interest me more, and showed me large-format pictures of motorbikes and scantily clad men and women. When he saw that I didn't like those either, he pointed out a stand with pictures that, he said, were more for the heart. Pictures for the heart showed the faces of girls against shimmering violet and blue backgrounds, the girls had huge eyes and mouths, and a huge tear shining on one cheek. I left the shop in alarm. No photo or picture had ever reminded me of the mother of my daughter so much as those pictures.

Nelly didn't radiate any such beauty. I wouldn't have come close to such beauty a second time. Nelly had covered her despair and her pain with a cloak, and that cloak hid her figure.

The sky cleared in one place, the sun made the grey look like a wall, a yellow grey. On the way out I asked whether I had any post. The porter handed me two letters, and I felt his eyes on my back, as if he knew for certain that this was the first time I had left the grounds of the camp for months.

Three people were waiting at the telephone kiosk outside the camp. They were standing in line, and I joined them. I opened the first letter. It was from a firm called Schielow, *Your Expert for Alarm Systems*, and the wording was similar to the countless other letters I had already had: *Dear Herr Pischke, we regret to inform you that we cannot consider you for our vacant post as an electrician.* The next sentence seemed to me strange: *As direct contact with the customers is necessary in our firm, and confidence and security are the basis of our success, we do not, unfortunately, feel able to employ you.* But the last sentence was extremely unusual: *We do not, of course, have to reject your application in view of your police record, but above all because your professional practice as an electrician is obviously more than fifteen years in the past.* The emphasis with which the former argument was ruled out made it impossible for me to overlook it. My two periods of imprisonment, a good four years in all, were certainly the trouble. Where did it specify the reasons anyone had for being in prison? And ultimately there was no reason cancelling out that fact.

However red Lenin's head might be. If I had made it to the border but not a centimetre further, that was due almost entirely to the watchfulness of the People's Police.

A woman came out of the telephone kiosk, and one of the people waiting went into it. Two men came along from the porter's lodge and got behind me in the queue.

The second letter contained a handwritten note. *Get out of here, you nasty little snoop, before you get crushed underfoot by accident.* There was no sender's name on the envelope, no stamp. It must have been handed in at the porter's lodge by the writer in person. I tore it into little pieces. The father of her children, Nelly said, had *disappeared*. If he could disappear, then so could I. There were various ways to do it. But only one of ensuring that you didn't have to bear yourself any more.

I had got the rope for the old lady who was my neighbour. A young man like me, she had said, must surely know where to get hold of a good stout rope, and she had tried to press a tenner into my hand. But I wasn't letting anyone pay me for such services. I found the rope in the cellar containing the boiler for the central heating. It was two centimetres thick, which seemed to her thin. She held it in her hands and seemed to be weighing it up. Then her disappointment gave way to a curious tenderness, and she caressed the rope. She would need to be able to tie a loop and make a good knot, I explained, and I was going to show her what I meant, but she wouldn't let go of it. When she asked if a rope like that might not break, I had shaken my head confidently. She could rely on it, I told her. And so she could.

Next day, when you could still see the tracks left by the fire-fighters in the snow outside the block, I brought a rubbish bag down. On top of the dustbin lay ironed nightdresses of firm linen trimmed with handmade lace. I put the nightdresses aside and found stockings rolled up, large pairs of panties, as well as a sewing box with its contents, and thought that her other garments must already be in the old-clothes store. The camp management had no use for her other household goods. They were put in the bin and consigned to the past. Beneath a watercolour painted in a craftsman-like style, a seascape with dunes and a wooden pier, lay a sponge bag, two framed photographs with the glass still intact, and a biscuit tin that already had several dents in it. The photographs showed a man in uniform and the same man in a tailcoat with his wife and little daughter. I took the biscuit tin and hid it under my jacket. Up in my room I opened it. Pressed violets and faded rose petals lay among hand-embroidered mats and tray cloths, but also a letter that a mother had written to her son. I found a photograph on cardboard, showing a plump naked girl who was barely covering herself with a dark animal fur. She was old now, because the photograph was old, old as my mother might be, old as the woman for whom I had found the rope. And yet I had to think of the daughter they were going to bring me. Without wanting to, I wondered what the girl supposed to be my daughter looked like. I was afraid she might have her mother's beauty. I was even more afraid I might not recognise her.

Who could have had any interest in buying her freedom? It was conceivable that the government wanted someone else to be free, and in return had to take not only a busload of major or minor offenders from the government on the other side but also a few children for whom they had no use there. The girl could have committed a criminal offence herself, she could be sick or disobedient, and finally it wasn't out of the question that after a life begun with her mother, another cut short in her grand-mother's house, and a temporary one in the home, she herself wanted a life at the side of a father who was unknown to her but at least lived in the West. I couldn't hold that against her, but even less could I offer her such a life.

The queue waiting outside the telephone kiosk had dispersed, the men and women were standing in a circle talking to each other. When the door of the phone box opened, I stayed where I was. I didn't want to push my way forward. The note with the number of the children's home had turned damp in my hand, the blue ink was smeared, and the numbers were almost illegible.

I took a handkerchief out of my jacket pocket and wiped my hands. I rubbed them, but the blue ink wouldn't come off; it seemed to be spreading, and the embroidered handkerchief was taking on the colour as well. Although the rose petals were faded, they gave off the aroma of the old woman for whom I had got a rope, which she had used to jump into the tree right outside my window. Her death soothed me, and made the rushing in my ears sound less like the distant surf of ocean breakers, more like a splashing, the pleasant swell of that northern sea I thought I had recognised in the craftsman-like watercolour. The Baltic was breaking in my ears, its waves lapping gently on the shore of my eardrum, and drowning one ear until it bubbled and finally cleared with a plop. Then silence set in.

The people outside the phone box shuffled from foot to foot. More of them had arrived. The phone box itself was empty. Obviously these people had given up waiting. The thick sheet of ice on the paving stones forced me to put one foot slowly in front of the other. A metre from the phone box I stopped and looked round; one of those standing there had been watching me on my way to the phone box. He turned his back to me. The silence in my ear was going away. I thought I heard the whispers and murmurs of the crowd as they looked askance at me in turn. They were standing close to each other, shoulders touching. The whispering never stopped, and the door to the phone box was standing open.

'What's the matter? Don't you want to use the phone?' one of them called to me.

A rustling noise went through their coats, or was the sound only in my ear? The murmuring and muttering, the whispering and rustling. One man looked over his shoulder at me and moved his head in a way that I understood as a challenge. I took a step and slipped into the kiosk.

As I dialled I heard rattling on the line, and then nothing for quite a long time. My heart was beating in my ears and against the receiver. I heard the engaged tone. I tried again, and waited after the dialling code. I tried dialling through the engaged tone until the dialling code was released and I could dial the rest of the digits. Again, I heard nothing at all for a while, then a rustle on the line, a crackling, a whispering. Perhaps the whispering came from outside, or perhaps it had been caught in my ear and was nothing but a trick of the mind.

Suddenly I heard the familiar ringing tone. My heart raced.

The receiver was raised. A man's voice said something that I couldn't make out.

For inexplicable reasons, I had counted on hearing a female voice, and I couldn't imagine that this man was on the staff of the children's home.

'Hello?'

Sometimes State Security came on the line.

'Hello?' the voice at the other end of the line asked impatiently.

Quickly, I hung up. I turned round and looked at the people standing in a circle, looking my way now and then as if they were still waiting after all. I dialled again. I heard a ringing tone once more, and this time a woman answered.

Even before I could say anything I heard a click on the line, and then the tone for the end of the call. The money went through. With the receiver in my hand, I fed more coins into the phone. I dialled the last number but one, then pressed the stand of the receiver down and collected the coins from the little drawer. Outside, more people had gathered. At my first step out of the kiosk I slipped, lost my footing, and fell full length on the ice. A foot kicked me in the ribs, another in my stomach.

'Scum,' I heard, and then, 'Snitch.' With difficulty, I managed to get up on all fours, but then I felt a blow on the back of my neck. 'Traitor.' My forehead hit the ice. The cold felt good, but all the same I tried to get up. 'Arsehole.' A woman's face appeared above me, her cheeks bulging, and she spat in the middle of my face. 'Get out of here, you piece of filth. Bastard. Snoop.' She seemed to have an endless supply of saliva in her body. As if in slow motion, I saw her mouth open and close, fluid came out, was distorted in the air between her face and mine, stretched out at length, gave off air bubbles and folded itself together, its structure was drawn out, came closer, the woman was a spit machine, and it splashed into my face. 'Stasi bastard.' A kick in my crotch, and the pain went through my back and up my neck to my head. I was burning inside, something cracked, and I thought I heard wood burning. My spine went over backwards, the pain was hot until it burned and then burned out. Someone took his foot off my hand, off my fingers. I still couldn't move them.

I had curled up like a woodlouse and thought: My armour may be hard enough, but it is soft too. It was a good thing that I didn't feel the pain any more; I consisted of little else but pain. The voices moved away. But I felt something warm again, and tried to make out what it was. One man was still standing beside me, and I heard another man calling to him to come away. The warmth went through my trousers and pullover and flowed over my face. I thought I saw the man stuffing his prick back into his trousers, turning and walking away, but I wasn't sure. I lay there waiting to find out what I felt, but there was nothing.

I didn't stop thinking. I was trying to register details so as to stay awake. The warmth turned cold as ice.

Four small boots stopped before my eyes. A face pushed itself in front of mine.

'What are you doing there?' The little girl looked at me curiously.

'He's dead,' said the other child, nudging my shoulder with his boot.

'Then we must fetch someone.' The girl looked at my face again. I wanted to tell her that they didn't have to fetch anyone, I lived here and I was sure I could get home alone, but my tongue felt heavy. The little girl screamed, 'He moved, he moved!'

A woman with a dog was coming closer. I felt the dog's nose on my face. A tongue licked my lips, but however hard the woman tried to call her dog back he wouldn't obey, and it seemed to be stronger than her. She came over, bent down, put it on a leash and hauled it away.

A pair of rubber boots stopped, a small suitcase was put down, and a wet fur passed over my face. 'Come along, get up.' The elderly woman with the Polish accent held out her hand. I propped myself on an elbow and stood up, bent over but with both feet on the ground, feeling no pain, only cold and heat and the ground under my feet and the rushing in my ears, like leaves rustling in a birch wood. The woman was no taller than me. My right arm wouldn't obey me; I held my left hand out to her. I thanked her, but she dismissed my thanks, and just smiled surreptitiously. She picked up her leather suitcase and crossed the road. Strangely small feet and small footsteps showed under the massive fur coat, but she did not totter, she tripped along. At the bus stop she sat down, put her suitcase on her lap and waited.

The receiver was still warm; it couldn't be too long since someone had been holding it. My slow tongue would obey me. 'Ah', I said as I dialled. A good thing telephone kiosks were so small; you could lean comfortably against the wall and it wasn't very likely you would fall over. I held the receiver firmly in my left hand, because my right hand couldn't get a proper grip.

'Hello?'

'My name is Pischke. Hans Pischke.'

'Yes?'

'Pischke.'

'Yes, hello, is there someone there?'

My tongue was swelling, getting so thick that it entirely filled my mouth cavity.

I listened to the ringtone on the line for a while. Perhaps my arm just felt too heavy to put the receiver back on its rest. Something smelled bad. I pushed the door open with my shoulder and dropped the receiver, which banged against the wall under the phone, but I went on walking. The ground under the soles of my shoes felt slippery. I wiped my face with the back of my left hand, something wet and bad, the woman's saliva was reddish and sticky. For the first time since I could think, I remembered how, when I was a little boy, my mother had licked my snotty nose clean with her tongue. Apparently we didn't have any handkerchiefs. The bad smell clung to me like a memory.

If everyone had the same sense of honour for the lives of others as the old woman who had asked me for a rope and hanged herself in the tree did for her own, I wouldn't have had to go this way, I wouldn't have had to pass the porter again, get out of the sight of women and children and away from the dog's muzzle. But these people were just amateurs; they began their work on me and didn't follow it through to the end, leaving me to lie there alive. Beginners without any conscience. The rushing in my ears swelled, it sprayed and foamed. I put one foot in front of another and stopped, because I had pulled a sinew. They hadn't torn off one of my legs or even just broken it. They hadn't wanted to kill me and release me, they had only wanted to torment me. They weren't beginners after all, they were the sort who had no conscience about hunting people down. Contempt overcame me. But I was tired of fighting back. My contempt gave way to disappointment and nausea. Anyone confused and stupid enough to take me for a Stasi informer in the GDR was certainly not in a position to release me from breathing. Hunters needed to be part of a pack and couldn't get out of it. My breathing came heavily, that was all, and when the air pressed against my ribs on the inside I felt something like pain again for the first time.

Collective confusion led only too easily to plots directed at random against things and creatures, and it might have been nothing but chance that they had made me, of all people, the target and subject of their confusion.

The porter did not look up as I passed him.

A fat woman stood in my way. Horrified, she clapped her hand to her mouth. 'My God, what have you been doing?' I avoided her, as I avoided all those women who spoke to me in the laundry and outside the management offices; they followed me under cover of darkness, their kindly eyes lay in wait for me.

'Stop,' I heard her call, but I didn't wait, I was not going to hesitate a moment longer, my patience was exhausted.

The matchstick was no longer stuck in the door frame, or perhaps it hadn't fallen out until I opened the door. I picked it up from the linoleum with my left hand and put it in my trouser pocket. I fetched a basin of water from the bathroom and locked the door behind me. She was supposed to be coming on Monday. They said her name was Doreen. It was supposed to make me happy. It made me shiver. I took off all my clothes, wet or dry, folded them up and put them on the bed. I put on my pyjamas and my striped dressing gown over them. While I dipped my face in lukewarm water and felt for my eyebrows with my left hand, rubbed my nose and rolled my eyes in their sockets to help me relax, my right hand hung down beside me. The baby was crying. I dried my face with one of the embroidered cloths that smelled of roses and violets and the old lady who had been my neighbour.

I dabbed my eyelids and eyebrows. Once, long ago, I had thought I could change the world, I had felt great in my mind, at least as a part of the world. I cautiously felt my nostrils. I had believed in victory and personal freedom. But anyone who won a victory was left alive, and I didn't feel much like that any more. I couldn't imagine what the girl who was supposed to be my daughter looked like, and I didn't want to. I wasn't going to open the door to some strange girl and hear her asking me questions. I would never tell anyone about the failure of my flight to the West. I didn't want to tell anyone anything, I didn't want to know any more. Certainly not who might have wanted to ransom her and me. Ultimately I might have found myself in a bus full of long-term prisoners being shipped to the West, thrown in as a free gift with a single person who really was loved and wanted there, or at least whose presence was desirable, a bus full of prisoners whom the West simply had to accept to get the one person they wanted.

The water had gone cold. Several hours must have passed, and I was still washing and drying my face, cleansing my body to get rid of what had first been the warmth and later the cold of my skin. The ticking of my watch made me look up. I had put it on the bed with my clothes. I was sitting in my pyjamas and dressing gown, bending over the basin, and dipped my face flannel in the water.

'Open up!' Someone was shaking my door. The baby was crying. 'Open this door at once or it will be your fault.' Nothing would be my fault, no one but me was to blame for my life, however long my neighbour shook the door. I put the corner of the towel in my ear and let it suck up water.

The door opened with a metallic click, and the baby's father, carrying the baby and holding his wife's hand, stumbled into my room. Something fell on the floor. He must have broken the lock out of the door. For a second the baby held its breath, then it started howling again.

'Here, there's milk in the kitchen.' My fully dressed but still beer-bellied neighbour dumped the baby on my lap. 'We'll be back in an hour, two at the latest.' Before I could work out what he meant, he hauled his wife out of the apartment after him and ran down the stairs. The rushing in my ears was joined by a knocking noise: it knocked and knocked and knocked. As soon as the front door of the apartment had latched into place the baby stopped screaming. It weighed alarmingly little. I raised it in the air with my left arm and then cautiously put it back on my lap. Where could I put it? The moment I sat it on the floor or the bed, it fell sideways or backwards and started crying again. As soon as it was on my lap it kept quiet and watched me. Only the ticking of my watch could be heard, no rushing in my ears, no clicking and knocking, not even a rustle. My watch was still lying on my carefully folded clothes. I put the baby on the table in front of me. Carefully, I stretched my left arm out and reached the watch with my fingertips. The baby was watching every move I made – and when I made the wrong move it began crying.

It was ten past eight; a sleepless night was shorter than one that you had slept right through. Daylight would soon be falling through the curtains. I thought of somewhere I could take the baby. I got my clothes on, put my jacket over them, and went out past the blocks of buildings carrying the baby. I didn't know exactly which was Nelly's apartment, I only thought I recognised the entrance.

After a few minutes the front door of the building opened and a woman came out. 'What are you doing with that child? It'll catch its death of cold.'

I pushed past her into the building. Sure enough, the baby was wearing nothing except for its vest and romper suit, no jacket, no cap, no shoes. Though maybe it didn't need shoes yet. The light in the corridor went out. I leaned against the radiator on the wall and kept still. As long as the baby didn't cry everything was all right. Upstairs a door opened, a light came on, and heavy steps came down the stairs. The man coming down didn't even look at me; he just wanted to get past.

'Excuse me, do you know a young woman who lives here with her two children?'

'Nelly? Second floor on the left.' He opened the door of the building and disappeared. He could have been with her.

On the second floor I pushed the doorbell with my elbow. It made a buzzing sound, just like mine and probably all the other doorbells in the camp.

A woman I didn't know opened the door.

'Excuse me, I thought . . . doesn't someone live here called –'

'Nelly? Yes, she lives here.' She pointed to the door of a room and let me into the corridor. 'Well, what have we here? Oh, how cute! Looks like you, too!' The woman followed me to Nelly's door. She waited for me to knock, but my right arm still wasn't working, and I was holding the baby in the crook of my left arm. I kicked the wood, and the woman, shaking her head, disappeared through a door that she left ajar. She'd be listening. I had to knock by kicking the wood again. I thought I heard voices on the other side of the door. Perhaps Nelly had a radio set. By now it was eight thirty, and her children must be at school. Just as I was raising my leg for the third time to knock, the door was opened a crack and Nelly's face appeared.

'What are you doing here?'

'This is my neighbours' baby.' I held it out to her, with my right arm hanging limp by my side.

'Have you been in a fight?' She stretched her arm through the slightly open doorway, touched my lips and, fleetingly, my eyebrows.

'Can you take it, please?' I held the baby against the crack in the door.

271

'What?' She looked at me in surprise, and what I could see of her face in the doorway was narrower.

'Please let me in.'

'I'm sorry, but this is a really bad time.'

'Please.'

'No.' She closed the door a little more, and now I could see only half of her face.

'Just for a little while.' It didn't seem as if the baby impressed her in the least.

'Can't you see it's no good? I don't have any clothes on, I don't want to let you in at the moment.' Her one eye looked at me with a familiar expression, and winked as if to tell me something. The door closed. The other door through which the woman who shared her apartment had disappeared was also closed. I felt for the light switch in the almost dark corridor.

It was none of my business what Nelly did at eight thirty in the morning while her children were at school learning writing and arithmetic, or why she was hiding naked behind her door and wouldn't let me in. Perhaps she was ill and didn't feel good. She coughed a lot, a hoarse cough.

Before I left the building I tried to hide the baby under my jacket. But the baby stretched and showed the curve of its back. It was crying. It didn't think much of the warmth and darkness of my jacket. So I went over the small patch of icy ground and took the baby back to my apartment, where I put it on my bed and let it howl.

Why should I let a baby disturb me while I went about the things I had to do? I carefully folded the embroidered cloths with my left hand, taking care that the corners touched, before I smelled them and put them back in the biscuit tin. I took only the used cloths into the kitchen, soaked them in cold water, wrung them out and took them out of the sink one by one. The fabric, previously so smooth, was ugly and crumpled now. I didn't have time to go over to the laundry and iron the cloths there. The sight of them bothered me so much that I stuffed them into a bag, which wasn't very easy with my left hand, and threw them away with the rubbish. My packet of crispbread was standing in the cupboard where it ought to be; no unauthorised hand had been interfering with it overnight, and I saw with a sense of satisfaction that the last slice was just enough for a meal. I folded the empty packaging and threw that away as well.

As soon as I opened the door of my room, the baby, who was still lying on its back, turned its face to me and followed all my movements. The door wouldn't close any more; my neighbour had destroyed the lock when he forced it open. I put the knife to the right of my breakfast plate, exactly parallel to it at a distance of a finger's breadth, with the cutting edge of the blade inward.

The water was boiling. Opposite my table setting I put out my hand mirror, soap and worn-out shaving brush. I placed my razor and two blades beside the small basin of water. I cleaned the large basin until my left hand felt tired, unused as it was to doing all these things on its own. I heard the child's crying at the same time as the water coming to the boil. I didn't think of it as a baby any more, now that I had looked into its eyes and seen how greedily and demandingly it was searching its surroundings, I felt it was a larger human being, a child, with the demands of a human being that didn't cry just because it could cry but because it wanted to cry. The hot water left a foamy top on the Nescafé.

'Has she been crying all this time?' The child's father had knocked and come in before I could put the mini-boiler down and open the door to him.

'Who?'

'The little one, of course.' He picked the child up from the bed, shaking his head as if it were unusual for her to cry, and hugged her close like a part of his body that had been missing for a long time.

'The child may be hungry, but my crispbread is finished apart from the last slice.'

He turned to his wife, who had stayed in the doorway. I wiped the handle of my razor with my handkerchief, but my one-handed pressure wasn't enough to clean the grooves as well.

'You'd better watch out,' said the man, waving a menacing finger at me. 'There's something going on. If I were you I'd get out of here.' The threat became a warning and I took it as confirmation of my feeling that he wanted to warn a partner, an accomplice for whom he felt sorry, not because he felt personally close to me but because, as he saw it, I might belong to the same organisation as he did. Someone must have confided to him the suspicion that I was a member of the Stasi.

He caressed the child's head. 'Don't take too much time about it, they're not at the door yet.' He was uneasily chewing a matchstick, shifting it from corner to corner of his mouth with his teeth. Perhaps the same matchstick had once been jammed into my door. I saw sparks of fear in his heavy, battered face, and thought about his hints, the threat and the warning, until they fell into place, and he was making a demand on me, an anxious request for fear that the boat in which he was sitting might capsize if anyone was killed in it or forcibly torn out of it. You didn't want to capsize, particularly not with a child in your arms and a wife in tow who would probably do all she could to avoid the lifebelt, who would want to sink as quickly and quietly as possible.

'If you'd leave me in peace now – I have something to do.' I had put my left hand on the door handle, and was waiting until he took the last step backwards.

He nodded to me and left. A room with a closed door, a room where I was alone, sent a pleasurable shudder running down my back. I pushed the curtain aside, opened the window and sat down in the window frame. The first cigarette made me agreeably dizzy. Down below, the crows were mobbing a rather larger black bird that obviously couldn't fly any more. They hopped over to it and pecked at the frozen ground, and as if it felt threatened by their movements it hopped sideways to get to safety. The crows went after it. I ground out my cigarette on the windowsill and left the cigarette end lying there. A few snowflakes were dancing outside the window. I pulled my chair back and sat down to eat breakfast, trying to rearrange the noises in my ears into a kind of music. A sparrow came down on the windowsill and investigated the cigarette end. The window closed. Alarmed, the sparrow flew up, one wing brushing past the pane. The snowflakes grew larger, the snow was falling faster and more thickly, and the cawing of the grey-black birds was muted. The idea that I could no longer entertain any hope, let alone expect release, filled me with great calm. There would be no more clicking and snapping in my ears, no doors opening and closing, no more coming and going.

A second sparrow flew along, snapped up the cigarette end in its flight, and let it drop a moment later. The windowsill cleaned itself that way.

I left the last sip of coffee in my cup, took the crockery into the kitchen and rinsed it. The key would still turn, but I couldn't lock the door of my room. The child in the next room was crying and everything seemed the same as usual. A draught of air made my door rattle. Back and forth, back and forth. I could hardly go into every room and close the windows. Mine had let draughts in ever since I had been here. When it rained, a narrow rivulet ran from the outermost right end of the windowsill along the wall, beside the radiator and down to the floor. Now and then the door rattled; as soon as I was hoping, after a pause of any length, that it had been the last, along came another. It could send you crazy. Crazier than the crying of the child, because by now I was used to its regularity. One-armed, I could move the wardrobe across the doorway only with difficulty. The dirt perhaps of decades, and accumulated by hundreds of occupants who had stayed in this small half-room before me, stuck to the floor and you could clearly see the outline of the wardrobe where the linoleum was still a strong and pristine grey. Snow was driving so hard outside the window that you could see hardly anything of the block opposite. The mini-boiler sent fine little bubbles rising up. Its glow lit the pan of water on the inside, and I held my hand over the pan, moved my cold left hand, bent each finger separately and then all of them together. The water turned white as if it were foaming and drawing itself together. The heat was exerting pressure on the water. In tiny places the surface rose, turned, exploded, broke and blew bubbles. I took the plug out and poured the boiling water into the large basin, sat down at the table and began to shave, as usual in the morning. I couldn't begin the day unshaven; the mere idea made my skin crawl. The man who had made political ideas his own, and had made his own ideas political: how excited he had been to climb Lenin's bronze head, up its armour and into the hollow space inside, and how much he had felt himself, entirely himself, in that excitement – he seemed to me a different man now. I had become strange to myself, where days could not be measured out in rituals, hours did not pass in rituals. The razor blade scraped my skin. This stranger might have a daughter called Doreen. The skin of my chin felt smooth; another man had been reminded of Czech fairy-tale princesses who promised to live in another world and stay there, if you made no mistake in dealing with them; it passed smoothly over the skin above the mouth, and there were the recurrent dreams at night of women who sat in a wicker chair beside the sea, and could have been my own mother but for the tracks of bird's feet that they left behind, and smoothly over the throat; another man who sometimes looked out of my eyes and had made use of my rituals. That other man would never get into me again, and the memory of his thoughts would remain that of someone familiar, but copied only the past. How painlessly a man could harbour broken bones in him I knew only since yesterday evening, and thanks to the man who was hunting me. Although physical sensitivity had set in over-night I felt no pain. I had disappeared, without any vain hopes of return. I washed the dirty blade in the water in the small basin, placed the razor, brush and soap in a straight line above it. The mirror was rather cloudy, but I could still see the face of the man who was hardly me any more. The water in the large basin had reached hand temperature. I could do nothing with my right hand, it wouldn't move, the blade kept falling from my hand and into the basin. Only with my left hand could I press and cut, and watch, with the other man's eyes, as streaks of red mingled with the water in the basin, traces of red ink, until the water was all red. A warm dizziness climbed up me. I put the razor blade in my mouth, held it firmly between my teeth and pressed it into my skin; inside the tongue touched it, rubbed until the skin of the left wrist also gave way, opened and stung as it slipped into the water next to the right hand – a happy, gentle tingling in water of body temperature. All of me became the past, so clear was the stinging and extinction in water that would soon be below body temperature, and the stinging sensa-tion streamed away at its leisure.

Nelly Senff wants to say yes

In the canteen, they were serving goose for everyone. Goose with gravy, red cabbage and dumplings, all you could eat.

Two police officers were walking along the path outside the block down below, leading the woman with bright red hair and gleaming silvery trousers between them. They were followed, at a little distance, by John Bird, his head hunched down between his shoulders and leaning forward, as if he found it distasteful to be still walking around the camp. He was smiling; perhaps he was glad she had been caught.

Vładisłav Jabłonovski had been sitting at one of the long tables in the canteen since morning, stirring a cup of coffee although he took neither milk nor sugar.

'Oh, there you are, Nelly,' he said when I came in for a moment at midday to get some butter. It was as if he had been waiting there ever since he asked me to dance with him months ago, as if we had a date and I was only two minutes late for it.

'I'm just getting some butter. My children are waiting for me upstairs.'

He nodded uncertainly, and sighed.

'Shall we see each other at the party this evening?'

At a loss, the old man looked at me. He was watching several women decorating the hall. They were putting stepladders on the tables, climbing them and hanging garlands up among the lights.

'Where's your daughter?' I asked him.

'Gone.'

'Gone?'

'Gone off again. When she still wasn't back at ten in the evening I looked under the bed, but there was nothing there.'

'Would you have expected to find her under the bed?' I had to laugh.

'Her gumboots were gone, and so was our suitcase.'

'Where is she, then?'

Vładisłav Jabłonovski stirred his coffee and seemed to be thinking. But then he said, 'No idea. I certainly won't go looking for her.'

I sat down beside him and asked more questions. In the days after that, he said, several people delegated by the camp management and other authorities had been to see him and question him. Vładisłav Jabłonovski couldn't give them any answers, but he told them how hungry he got because, after all, he didn't know where to go to find food. He didn't know about the canteen. He also talked about his digestive troubles. It was difficult to understand him, said the male delegates, putting it down to his Polish origin. But there was a woman among them who had been watching him as he talked, and she asked him to open his mouth wide, please. She didn't utter a cry of horror, but calmly asked her male companions to take a look inside Jabłonovski's mouth. Several teeth were missing, and the woman said she would get in touch with a dentist, no wonder he had trouble with his digestion.

Vładisłav Jabłonovski didn't miss his daughter. For the last few days a young woman from an integration authority had visited him instead, to ask how he was doing. She explained what the ration coupons were for, and went to the old-clothes centre with him. They would have to see if he could still look after himself on his own, she said, and mentioned a care home where a lot of nice people lived. She found him a pair of trousers and a jacket, and told him to come to the canteen next day. He hadn't even known it was Christmas, and since he had forgotten exactly when he was to come to the canteen he had been sitting at the long table since eleven o'clock.

He watched people coming to get plates of soup and then eating it. One man asked about the goose, but they told him there wouldn't be goose until the party for everyone began at six. Later a man arrived with cardboard boxes. The women unpacked stars made of silver foil, branches and candles. They put arrangements of spruce twigs and varnished rosehips out on the tables. When they climbed stepladders to hang up the garlands Vładisłav Jabłonovski whistled softly to himself; the women took no notice of him but let him sit there stirring his coffee. I saw him take a bottle of vodka out of his jacket pocket and stir the last few drops into his cup. He stirred the coffee, whistling quietly. The women took no notice of him, they let him sit there, stirring his cup, and now and then they glanced at the big clock hanging on the wall. Music rang out from the loudspeakers, and one of the women sang along with almost every carol. Vładisłav Jabłonovski smiled, a smile that looked vacant and went on and on. He was probably remembering how he had danced with Cilly Auerbach, and perhaps his dance with me crossed his mind as well. But he sat there and didn't ask any of the women to dance.

A man came in, wished the women assistants a happy Christmas and thanked them for their help on this very special day. The women put their coats on. He handed out little bags to them and told them to hurry home to their families now.

'Well,' I said to Vładisłav Jabłonovski, 'see you this evening, then.'

I got some butter. Ahead of me in the queue a woman was helping the pastor who officiated in the camp. She looked after children, ran errands for him and ironed his laundry. She was telling another woman how a man from Block D had been brought back from hospital to the camp. He hadn't slashed his wrists efficiently enough; he had cut across the arteries rather than lengthwise, and his loss of blood had left him unconscious. That was how the police found him. They wanted to talk to him about Grit Mehring, and had to force the door of his room open, because he seemed to have pushed a wardrobe across it, and was lying on the floor in a strange, contorted position. He was taken to hospital, and the pastor insisted on going to fetch him in person three days later. She, the woman I overheard, was supposed to go with the pastor, as she sometimes did on errands that took him outside the camp. The man had not wanted to see the pastor, indeed did not fundamentally want to see anything at all, and expressed his disappointment on finding that all around him had not stayed black by maintaining an iron silence. The pastor had told Hans that he had experience of such situations; he placed a hand on his head and talked to him. He brought Pischke back to the camp in his VW minibus, talking to him all the way and offering assurances of the beauty of life. He also said that Hans wouldn't be alone any longer now, his daughter had arrived that morning and he, the pastor, would entertain the two of them in his official apartment all that day, there would be tea and biscuits, and in the evening they would all go over to the canteen together for the Christmas party. Hans, apparently, had sat in the passenger seat of the minibus saying nothing.

It had snowed all day, large snowflakes, but none of the snow settled.

I made the children bread and butter with salt on it, and crawled into the bottom bunk of the bed with them. They wanted me to read them the story of the *Snow Queen*, the same as every year. It was getting dark.

Later I took Aleksei and Katya, both of them holding my hands, to the canteen. Large Christmas stars hung in the lighted windows, shining with a pink glow. One of them was blinking on and off; there must be something wrong with the contact. A woman who presumably belonged to the camp management was standing in the doorway welcoming new arrivals, shaking hands with adults, patting children on the head. Two young men stood beside her answering questions about where guests were to sit and when there would be party food. All the children's eyes were drawn to the plates, which had brightly coloured paper bags on them. I kept seeing a small hand reaching out to investigate one of the bags, but not daring to take it. Neon lighting kept its chilly watch on the assembled people. The pastor walked about under the neon tubes, taking any hand he could get hold of in his own white hands and shaking it, while he kept wishing the guests a happy Christmas. At the front of the hall his wife was organising children into a group and trying to shake, if possible, as many hands as her husband. Hans was sitting at one of the long tables, in the far corner by the window. I saw him at once, rolling himself a cigarette. His head was bent, and his hair was white where the hairline receded from his temples. I felt an instinctive urge to say *yes* to him, call out a *yes* that would echo through the whole hall. But he hadn't asked me anything, and I didn't think he was going to ask any question requiring that answer. Holding my children's hands, I pushed past the people and sat down opposite Hans at the table.

'How are you?'

'All right.' Without looking at me, he licked the paper and stuck his cigarette together. 'Would you like one?' Hans held out the cigarette to me across the table.

'No, I only smoke sometimes. Not today.'

A girl with a broad, rather swollen face was sitting next to Hans. He lit his cigarette. His pale shirt with its narrow stripes, made of a fabric so thin that you could clearly see the vest underneath it, emphasised his pallor and the heavy, bluish bags under his eyes.

'You look terrible.' I laid my arm on the table and stretched out my hand, hoping to reach his. But Hans needed to use both hands as he smoked. Every few metres along the tables there were paper plates with spiced Christmas biscuits and little coloured paper bags arranged in fan shapes on green napkins. It was a decorative arrangement that, at least at our table, seemed to make it impossible to take a single biscuit off a plate and eat it. Hans, who was still hunched over the table with his head, which was too large for him, between his shoulders, had propped his elbows on the tabletop and was clasping his cigarette in both hands. It was an awkward and pathetic position. He looked like an insect sucking nectar from the calyx of a flower. Only when it reached his lungs did the nectar seem to complete a change, emerging from his nostrils in thick, yellowish smoke. The cuffs of his shirtsleeves looked bulky, and a piece of muslin bandage was emerging from the cuff over his left wrist. Two women were walking round the tables, pouring mulled wine into paper cups.

Katya and Aleksei kept turning to look at the end of the hall where the pastor's wife had arranged the children into two rows by size. Aleksei's head was leaning on my shoulder, and I put my arm round him. Hans cast Aleksei a quick glance, and Aleksei cast one at Hans, then Hans ground out his cigarette and rolled another.

Once again he offered it to me, but I shook my head. He found matches and struck two before the third caught light.

'I'd like one, though,' said the ash-blonde girl with the broad face beside him, putting out her hand. He let her take it, and pushed the folder of matches across the table without looking at her. She had a fringe as straight as if someone had used a ruler when it was being cut. Hans pulled tobacco out of a packet and rolled it in the cigarette paper between his yellow fingers.

'Your daughter?' I asked.

Hans nodded. 'Doreen.'

Doreen was fully occupied with smoking her cigarette, and obviously didn't like to look at me and her father.

'Hello, Doreen.'

Doreen did not condescend to give me a glance, but turned her head and tried to keep the smoke in her lungs as long as she could.

'She was arrested today, but I expect you know that,' I said to Hans.

'Who was?'

'The woman calling herself Grit Mehring. It won't have been her real name.'

Hans shrugged, as if he didn't know who I was talking about and didn't care either.

'Apparently she was living in your block and spread that rumour about you.' Aleksei snuggled closer to my arm.

Hans calmly drew on his cigarette twice before looking down at the ashtray. 'What rumour?'

'You know what it was.' Then I wondered whether Hans really didn't know who or what I was talking about. He seemed to be ashamed of himself, not so much because of the suspicion in circulation – although word of the woman's arrest was being spread as quickly as her own rumour before – as because he felt uncomfortable sitting here, where he couldn't help seeing and being seen. I suppressed my cough until my eyes were watering, and my view of him was blurred. Then I said, softly but clearly,

'Hans, that's character assassination. Deliberate character assassination. You can bet she's with the Stasi herself.'

Hans's expression did not change. He went on smoking his cigarette until it was so short that it seemed to be burning his fingers, and then he put it out. He was not at ease with himself, but how was I to console him for that? He pressed saliva out through his front teeth, his mouth twisting as if he felt disgusted. I stood up and stroked his hair, but he turned his head away beneath my hand.

'Don't, Mama, he doesn't want it.' Aleksei pulled me down on the bench again and whispered in my ear. 'Can't you see he doesn't like being here?' I ran a finger over my son's mouth to keep him quiet, and dropped a kiss on his forehead.

The neon lighting on the ceiling went off, the carols coming over the loudspeakers fell silent. Only the chains of fairy lights and the Christmas stars in the windows were still shining. There were fairy lights even round the loudspeakers.

'*From heaven above to earth I come,*' began a children's choir. No one in the hall sang along; they all turned in their chairs to look at the children. We too turned on the bench, which meant turning our backs on Hans and his daughter.

'We have real candles at home,' said Katya, taking my other arm.

'At home,' I repeated.

The carol ended, the audience clapped like mad, the ceiling lights came on again. Instead of Santa Claus, a man in a suit with a sack over his shoulder appeared, followed by a woman in high-heeled shoes and a skirt suit, with a pointy red cap on her head. The man in the suit put the sack down on the floor. The camp manageress puffed into the microphone and introduced them as messengers from Santa Claus, Dr Rothe and his wife. They held hands and bowed briefly. I heard a voice behind me whispering something that sounded like *traitor*, and cautiously turned. Hans was looking at the table in front of him, and it wasn't clear to me whether he had said anything. Just as I was about to turn and look ahead again, he said, 'That's what they call you too.' I wasn't sure whether he had said *traitor*, and anyway it didn't seem as if he were speaking to anyone in particular. I hesitated. I didn't want to feel as if the epithet was addressed to me.

'I am sure everyone here in the reception camp will know about the Bears' Club. I'd like to introduce my wife to you. Last week my wife decided that from the beginning of the coming year she would work for you here in an honorary capacity. She will spend ten hours a week concerning herself with your needs and anxieties.' The familiar voice droned through the microphone as if he were master of ceremonies at a funfair. With a sweeping gesture, Dr Rothe indicated the woman beside him, and there was sporadic clapping in the front part of the hall.

Katya dug her elbow into my ribs. 'Isn't she the mother of that boy Olivier?'

'Shhh.' I heard murmuring behind me, and held both children close.

He only wanted to mention a few figures, Dr Rothe went on, to back up the good news of all the people in need whom his organisation had been able to help this year.

The camp management clapped, the pastor clapped, the women assistants clapped. Some of the camp inmates clapped as well. I ventured a glance over my shoulder, and saw Hans still clasping his cigarette in both hands. After every figure Dr Rothe inserted a pause pregnant with meaning, and waited for the applause. At every round of applause he waved his hand in thanks, beaming all over his face. I turned my head to the left, where Vładisław Jabłonovski was sitting in the place he had made his own, stirring the contents of his coffee cup. Once again he took a bottle out; this one was half full. He poured some vodka into his cup, stirred it and drank. What was his daughter about to say to me when I last saw her? She had been standing outside my door, and what she was saying began *I just wanted to*.

'And we have spent a sum of twenty thousand dollars for the disabled children of Bangkok alone.' Pause. The front rows applauded.

'Not to mention the soup kitchen in Mexico City, eight thousand dollars and fourteen volunteer helpers in all.' Applause.

'We're all traitors,' I heard Hans say distinctly behind me. I did not turn my head a centimetre. Dr Rothe went on, his hand passing over his lapel.

'And that, ladies and gentlemen, was only a modest selection of our activities.' He waited for the applause and then raised his arms to express gratitude and to calm the enthusiasm. 'Now I would like to hand over to my dear wife, and wish you all a happy Christmas.' Pause. Applause. His wife spoke into the microphone, but her voice was a whisper without amplification. Louder, louder, they called from the front rows. Her immaculate legs shimmered in mother-of-pearl-coloured tights. She tapped the microphone with her fingers, laughed, and her entire face consisted of her mouth and her radiant white teeth. After a short consultation with the pastor, Dr Rothe leaned over to his wife and said something that she clearly didn't understand. She frowned. Suddenly Dr Rothe's loud and impatient voice rang out from the microphone. '*Turn it on*, Sylvia.'

Frau Rothe apologised, whether for the microphone, herself or her husband I couldn't be sure. She said it was her good fortune to lead her life at the side of a man who set such a fine example, committing himself pro bono to human beings in need. Once again her microphone failed, and an assistant moved it aside. He indicated to Frau Rothe that there was something wrong with the microphone and she should use her husband's. She shyly stepped up beside Dr Rothe. Her voice sounded quite different coming from his microphone, unexpectedly soft and gentle. Her dear husband was generous, she said, even with his private fortune.

I heard a caustic laugh behind me, someone hissed through his teeth, and then I recognised the voice of Hans, saying louder than was necessary, 'Generous with his private fortune, huh, a man still sitting on a private fortune thirty years after the war who doesn't even have to work? I guess it just about pays for the tailor-made suits.' His laugh died away, but no one turned to look at him. Frau Rothe patted her firmly waved hair with her mother-of-pearl fingernails. It was a good thing she was so far away from us. She was now, she said, going to ask every child in the hall to come forward, recite a short Christmas poem, and get one of the lovely, pretty little presents out of the sack.

The children rushed forward. They formed a neat crocodile as if they had been practising, and one after another they recited a poem. Some of the children sang a short song. Katya and Aleksei helped each other to get through the rows and arrive, but not in front. Doreen waited a little longer and then, with ponderous steps, moved a few metres forward; for a long time she was last in the long crocodile that reached to the far end of the hall.

When it was Katya's turn she stammered.

'Well, what sweet little poem are you going to recite?' Frau Rothe bent down to Katya and held the microphone right in front of her mouth.

'Dear Father Christmas . . .' Katya paused, and got some applause from a single member of the audience, one sitting close to us, almost behind me – Hans, whose cigarette was stuck in the corner of his mouth and held his arms above his head, clapping loudly and all by himself.

'And how does the poem go on, dear?' Frau Rothe tried to conceal her impatience.

'I don't remember.' Katya turned to one side, where Dr Rothe and the pastor were standing and looking at her expectantly.

'Then maybe you'd like to sing a pretty song?' Frau Rothe straightened up and held the microphone in front of Katya's mouth from above.

'I don't know any songs.'

'None at all?' Frau Rothe made her voice sound incredulous. Katya slowly shook her head, looked at the ceiling, and her face was bathed in neon light.

'Oh how joyfully . . .' Frau Rothe sang the first line and waited for Katya to go on, but Katya shook her head vigorously.

'Then maybe we need Santa's naughty companion with his switch to beat her,' said Dr Rothe to his wife, joining in.

Katya crumpled up her face with her hands, blew out her cheeks and narrowed her eyes. She looked as if she were about to perform in a pantomime. She sang into the microphone: 'Hansel and Gretel got lost, we are told, in the forest so dark and so bitterly cold. They came to a lov-er-ly gingerbread house, who do you think's nibbling it, only a mouse.' Out of breath, Katya looked straight ahead. No one clapped, all was quiet in the hall. 'Push her in the oven, push her in, do,' she half sang, half chanted.

Dr Rothe looked restlessly at his watch. 'That's enough, girl, that's enough.' He put his hand in the sack and handed his wife a small packet, which she gave to Katya. Katya took the present with one hand, but with the other she clutched Frau Rothe's hand holding the microphone. She sang: 'Hansel I will roast, until he's crisp as toast, so the witch said, but they killed her stone dead.' I could clearly hear her breathing out, and she bobbed an awkward curtsy.

I turned to Hans, who was looking straight through me at just below my eye level. All the same I put my arm on the table. I tempted him with my fingers, but he took no notice, only drew on his cigarette and glanced aside so as not have anyone look him full in the face. Suddenly he put his head back again and stared at me. The audience was giving Katya hesitant applause.

'Well, that was . . . how can I put it? That was charming!' said Frau Rothe, hastily laughing.

'Delightful,' added Dr Rothe. 'But now we must hurry, children. Are you next in line? Can you recite us a really short poem?'

Hans looked at me sadly and said, quietly but distinctly, 'Aren't you one of them?'

'One of what?'

'A traitor.'

'What do you mean?'

'Well, aren't we? You, I, all those people over there. Never mind if we moved, fled the country, lost citizenship – we still didn't stay, we didn't stay put to fight.'

'Why would we fight?'

Sadly, Hans shook his head. He seemed to deplore the fact that I couldn't follow him. 'People who mean things seriously don't run away, they stay and fight, don't they?' Hans laughed out loud; his laughter sounded cynical, malicious, and I saw him plucking at the muslin bandage on his right wrist. Up to that point I had believed I could follow his train of thought and just didn't want to. But with that dark laughter, if not before, he seemed to be betraying himself, becoming a traitor to himself, to his wish not to be here any more, to the gravity and absolute truth of that wish. Hans laughed, and while his eyes did look at me, he did not appear to see me any more. He drank his mulled wine in a single draught and lowered his gaze to the cup; his black laughter died away.

Behind me, I heard Aleksei start singing. *'Joy, oh spark of fire divine, daughter of Elysium.'* Compared to Schiller's 'Song of the Bell' he probably did think the 'Ode to Joy' was a short poem.

To shield Hans from my gaze, I turned round to look forward again. Vładisław Jabłonovski seemed to have fallen asleep over his coffee. His head lay on his chest, his breath was calm and even. *I just wanted to say goodbye*, that was what his daughter had said to me a few days ago. Katya set off on her way back with her present. Dr Rothe and his wife were listening to Aleksei.

> *'Joy is drunk by all creation*
> *At Mother Nature's lovely breast.*
> *Both just and unjust, in elation,*
> *Trace rosy paths at her behest,*
> *To wine and kisses beyond measure,*
> *To friends who the same way have trod.*
> *Even worms know sensuous pleasure*
> *And the cherub lives with God.'*

When Frau Rothe heard the phrase *sensuous pleasure* in a little boy's mouth, she involuntarily burst out laughing. After the line about God, Dr Rothe thought, or anyway decided, that the short poem had better be cut even shorter.

'Thank you, thank you, little man,' he said, thrusting a present into Aleksei's arms. He grabbed him by the shoulders and sent him off the stage and on his way back.

'Well, children, we don't have much time left. We don't want to listen to poetry all evening, do we?' He laughed. This time he wasn't waiting for applause, but taking the next package out of the sack and pressing it into a girl's hand for the rhyming couplet she had delivered. The two of them dealt briskly with the last few children, and Doreen didn't have to recite a poem at all.

Before she could open her mouth, the pastor handed her a present, while Dr Rothe was already helping his wife into her coat and saying goodnight to the management, the pastor and a few other people. Doreen held her present as if it were very fragile. Then she stumbled and fell full length. Perhaps she had fallen over the chain of fairy lights, but anyway she brought the Christmas tree down with her. The light flickered briefly, then all the chains of fairy lights and all the stars in the hall went out. Only the neon lighting was still on, and while a few women clustered round the girl to help her up, Dr Rothe and his wife were disappearing through the doorway. A little later the festive lights came on again. Someone must have changed the fuse. The women assistants had difficulty in standing the tree up again. A few glass baubles were broken, and the chain of lights on the tree stayed dark.

I saw Doreen fending off the hands of the pastor and his wife. Leaving the two of them behind, she made a beeline for the trolley of food. The women assistants had gathered there, and were serving goose with red cabbage and dumplings to the party guests. Knives and forks clattered. There was not much talking. I whispered to Hans, 'Do you want something too?' But he said nothing. His daughter resembled him only in her taciturnity. Even seated, she was a head taller than Hans. She had loaded her plate, and was devouring the dumplings almost whole. Only now was there a smell of burnt plastic in the air. I pushed past shoulders and voices; no one else seemed to notice the smell of something smouldering. The ends of the queues were constantly replenished, and I gave up any idea of joining one of them myself. Undecided, I looked round. The Christmas tree seemed to be giving off smoke. I went closer to it. It was crackling. Something was shining and flashing. Sparks were dancing round the tree. Burnt matter rose lightly into the air, floated upwards, glowing, and went out. More and more embers came away from the tree and reeled gently in the air above the guests' heads. There was a smell of evergreen needles. I saw the pastor's wife take a step towards the tree, as if in slow motion, and then two steps backwards. She waved her arms about, hitting one of the assistants, who pulled her back from the burning tree again. The groups of people who had been waiting in orderly lines by the food trolley just now dispersed. Only the children were shouting, but with cheerful excitement rather than in panic. The grown-ups formed a circle round the fire and watched in silence as the sparks grew to become flames. The crackling turned to fluttering and rushing sounds.

Only once did I succeed in glancing at the far corner of the hall through the dense crowd of people. Hans had folded his hands in front of his mouth. Perhaps he was laughing. His dark eyes reflected the firelight.